Electric

**Also available from Alyson Books
by Nicole Foster**

Awakening the Virgin: True Tales of Seduction

Electric

best lesbian
erotic
fiction

edited by nicole foster

alyson books
los angeles | new york

© 1999 BY NICOLE FOSTER. AUTHORS RETAIN RIGHTS TO THEIR INDIVIDUAL PIECES OF WORK. ALL RIGHTS RESERVED.

MANUFACTURED IN THE UNITED STATES OF AMERICA.

THIS TRADE PAPERBACK ORIGINAL IS PUBLISHED BY ALYSON PUBLICATIONS, P.O. BOX 4371, LOS ANGELES, CALIFORNIA 90078-4371.
DISTRIBUTION IN THE UNITED KINGDOM BY
TURNAROUND PUBLISHER SERVICES LTD.,
UNIT 3 OLYMPIA TRADING ESTATE, COBURG ROAD, WOOD GREEN,
LONDON N22 6TZ ENGLAND.

FIRST EDITION: AUGUST 1999

01 02 03 **a** 10 9 8 7 6 5 4 3 2

ISBN 1-55583-500-7

PS'
648
.L47
E43
1999

LIBRARY OF CONGRESS CATALOGING-IN-PUBLICATION DATA
ELECTRIC : BEST LESBIAN EROTIC FICTION / EDITED BY NICOLE
FOSTER.—1ST ED.
    ISBN 1-55583-500-7
    1. LESBIANS—SEXUAL BEHAVIOR—FICTION. 2. AMERICAN
FICTION—WOMEN AUTHORS. 3. EROTIC STORIES, AMERICAN.
I. FOSTER, NICOLE.
PS648.L47E43 1999
813'.01083538'086643—DC21   99-11709 CIP

CREDITS
•COVER PHOTOGRAPHS BY ANGELA WYANT.
•"CACTUS LOVE" APPEARED IN A SLIGHTLY DIFFERENT FORM IN *ON OUR BACKS,* VOLUME 5, NUMBER 4 (MARCH–APRIL 1989).
•"ME AND MY APPETITE" APPEARED IN *EVERY WOMAN'S DREAM.* © 1994 BY LESLÉA NEWMAN. REPRINTED BY PERMISSION OF THE AUTHOR.
•"MERRY CHRISTMAS, KATHERINE" APPEARED IN A SLIGHTLY DIFFERENT FORM IN *ARIZONA LITERARY MAGAZINE,* 1986.
•"THE COMMON PRICE OF PASSION" BY JESS WELLS IS EXCERPTED FROM A NOVEL OF THE SAME TITLE.
•"THE PLACE BEFORE LANGUAGE" APPEARED IN AN EXPANDED VERSION AS A NOVELLA IN THE FICTION COLLECTION *SWEAT* BY LUCY JANE BLEDSOE (SEAL PRESS, 1995).

Contents

Introduction

One French babe. Two German vixens. A mean strip-
per. A no-nonsense card shark named Johnny. A daddy
with a unique approach to parenting. A luscious professor with an awesome grading system. A splendidly
naughty cast of characters with enough hot plots and intrigue to make even Shakespeare break into a sweat.
That's what you'll find in this collection of Alyson's best
lesbian erotic fiction of the past ten years.

Electric. The 25 stories in this book *breathe* electricity—and I'm not talking Amana, KitchenAid, or
Maytag. Just what makes a sexual encounter electric?
Ask any of the eager women in these stories, and you
won't have the strength to ask again. Ask Neny from
"Disco Nights," and she'll spread out a meal that will
have you coming back for seconds—and thirds and
fourths. Ask Windy Sands from "Cactus Love," and
she'll get her Arizona trailer rockin' (so don't come
a knockin') in no time. Ask a certain daring stone

butch, and she'll turn the white walls of "The Ladies Room" a blushing pink.

How about dunkin' your doughnut with Sally and Sonny ("Me and My Appetite") in the Macy's dressing room? Follow the sexpot's lead in "Hot Wheels," and do a solo rev in the front seat of your sun-baked car. Learn to make beautiful music with a flirtatious camper, and you'll no longer be "The Festival Virgin."

These aren't just the best stories—they're the *steamiest, spiciest, loveliest, sizzlingest, and funnest.* Including respected and talented writers such as Lucy Jane Bledsoe, Wendy Caster, Linnea Due, Bonnie J. Morris, Lesléa Newman, Mariana Romo-Carmona, Marcy Sheiner, Robin Sweeney, and Jess Wells, this volume is a welcome—make that sensational—addition to any self-respecting erotica connoisseur's well-thumbed collection. So put on the Luther Vandross, dig those candles out of the junk drawer, make yourself comfortable, and get ready for the best—because the best is yet to come.

Nicole Foster
Spring 1999

Electric

Disco Nights

by Mariana Romo-Carmona

Neny was a timid girl, especially each time she walked into the Evergreen, the new bar where the jukebox was stocked with all the latest disco and a woman might ask her to dance as soon as she took off her coat. She'd have to shrug and smile and pretend she was sore from playing softball so she could slide away from all the glittery women, the after-work crowd in their two-piece office suits that so easily became disco skirts. It wasn't that she didn't like disco; it was easier to dance to than salsa anyway, and she was the only Latina west of the Connecticut River who couldn't do salsa, lead or follow. But she was shy.

She almost wanted to return to the old bar, The Lib, where the jukebox had hardly anything she'd want to hear, except maybe Patsy Cline. But when Neny walked into the dark hovel, nobody even looked at her, and she was safe. There was no dancing at The Lib anyhow, except maybe by the pool table between games, when all the butches would take a break and hold their femme girlfriends tight, their cigarettes lining the edge of the table, burning holes into the wood. And that wasn't dancing—it was hugging, making out; it was feeling the length and breadth of the women they loved for a few minutes before getting back to the inter- minable tournament. Not a bad way to be, but Neny had been lured to the new place too, like all the other younger dykes: to the bigger space; to the frozen, pretty drinks; to the bathroom with a big mirror in it; to the friendlier atmos- phere. The new bar made everyone feel like the Dark Ages were over and people could be young and queer if they wanted to, without having to hide in some joint where the bouncer was a man. At least at the Evergreen, the bouncer was a woman: Marylou, with her pack of Camels rolled up into the sleeve of her T-shirt.

So this evening Neny rode around on the bike once more, once around the block, feeling her legs getting crampy since she'd been riding for two hours already, waiting for it to get dark so she could get to the bar. It was the summer days, so long since she had nothing to do but work at the bakery with her mother, play softball with the jock girls, go to the bar, and fantasize about somebody, because Neny had decided she'd never fall in love for real again. It hurt too much. She was too easy, too soft, with her baby face, freckles, and black spiky hair that no amount of Dippity-Do was going to tame, and her big hands, brown arms, all achy for a girl to hold, achy for a woman. She had to stop this fantasizing and riding around at the same time, though; it didn't take much for Neny to get all excited on the bike, riding over the Hartford streets, mak- ing her underwear so wet she'd have to go home and change before going into the Evergreen.

She locked her bike on the fence and took her cigarettes out of the seat pouch. Neny didn't smoke much, but she was tall and lanky, and what was she going to do? She had to smoke to hold something, since she looked horrible in a disco dress holding a purse. She fixed her purple bandanna in the back pocket of her jeans and prepared herself to saunter in. Marylou was watching from the door.

"That's $2," she told Neny.

"What?" Neny's heart nearly stopped.

"Just teasing you, kid! You're never here late enough for me to charge you cover. Get in there and watch you don't eat all the peanuts off the bar before the customers arrive."

Marylou could be cruel. She slapped Neny's behind as she walked in. Neny tried to play it cool, peering inside for some-one she knew, but then she could hardly see anything since her eyes hadn't adjusted to the darkness of the bar.

By 11:30 the place was so crowded there was a constant line by the bathroom and nobody could move more than five inches in any direction on the dance floor. There was a choice of stand-ing or dancing in line, which worked well when everybody was doing the hustle, and there was no difference between the women dancing and the ones just standing there, holding a beer, watching. That's what Neny waited for, when there would be no pressure and she could pretend to sway while trying to learn the steps, pushed by the feminine wave that carried her to and fro.

Meanwhile, the music had reached the level where only short bursts of conversation were possible. Donna Summer crooned about getting some hot stuff this evening, along with everybody else in the bar, including Neny, who was nursing her second beer and beginning to feel bold.

Mouthing the words to the song, Neny was suddenly enveloped from behind by Alma, the hottest dancer and the nattiest dresser in the place. Even the jock girls acknowledged that Alma cleaned up good when she got out of work and headed for the bar.

One song glided into another, and everybody oohed and sighed in unison.

"Come on, dance with me, Neny!" Alma was wearing a pale blue polyester dress that shimmered and hugged her body like a glove—a pair of them, one over each breast, thought Neny, feeling a little dizzy. Around her smooth neck, Alma had three long gold chains, which twirled when she did and then nestled conveniently when she shimmied, golden brown arms by her side, a little salsa shake of the shoulders for good measure. Neny lost her mind and did what Alma told her, letting herself be led until the last echoes of the famous Donna Summer orgasm had stopped ringing in her ears. Alma twirled Neny one last time and, seizing her by the shoulders, placed a coral kiss right on her lips, saying, "Thank you, Neny. That was great!" before disappearing toward the bathroom line. Neny was heartbroken but elated, and now, with nothing to do, she decided to head for the rest room.

This time she got in surprisingly quickly. Alma wasn't there, and one stall was actually free, the other filled with seven girls sniffing coke and gossiping. And the only woman sitting on the bathroom vanity, looking into the mirror to apply more mascara, was Evelina, who acknowledged Neny with a weak "Hey" and went back to the tissues and makeup.

Neny used the rest room and considered she'd done OK for the evening. She might as well go home and fantasize some more.

"Hey, Neny, *pásame un poco de toilet paper, por favor.*" A hand reached out under the stall to her right. Neny wadded up some to give her.

"Why don't you speak English—you're in America now." Neny recognized the voice of Karen, the pitcher from her softball team.

"Listen, *gringuita,*" came the response. "You're in here doing coke with us, so you gotta speak Spanish, OK?"

"OK."

"Hey, Neny, you wanna do a line, *m'hija?*"

"No, *gracias,* Quela, you know that stuff makes me nervous." Neny zipped up her jeans and went to wash her hands. Evelina was still there, blowing her nose.

"Evelina."

"Neny."

"Evelina, you crying?"

"Nope," said Evelina, tears streaming down her face and ruining her mascara. Her round face and full lips were all flushed and pouty, making her look like a sad little girl. Neny wanted to hug Evelina, to comfort her somehow, but she wasn't sure if she should.

"Well, where's Carmen?"

"At work. She'll be here soon," Evelina sniffed.

"OK, don't cry. Coming to the game on Sunday?"

But the answer was obliterated by the magnificent seven exiting the stall, high as kites and ready to party.

"Ooh, girl!"

"Tell me 'bout it—"

Neny was hungry and decided to make one last pass by the bar to see if there were any peanuts or Chex mix left. It was before 1 o'clock, and she knew that things were just beginning to get good, but she couldn't hang with it. The jock girls called her over from a table to sit with them, but she just gave them a practiced smile and took refuge by the barstools. The black girls had arrived, and there was some hot dancing going on between them and the Italian regulars. The peanut bowls were empty, and Neny felt deflated. She didn't belong anywhere. She *could* run and steal bases, though; that was her calling in life.

Just then the music ended and there was a lull in the heated night. Neny looked up and saw Carmen, Evelina's girlfriend, walking in the bar. Alma and Quela joined her.

"Awright! The Latin mafia is here!" one of the regulars yelled near the bathroom. "Now we're gonna get some music!"

Indeed, Carmen and company squared shoulders and sauntered to the bar to talk to the manager. Carmen, with her square face and square haircut and square manners, who always got exactly what she wanted. Alma and Quela simply crossed their arms and waited patiently by the bar. A new bowl of Chex mix appeared magically on the counter. Neny knew that even though the manager, Gloria from Peoria, the toughest dyke in the free world and a loyal fan of Barbra Streisand—hence the name of the bar—would dig in her heels for a while, claiming that salsa was too new and nobody really knew how to dance to it, eventually Carmen would prevail. If Gloria authorized the playing of three Latin tunes, it was a major victory. It was also the only time Neny felt proud, and giddy, even if she couldn't dance.

Neny stayed for as long as her growling stomach let her. It was a three-tune night, and Carmen was soon holding her adorable girlfriend, Evelina, and twirling her, leading her in an increasingly complicated set of erotic passes and sweeps that showed off Evelina's curves, generous and graceful, and Carmen's own practiced, steady moves that drove all the femme girls crazy. There was Alma, dancing up a storm with Quela, who came a close second to Carmen in terms of being *muy* butch and impenetrable. *And to think I got a kiss from Alma tonight,* thought Neny. Then all the others lost their fear and joined in, swinging, shaking, and shimmying their booties for all it was worth, until Gloria deemed it was time to bring back the Bee Gees and calm everybody down.

"Wow, Carmen is hot!" someone said to Neny's right.

"Nah, it's Evelina who's hot!" said the woman to her left. Neny was stuck in between a serious gossip session because, as usual, people didn't even know she was there. She stood still.

"Yeah, but Carmen knows what she's doing: She calls the shots."

"When they're dancing, OK, I agree with you. But when you get them in the sack, I hear she's a yawn."

"You're kidding!"

"Nope. She's the kind who rolls over and hands her lover a vibrator."

"No!"

Neny's ears were burning. She wondered if that was why Evelina was crying in the bathroom. *Enough,* she told herself, *it's late and Mami's going to wake me up at 6 to go to the bakery.* It was time to go home.

The afternoon light streamed in and bathed the room in waves from the rain on the windows. Evelina slid her hips a little farther under Carmen's hands, raised her right thigh higher, and waited for her girlfriend's breathing to get a little more rapid. She thought this might be the time; she felt excited and wet, all elastic with desire and tenderness. She felt generous and open, but then everything about her was that way: her spirit, her body, rounded, soft, from her breasts to the smooth heels of her size 5½ feet.

"Evelina?" Carmen was happy, her square jaw and her shiny black hair nestled in the curve between Evelina's neck and the rising line of Evelina's breast. Carmen grasped Evelina's hips and gently turned her over on top of herself, sighing languorously at the silky impact of their skin blending together. Carmen closed her eyes and let Evelina take over. Evelina opened hers and took in Carmen's features, smiling placidly, her dark eyebrows perfectly shaped against her light skin, turning her head against the pillow and showing off the profile that Evelina had once thought noble. No, it wasn't going to be this time.

Everyone thought Carmen was such a butch and envied Evelina for having it so good, but there was much more to it than having it good, thought Evelina, as she initiated the familiar journey down Carmen's body. First here, then there, then some kissing around the belly button and she would be screaming with those short little yells. Damn it, why did it have to be so easy? Evelina wrapped her arms around Carmen and lost herself in the moment, feeling again open and giving. It was, after all, something in her power to give and to do it well: to slide her breasts on Carmen's, to let her hair down to tickle the inside of Carmen's well-toned thighs, to tease along those legs with her tongue until she herself was ready to dip her tongue in the right place and move it fast, slow, sideways, up and down, then still, then push once, twice—that's it.

She placed her head slowly down on Carmen's breast, feeling satisfied but still excited, waiting.

"Mmm, baby, that was so nice," whispered Carmen.

Evelina slid up on the bed, brushing against her lover's body, opening her brown eyes and reclining her face on Carmen's shoulder.

"Carmen?" She cooed, placing Carmen's right hand against her mound.

"Oh, Evelina, you know I can't get into that now. I gotta get to work, babe." Carmen slid out of the bed and headed toward the bathroom.

"But, Carmen, I want—" Evelina began.

"You want me to pay the bills, don't you, honey? Come on, you know where the vibrator is. I'll see you tonight."

Slam, went the front door, and crash, went the vibrator against the full-length bedroom mirror.

"Pay the damn bills," yelled Evelina to herself, because Carmen was gone and there was no one else to yell at. "Well, maybe I should quit the damn Wilbur Beauty Academy and enroll at Trinity College; then she can really pay some damn bills." Evelina put on her white terry-cloth robe and went to the kitchen to get herself a piece of Italian bread and butter. She pulled the butter dish out of the refrigerator, then sat on the counter, as was her habit, dangling her feet, reaching for the bread and the fresh smell that came out of the paper bag. She opened the pink butter dish so the butter would soften, but she couldn't wait. She thought she'd call Alma to talk about her troubles, so she picked up the green wall phone but realized Alma wouldn't be home. She herself should be at the school, practicing the Vidal Sassoon bob, but she'd stayed home, hoping… Evelina got down off the counter, stuffing a soft piece of bread into her mouth, thinking she should go in the bedroom and clean up all the glass from the broken mirror, then maybe take a bath to calm down.

It was completely dark out, and the candle had burned all the way down. Evelina didn't know how long she'd been in the bathtub, but the water had cooled considerably. She thought she'd get out, yet she wanted to lie there a little longer, spreading the droplets of water and bath oil over her cinnamon knees, her rounded belly, the breasts that spilled easily over her rib cage and got tickled by the edges of the warm water. She had cleaned the apartment, picked up all the glass and tried the vibrator even, but it was broken. Good, she thought. Ever since Carmen had gotten to be the manager at the steak house on the Silas Deane Highway, there was no point in going to bed with her. What was the point? Evelina asked herself. Her girlfriend got more of a kick from getting people to do things than from sex. The guys at the grill, the wine steward, the waitresses, even Gloria from Peoria at the Evergreen. She just liked to give orders, play the butch, but when she got into bed…nothing.

But Evelina had felt sorry too for breaking the mirror. She'd started to make zucchini bread from scratch; a special corn dish, *pasteles*; and beef stew Cuban–style, just to please Carmen. She sat up in the bathtub, thinking about the mess she'd left on the kitchen table, on the counters, all the plantains, corn husks, and the zucchini. She squeezed off the water from her hair, wrapped the long curls into a towel, and stepped back into the white robe. Just then, the doorbell rang.

"Who is it?" She ran on her bare feet, calling toward the door.

"Um," said Neny when Evelina opened it.

"Oh, it's you. What's wrong?"

"Nothing. I thought I'd see if, I mean last night, and you know, well, practice was rained out. I can come back if you—"

"Oh, get in here—I don't care. Come in and keep me company."

"Where's Carmen?" Neny asked, looking all around.

"Is that all you can say? She's at work, where she always is. Come in the kitchen; I'm making bread."

"What's with all the *guineos*?" Neny took off her leather cap, adjusted the lace on her sneakers, then plunged her hands into the pockets of her shorts. Evelina's robe was opening, and Neny could see the cleavage that existed only in her fantasies.

"That was going to be *pasteles*. Sit down, I'll make you some *café con leche*."

"Why were you crying last night?" Neny asked, thinking she'd gone crazy. What else would she be doing asking a question like that?

Evelina stopped on her way to the stove. She turned around and looked at Neny, who looked back at her with concern in her sweet, freckled face. "*Ay*, Neny!" She rushed into Neny's arms and hugged her gratefully. "You're so sweet!"

Neny held Evelina for the longest time, smelling the bath oil on her neck and the shampoo from her hair when the towel fell off and feeling the warmth that came through Evelina's robe.

Without knowing why, Neny started to kiss Evelina's hair, saying softly to her, "It's OK, Evelina, I'm here, I'm here."

Until the phone rang. Evelina jumped out of Neny's arms to get it. Neny wanted to apologize for something, but she didn't know what. Maybe there was nothing. She watched Evelina spring up on the counter to get the phone. It was Alma. Neny sat down on a chair and watched.

After a few minutes Neny was intently watching Evelina on the phone because it was a beautiful sight to see. Evelina was completely absorbed in the call, looking away, twirling her hair with her left hand while she held the phone with her right. She had raised her left knee up, and her small left foot was planted flat on the counter. Her left arm rested on her knee, and the robe had slipped down the side of her leg, but nothing, nothing showed. Neny couldn't see how this was possible. She looked again. Nothing. *The robe is open at the neck and at least Evelina's breasts must be in there,* thought Neny.

"Alma, why didn't you tell me about this?" Evelina was saying. "Oh, wow, that's crazy!" And then she saw Neny looking at her, realizing that she was sitting on the counter the way she always did. But now she was in her robe, naked. A rush of her upbringing invaded her momentarily, then left her. She looked at Neny, eyes half-closed and those long eyelashes shading the girl's pretty, freckled face. Evelina switched the phone from one hand to the other, stretching, letting the robe fall a little more open until her right breast was completely visible. Neny froze on the chair. Evelina stretched her back and started to raise her right leg up the counter. Neny almost fell off her chair then.

"Oh, please, you don't expect me to believe that!" Evelina said into the phone. Neny got up and walked toward her. Evelina kept talking. Neny looked into Evelina's eyes and waited.

"Mmm-hmm…?" said Evelina and switched the phone back to her right hand, leaving her neck exposed. Neny bent to kiss it, and she was hooked. There was no way she could lift her face from that neck, from Evelina's shoulder, any more than she could deny her own name. So she steadied herself by reaching for Evelina's breasts and trying to be as quiet as she could. It was a tacit agreement.

"Ooh, no!" cried Evelina into the phone, because she didn't have to be quiet at all. She felt Neny's hands gyrating slowly over her breasts, the girl's thumbs and forefingers pulling gently on her nipples with such precision, Evelina was amazed she couldn't remember ever having looked at Neny before, not this way, definitely not this way.

"Oh, stop!" she gasped into Alma's ear, who chattered on, unconcerned and totally uninformed. Neny felt she was about to start moaning loudly, so she bent down lower and began to roll her tongue over Evelina's breasts, wrapping it around each nipple and sucking as though the nipple were a raisin protruding out of a cinnamon roll. On the phone, Evelina was talking fast, God only knew about what, but it seemed to steady her, and Neny kept licking and sucking until she was too dizzy to stand up.

"Girl, you better tell me everything!" Evelina commanded, and Neny knelt on the floor and undid the robe quickly, taking hold of Evelina's left leg and placing it over her shoulder in case Evelina got tired.

"Go on—" said Evelina, and Neny didn't wait to bury her face in paradise. Evelina's black pubic hair was wet, very silky, and tasted and smelled like a cornucopia of flavors. Salt, bath oil, tangy wetness.

"Oh, my God! I can't stand it!" said Evelina weakly, supporting herself on Neny's shoulders. "Hurry up, get to the point!" And Neny did, twirling her tongue again, only more gently, to find Evelina's clitoris.

"That's it, *muchacha,* you're killin' me!" cried Evelina, and then she was quiet for a long time while Neny applied pressure and long strokes on the sides of her labia, her clitoris, the edges of her vagina. Evelina was so turned on she wanted to explode, and yet she didn't want the moment to end. She felt every part of her body sizzling in an erotic vibration that sent her higher each second, and she wanted to play it to the hilt, but she knew she was either going to have to stop or lose consciousness or come and end everything right there. She slammed the phone in the cradle in the middle of Alma's question about her state of mind and hoisted herself with both hands to get closer to Neny's mouth. Except her left hand landed in the butter dish and sent the cover flying across the kitchen floor.

"Uh?" said Neny, her mouth moving kind of slow.

"It's just the butter," Evelina told her, contemplating the gob of it she had on her fingers.

Neny got up again and kissed Evelina, who tasted her own juices and decided to spread the butter on Neny's face and neck, then her own breasts. Neny's knees buckled watching the spreading of the butter, pleading, "Evelina, I have to make you come!" She picked Evelina up in her arms and stumbled to the table, where she tried to make some room, but Evelina didn't care. The robe served well enough, and she laid her head carefully on an ear of corn, while Neny straddled her and held her steady with those long legs of hers. Evelina now moaned and sighed freely and let Neny spread the rest of the butter all over her until she got to licking again, gasping for air because the girl was too excited for words.

"Faster, faster, Neny!" sighed Evelina, and Neny obliged, considering at the same time one of the zucchinis on the table. But since she already had so much butter on her hands, she easily pushed three fingers into Evelina's vagina without taking her mouth off her once. *It is amazing how a table facilitates matters,* Neny thought, but she didn't have much time to ponder because Evelina was coming in waves, and Neny wanted to make sure she caught every one with her tongue.

After a few seconds Neny lifted Evelina off the table and held her on her lap, both of them sitting on a chair, each stroking the other's face, kissing, and sighing slowly.

"Evelina?"

"Hmm?"

"Nothing, I just wanted to say your name."

"Mmm."

"Neny?"

"Yeah?"

"You're going to have to go, baby. I gotta clean this place up."

"I know."

"I'm sorry. I wanted to…" Evelina started to say, because she knew how it felt to be left wanting.

"Oh, don't worry about me; one turn around the block on the bicycle and I'll be off!" Neny laughed. Evelina joined her.

Maybe tonight was her night, after all. When Neny left, Evelina stood in the kitchen for a while, surveying the mess. She wanted to laugh, to dance perhaps. She went into the bathroom to take another bath.

Carmen's turquoise Datsun turned into the driveway with the wipers on. The headlights went off, and the door opened as Carmen got out. She'd had a good night at the steak house, and she was in a good mood. She looked up and saw that the outside light was out and made a note to change the bulb while she jangled the keys to her first-floor apartment in her hands. But inside the lights were off in the living room too and in the kitchen, so she turned them on.

"Evelina?" she called. There were corn cobs on the table. Zucchini on the floor. *That's odd,* she thought, and went to get a beer. Then she saw the counter. "Evelina?" she called again. "What happened to the butter?"

The rain had stopped, but the seat on Neny's bicycle was all wet. She retrieved it from under the skinny tree where she'd locked it up a block from Evelina's apartment and wiped the leather with her sleeve. She headed home, taking the long way around down Asylum Avenue, and then deciding to do a turn around Bushnell Park. The streetlights had a haze of moisture and moonlight glowing around them, the park benches glistened with raindrops, and the puddles on the brick sidewalks splashed when the tires of Neny's bicycle rode over them. Her legs felt warm, not cramped at all, and her hands felt powerful somehow as she watched her fingers gently squeezing the brakes and changing gears. There was a smile on her face.

Eating Out at Café Z

by Deborah Abbott

"But, Val," said Judith, her blue eyes wide, looking straight into Val's hazel ones from across the table at Café Z, "don't you miss cock?"

Judith certainly hadn't changed, thought Val. Even 20 years after being sophomores in the dorms together, where Val had yet to discover girls and was busy fucking boys, Judith retained her frankness. Val liked that, and though the question itself was hardly original, she had grown to expect it when coming out to friends.

Val took her time to respond, kept her hold on Judith's gaze, let silence hang on Judith's question. Then Val said slowly, letting each word roll off her tongue while raising one hand and curling her fingers into a fist, "I never found a cock…to fill me…like this."

Judith choked on her Caesar salad, gulped chardonnay, choked some more. Val laughed. She watched as Judith struggled to regain her composure, dabbed at her mouth with the linen napkin. It was clear she had been unnerved and hated that it showed.

"I never found one either," Val continued, "to outlast me. Always ended something like this." Val stabbed a leaf of romaine, held it between them, limp and dripping Roquefort. Judith laughed then herself.

"My question for *you* is," said Val, passing the wilted green lettuce over her lips and irreverently grinding it between her teeth, "do you really want to go to your grave never having eaten pussy?"

Judith blushed, put her hands to her face to hide the irrepressible response, but her ten bright red nails only emphasized the color in her cheeks. Judith recovered quicker this time and would not be outdone.

"How do you know I haven't," she said, with only the briefest pause, "eaten pussy?"

A pair of businessmen at the next table turned their heads sharply in Val and Judith's direction. Val grinned at them and winked.

"Because you wouldn't have asked such a stupid question. About cock," Val answered.

"Oh, no?" Judith said, cheeks flushed again, from the wine or conversation or both. "Maybe I just prefer a big hard-on."

"Well, maybe you've never had a big strap-on," Val shot back. "Choice of colors. Choice of—" Val began to explain, but Judith cut her off.

"It can't be like the real thing," Judith said while she poured more chardonnay, brought the glass to her lips, and let the shimmery liquid slip inside, leaving lipstick prints at the edges.

"You're right," Val said, grinning again, leaning toward Judith, so close she could pick up the scent of Judith's perfume.

"You're right, Judith. It's completely unlike the real thing. It's unnatural. Abnormal as hell. Really, really fucking sick."

Val was feeling good, like she'd regained her ground, until she suddenly noticed lace peeking from the V of Judith's blouse, creamy lace set against her lovely brown skin. In spite of herself, Val felt her cunt give a powerful squeeze.

"Anyway," Val continued, "don't knock it if you haven't tried it." Val was disgusted with herself for resorting to that old tired line, but she was desperate for words to cover up what had just happened between her legs.

"OK," said Judith, her turn to look Val full in the eyes.

"OK?" Val asked, one eyebrow raised, confused at Judith's meaning.

"OK, I'll try it," Judith answered.

Val felt her heart fall and land somewhere under the table, along with the fork she had dropped a moment ago. *Oh, shit,* she thought, *Judith has gone off and trumped me. If I don't take her up on her dare, she'll have me for sure. On the other hand, here I am, a femme, admittedly a broad-shouldered butchy kind of femme, sitting across the table from one very, very femmy kind of femme.* Val had always proclaimed loudly that polished nails and shaved legs were her two major turnoffs, yet here was Judith, with ten fire-engine-red claws, wearing heels and Hanes. Here was Judith, her old dormie, straight as the asparagus spear lying untouched on her plate, propositioning Val. Val had always been sure that it took at least a femmy butch to get her off. But the damp spot spreading across her panties was throwing that theory all to hell.

Pride was pride, Val conceded, and said to Judith, "I believe you should excuse yourself to the ladies' room. With all that wine…you must need…to relieve yourself."

Judith didn't miss a beat. She stood, set her napkin down on the table, and started to the rest room. Judith was a little tipsy, but Val was stone sober. To keep herself from chickening out, Val concentrated on the image of Judith's brown breasts framed by the lace. She had to confess she'd had no experience whatsoever with slips, only with tank tops, which tore off with one good yank. She followed Judith through the maze of tables, half hoping Judith would have a change of heart now that Val had accepted the challenge. Val tried to think of a way to salvage Judith's ego but came up empty. Walking behind her, Val remembered Judith from swim team. Judith had just told her she was still swimming. The thought of a woman's brown muscled back with pale crisscrossing strap lines never failed to turn her on.

Judith reached the door marked LADIES and held it open for Val. The bathroom was bigger than Val's studio, and certainly cleaner. Val took one look and smiled over their good fortune. Thank God—a handicapped stall. Plenty of room for two and bars to hold on to. No one tended to bang on the doors, figuring people with disabilities took hours to pee. Besides, Val could always stick the brace she wore on her right leg under the stall for proof. See, I qualify. Now leave me to my fucking, thank you very much. Val enjoyed this one little perk and cashed in on it as often as she had the chance.

Val pushed Judith into the stall, then latched the door behind them. She didn't let Judith turn around, wasn't sure she wanted Judith to kiss her. Although Val sometimes wore lipstick herself, she preferred to leave smudges, not have them left on her. And Judith was wearing deep crimson, only slightly dampened by her lunch.

"You're not gonna miss cock," Val whispered into Judith's ear, reminding Judith, preparing her.

"I'm not so sure," Judith whispered back, pulling her breath in sharply. "You guarantee it?"

"Guaranteed," Val said, "over my...lesbian body." Judith sounded hot already, and Val had second thoughts about Judith's lesbian virgin status. *In fact,* Val thought, *Judith sounds hotter than I do.* Suddenly Val felt her dyke credentials on the line. This motivated her like a slap to the jaw. *I'll be damned if I let some straight girl beat me to it,* Val told herself, feeling pure energy flood her body like adrenaline after a mile-long swim.

Val pinned Judith against the cool tile wall and pressed Judith's cheek to it. She unfurled her tongue against Judith's exposed throat, crawled into the hole of Judith's ear, retreated as quickly as she'd entered, and then sucked the lobe and the pearl earring at its tip, pretending it was the hard ball of Judith's clit. As Judith gasped, Val's own clit stood up.

"I'm gonna show you," Val whispered, plunging back into Judith's ear. She could tell this was one of Judith's hot spots by the way Judith started making low sounds in her throat, sounds that stirred something in Val too, making her shudder. "You won't regret it. Won't forget it. Won't look back, not even once. You won't even remember how to *spell* cock when I get through with you."

Val could tell Judith liked this, liked being talked to, liked being turned on by Val's tongue thrusting into her ear hole in this public place. Getting it on in girls' bathrooms was not something straight girls had usually done with boys.

Just as Val started to loosen her hold on Judith, to turn her around and work her tongue in the direction of Judith's warm brown breasts, the bathroom door slowly heaved open.

Judith stopped breathing, stared down at their four feet, then looked up at Val with unmistakable panic. Val took Judith by her waist, soundlessly lifting her until her feet straddled the toilet seat. Val held her finger to her lips, then took advantage of the moment to unbutton Judith's blouse. Val was eye level with Judith's breasts, which were full under layers of her silky slip and bra. Val began rubbing her face in slow motion all over that smooth laciness that smelled sweet like powder, like the inside of a lingerie drawer. *Oh, God,* she thought, a moan inadvertently escaping. Val liked this more than she could have guessed, could ever have admitted to anyone, almost to herself.

The woman who had entered the bathroom went into the stall next door. Val listened to her unbuckling her belt. *Good idea,* Val thought, and, synchronized with the stranger, unzipped Judith. Val pictured the stranger pulling her slacks down, down over a full round ass, saw panties slipping too, pictured the stranger letting herself down onto the seat, her legs spread, pussy exposed. Val's lips began throbbing at the thought.

Then Val heard the stranger's piss come splashing into the toilet bowl. Val had an incredible urge to stick her face under Judith's cunt and have her pee too. But she wasn't sure how to convey this to Judith and suspected this was too much indecency to ask of a straight girl who had no doubt never ventured far from the missionary position. Besides, Val wasn't keen on going back to the dining room with an earful of piss.

Judith was squatting on the seat, steadying herself with a hand on each of the metal bars. While the stranger flushed, Val got Judith's panties all the way down, till they were draped, sheer white, over her ankles. Without any warning Val pulled Judith's lips apart, found her clit, nearly forgot the sheet of plastic she always carried, paused to get it out and over the spot, and then, with the stiff tip of her tongue, went down on Judith. Judith let out a cry that was only half covered by the stranger's flush. It was the kind of cry that told Val that no one, no man, had ever eaten Judith with any finesse at all. The kind of cry that told Val she would soon have Judith, quite literally, in the palm of her hand.

The stranger was at the sink now. The hygienic type. Val heard the soap dispenser bang twice, pictured liquid squirting over the stranger's upturned palms, the stranger wringing her broad hands under the warm spray. Suddenly Val pictured one of those big bony hands plunging into her cunt, and at the mere suggestion of it, her pussy clenched, shooting wetness clear through her jeans.

Val's tongue kept playing with Judith's clit, and Judith kept making those deep, half-muffled cries. Val knew she was good at this, had been told so more than once, and had had a couple of decades to refine the technique. Not that it felt like technique with Judith. It was more like instinct. She was drawn to Judith like a wild dog keening to scent. She felt like she had known this woman's cunt before. She recognized the distinctness of its groove, recognized its hot, pungent odor. Which was crazy, Val knew, impossible.

Judith, who was now hanging by her hands from the upper edges of the stall, shifted. In pausing to look up at Judith's face, Val could see Judith struggle to keep from shaking the stall walls, struggle to hold back her cries, struggle to keep herself from arching away from Val's mouth. It was clear Judith was deep in struggle but deeper still in bliss.

Val knew Judith couldn't hold on much longer—in more ways than one. Val herself was soaked from her mouth on Judith and the thought of the stranger's slick hand up her. Judith was slick, Val could feel that. She brought out latex, took four fingers, way more than a cock's worth, and slid them into Judith. *Easy*, Val told herself, *easy, girl.* Judith's pussy strained against such a handful but clutched at the same time, like a lost child finally finding her mother. Val began fucking Judith, slow and steady. She looked up. Judith's eyes were closed, and she was breathing as quickly and quietly as she could through those crimson lips, which were shaped like the letter *o* and were as swollen as her cunt.

Oh, yes, oh, yes, Judith mouthed, lower than a whisper. Val could read her lips. Val kept working her up and down, with a rhythm that increased incrementally with each thrust, that went as deep as Val could go at this weird angle. Val took her eyes off Judith's face and put her mouth back on Judith's clit, which was now as hard as that pearl on her lobe. Even beneath the wrap Val could feel Judith's clit throbbing like the heart of a pearl oyster, pumping, straining, ready to burst.

The stranger was rinsing, rinsing for the longest time. *Some compulsive hand washer,* Val thought. No doubt she was listening to Judith's panting, Val's thrusting, Judith's juices sloshing. Val considered the possibility that the hand washer had taken her hands out from under the spigot, put one down her slacks, and was now lobbing away at her own cunt. *A kind of ménage à trois,* Val thought, liking the idea.

Judith came then, her cunt nearly breaking Val's four fingers as it spasmed. Her cunt held on to Val for dear life, squeezing and only slightly releasing, over and over, as if it had never come so powerfully before and might never come like this again and so had to keep this rapture going forever. The stall walls shuddered violently under Judith's grip, until she let go and collapsed over Val.

Val let Judith's orgasm wind its way down. When the pulse in Judith's cunt was faint and the muscles loosened their hold, Val finally pulled out, wiped a dripping, gloved hand on Judith's ass, found the nipple that was poking through the lace against her cheek, latched on, and sucked for a long, quiet minute.

The stranger was still involved in her hand-washing ritual but had progressed to drying, using the little drying machine. Judith had only half recovered, but Val was so hot and ready for sex herself that she seized the opportunity by grabbing Judith's hand and shoving it down her jeans.

Judith rose to the occasion, had no trouble finding Val's clit. Val was drenched, wet as any butch had ever made her. Val sat down on the floor, carrying Judith's hand with her, Judith's nipple still between her teeth. Val leaned back against the wall. She didn't give a damn what the stranger saw anymore and knew Judith was beyond caring. It was Val's turn to surrender; she was hoping Judith could pull it off, could carry her, because Val was longing to let go.

Val buried her face deeper in the silk and rubbed her cheeks back and forth over the cool cloth, losing herself in the sensation. Judith reached up with her free hand, brought one of her breasts up and out of the lace, and offered it to Val. Val accepted, her throat aching so badly she could barely swallow, the roof of her mouth pounding painfully with wanting Judith's uncovered tit. Val played with the firm, warm mound, licked at the puckered areola, then couldn't help herself any longer. She attached herself to Judith's stiff nipple like something helpless and half-starved, and sucked, hard, knowing Judith would have bruises for days after. But Judith seemed to understand Val's need and didn't protest. While Val sucked, Judith's finger rounded Val's clit, circled like she no doubt circled herself when there wasn't some cock nearby.

Then Judith took her breast away, brought her mouth to Val's, and gave Val a long kiss, her bold tongue pushing through the last of Val's resistance. It was hard to believe Judith hadn't been kissing girls all her life, but the thought of being first, of being Judith's very first lesbian kiss, made Val groan. She fleetingly remembered Judith's lipstick, which she knew was now smeared all over her own mouth. But Val didn't give a damn about the lipstick. Or about the stranger who was still drying her hands—or fucking herself with her hands or standing frozen in a state of horrified arousal just listening to Judith and Val fuck. Judith kissed her so long, so deeply, yet so tenderly, Val thought she would explode from excitement or lack of air. Judith's finger never stopped teasing her the whole time. Val realized she was just dying under this straight girl's hand, realized that this complete novice, total femme, cocksucking straight girl was taking her to some place no butch had ever taken her. It killed her to admit it, but it was true.

There was only one thing missing. Val grabbed a handful of Judith's hair and twisted her head so Judith's ear was next to her mouth. "Inside," Val whispered against Judith's lobe, taking one of her own hands and pressing at Judith's. But Judith hesitated, only circled lower, her fingers cautious, as though she were approaching the mouth of a cave, afraid to enter, afraid to find out what wild beast lived there.

"I need you," Val insisted, wrenching away from Judith's kiss, "*inside.*" Val needed Judith up her cunt so badly she could scream. She did scream, and pounded her hand once, hard, against the stall wall.

"Don't you know how," she gasped, her voice hoarse, "to fuck...a woman?"

As soon as she said it, Val realized that Judith *didn't* know how. And Judith said then, softly, almost like an apology, "No, Val, I don't. But show me. Will you show me? I want to...to fuck you."

Val believed her. Val took her own right hand, which trembled between them, and brought her fingers together like she was going to pray. And she was praying. Praying this straight girl was a fast learner, because she was so close to coming, and yet, without Judith inside her, so far away.

"Like this," Val demonstrated, "all of this. See?" Val slowly curled her fingers into a fist. "Just ball me. *Ball* me. You understand?" Val used that old term, *balling,* one they had used 20 years ago in the dorms. Val hoped Judith would remember, would relate to this. And as Judith made a fist, her nails curling into themselves, her hand *was* like a ball.

That's all the instruction Judith required. Val was so open, so wet, Judith could have dived, like she used to dive back on swim team, headfirst into Val. After a minute Judith found a good rhythm, and Val urged her on more, sinking her teeth into Judith's shoulder as a way of letting her know. Val's jeans were at her ankles, and she was pulling back on her thighs as Judith's forearm disappeared into her cunt.

Val could tell that Judith was getting into fisting her. Getting fucked by a woman was one thing, but fucking one was quite another. Judith, on her knees, picked up the pace, sweating and grunting from the effort, getting slick and hot again herself.

Val let go of her thighs, brought one hand to her rear, and plunged a finger up her asshole. The rush almost tore her in two. Then she took her free hand, spit on her forefinger, reached down and touched it to her clit with just the right pressure, just the way she liked it, and just like that she came. It was a massive orgasm. It seemed to take all of Judith's strength to hold on to Val and keep her from seizing all over the floor.

Judith kept working Val the whole time she came. As Val's head arched, the fluorescent globe on the ceiling, full as the moon, pierced her closed eyelids with a strong white light. As Val came, she howled like a dog leaning back on her haunches at the mouth of her own cave. With juices pouring out of her onto the tile floor, she howled into Judith's ear and the stranger's ear and maybe into all of Café Z. But Val didn't care. She knew nothing beyond her cunt's pounding and Judith's fist pounding, beyond sound and the penetrating light. And then Val knew too, with dead sureness in her wild-dog gut, that Judith wasn't now, wasn't ever, wasn't for a minute, missing cock.

Hot Wheels

by michon

She loves it when it's hot. Summer is made for her. She
was born in summer when the sun was at its highest. Her
body is made to receive heat.

She loves the heat so much that sometimes she just sits
in her car that's been baking under the sun. The air is hot
and humid, and the steering wheel burns her knees when
they touch it. The heat sucks the chill from her skin. It
raises the hair on her arms and unravels the knot between
her shoulders. She leans back, closes her eyes, and in-
hales/exhales.

Instinctively she lifts her hand to her chest. It lies between her breasts like a wilted flower, absorbing moisture
from her evaporating sweat. The pads of her fingers stick
to her skin, but she pulls her hand up to her neck, leaving
a yellow indentation where her fingers used to be. Her
hand strokes downward, smoothing the creases in her
neck, crossing the ribs in her tank top, down to the bottom of her shirt. She reaches four fingers under, resting

her thumb on top of the red cotton knit fabric. She draws spirals around her belly button with the uneven nail of her forefinger. The spiral forms a loop around her navel ring. She tugs.

It's heat-wave hot, but she doesn't roll down the windows. She just keeps inhaling/exhaling her available stock of air. Feeling the heat of her own breath cross her bottom lip is like tasting the heat of her flesh. Sweat builds at the rim of her hairline and in the cleft of her upper lip, but she can't lift her hand to wipe it away.

She doesn't want to distract herself, but she opens her eyes long enough to look around and wonder if people can see her. If they could, would she mind? Feeling safe from exposure, she lays her head back, closes her eyes, and allows her thighs to sink into the synthetic fibers of her zebra-print seat covers.

Belly button: right above the round of her belly. Her hand fondles the button of her 501s, slips the cool metal through the denim slit. She pulls the flat metal zipper down between her fingers to expose/to release her black burgundy wine passion flower.

Sweat trickles between dark crevices. It mixes with the scent of African violet body oil in her pits and behind her knees. The fragrance hovers in the car cabin like the aftertaste of black coffee clinging in her mouth. Inhale.

She slowly lifts the weight of her eyelashes. A glimpse of the bright buttercup sun burns her eyes: close.

Fingers tiptoe down, curl around the spiraling vines of her engorged bud. Lift. Push. Squeeze. The bud grows, darkens, and blooms with the rhythmic swirling of fingers pressed against it. Her pelvis pushes forward on the seat, and her thighs roll apart like the walk of a tumbleweed. Fingers swirl faster like the quick wrist strokes of blending creamy chocolate cake mix. Fingers slip between the ravines of the vulva. They slip inside like a tongue slips into a mouth.

Inhale/exhale/inhale/exhale/swirling/pulsing/throbbing/coming.

And she comes behind the shadow of closed lids flashing pink-purple-blue psychedelic circles. This ecstasy is like the slow flow of honey from a fallen jar. Lips slide and stick. Exhale.

She rolls down the window warm, dry air rushes in. It cools the sweat caught in her brow. She looks into the rearview mirror. The buttercup sun stares.

Пальцы двигаются быстрее, как-будто бьивают твоё любимое безе

Merry Christmas, Katherine

by Ouida Crozier

The buzzer sounded, jolting Katherine with its customary stridency and insistent message. She hated it and hurried to respond before the clamor could jangle her nerves again.

With irritation, she swung the door back—she had been expecting a quiet evening at home, alone—then hesitated, surprised. "Well, Judy...hello," she said, her voice that mixture of irritation and surprise, with a question at the end. Deliberately, she neither moved aside nor invited the young woman in.

Judy stood on the stoop, in shadow. It was snowing softly behind her, and wet flakes clung to her coat and dark hair. "May I come in, Dr. Nikles?"

Katherine stepped aside, nursing her feeling of being intruded upon, aware of being dressed in gown and robe and slippers, her hair pinned back. She felt vulnerable, and resentful, at the invasion of her privacy. She did not take well to unexpected, unannounced visits, whether from students or her peers. Few of her friends would have dared such an action.

Judy, however, was oblivious to this and walked right into the living room. She seemed to catch herself in the act of inspecting things and turned, focusing on Katherine.

"I apologize for barging in like this," she began, her hazel eyes fixed on Katherine's. Kate noticed that the pupils were dilated and wondered if Judy was intoxicated—she had never thought of the young woman as a user. "But," Judy went on steadily, "I felt I *had* to talk to you, and—" She paused, dropping her eyes for a moment. "I was afraid that if I called first, you might say no." As she looked up again, she seemed suddenly shy.

"Yes," Katherine responded, "I probably would have said no." She waited, ungivingly, for the rest.

As if to restore her intent, Judy opened her coat, slipped out of it, and pulled off her scarf, stuffing it into one sleeve, then folded the coat inside out and laid it on a chair near the door. She turned to Katherine again, a mixture of fear and defiance on her face.

The expression touched Kate, reminding her of herself at Judy's age, and she relented a little. She looked pointedly at Judy's boots, wet with the snow

"Well, you're here—you might as well take those off too. I'll heat some water for something hot to drink." She went into the small kitchen, a smile playing around the corners of her mouth at the gratitude she had glimpsed in Judy's eyes as she had given permission to stay. "What would you like?" she called.

In stocking feet, Judy came through the swinging door. Kate noticed how, in the girl's wet hair, gold highlights glistened under the bright kitchen lights. *Why am I thinking of her as a girl?* she chided herself. She must be at least 22 by now.

She reflected that in the perennial student garb of jeans and sweater Judy didn't *look* at all like a girl. *I must be getting old*, Kate sighed inwardly.

Now that she was welcomed, Judy perused her surroundings more freely while she murmured aloud. "Um, I guess...I guess I'll have...well, uh, what do you have, Dr. Nikles?"

Kate laughed. "I have coffee and decaf, instant. I have caffeine teas—jasmine and pekoe—and I have herbal almond, and some of that 'Zinger' stuff." She waited while Judy finished her visual tour.

"Hmm. I guess jasmine tea, please. I seldom get to drink it, and it's one of my favorites." Her voice, as usual, was just slightly breathy. Kate knew Judy smoked too much.

Katherine poured in silence, then handed Judy's cup to her. "Let's sit in here," she said, leading the way back into the living room. It was cozy with all the shades drawn and warmly lit—not a striking room but a comfortable one, and one that reflected Katherine's personality. She had recently painted, and she liked the new ambiance of the warm beige. The walls were hung with varied pictures in frames that displayed the natural wood: a poster of a Mojave girl, from an exhibit of early-American photography she had once attended; a watercolor done by a friend from a photo of her own of shrimpers in harbor; a miniature of a Renaissance painting of a woman in a richly blue gown; a David Hamilton nude. Plants, records, and books made up most of the rest of the contents of the room. Kate chose her favorite, much-used chair and sipped her decaf while Judy stood indecisively eyeing a nondescript couch some distance from where Katherine now reposed. Just as she was about to surrender herself to it, she spied a large pillow in the corner.

"May I use that to sit on?" she asked hopefully, moving toward it.

Kate nodded, beginning to feel exasperated. Her quiet evening was ticking away, forever lost to her.

Judy placed the pillow directly in front of Katherine, about four feet away, and settled herself on it. She stared into the tea as if she were reading something of great importance in the dried blossoms floating there. Just as Katherine drew breath to break the silence, Judy cleared her throat to speak. She addressed the cup of tea, but the words, obviously, were meant for Katherine.

"Dr. Nikles, I came here tonight because I need to be honest with you about something."

Oh, lord, Kate thought. *Here it comes—another student confession about some perceived transgression.*

"Dr. Nikles," Judy repeated, lifting her head, her dark pupils striking directly into Kate's eyes, "I...am in love with you."

There was a dead silence in the room as two pairs of eyes locked, vision wavering and dimming, and two hearts pounded—one in astonishment, the other with fear and passion. One could have heard the snow fall, had anyone been listening.

Oh, my God! thought Kate. *What* can *she be saying?* A sick feeling, familiar but not experienced in many years, washed over her as she sat staring at the girl whose eyes remained locked on hers. And with that wave came the unbidden thought, *How could she know? How could she possibly know?*

She drew breath. "Judy," she began softly.

"Dr. Nikles, please—listen to what I have to say."

"Judy," Kate tried again.

Judy put down her cup and raised herself on her knees. Now she was all of two feet away, her face just slightly below Katherine's line of vision. She rested on her heels, her hands gripping her thighs as if for strength or control. *I wonder which,* Kate mused.

"This is something I have not come to lightly—something it has taken me a long time to acknowledge and accept, something I had to work at coming to you with," She paused, and Katherine tried again.

"But, Judy—"

"Please!" Judy interrupted, fixing her with a look. "This is not high school, and although you have been my instructor and I your student, I am an adult and can freely make my own choices. I know what I am about." She paused again, and this time Kate thought better of trying to stop hen "I *am* in love with you. You are always somewhere in the back of my awareness, a comforting presence, an exciting and tantalizing absence. I find myself drafting letters and poems to you when I'm changing classes or doing laundry or in the shower. I can't stop thinking about you." Her voice had steadied and quieted as she had gone on, more sure now of being allowed her say. Her eyes, bright and intense with passion, softened, and she seemed to turn inward, attending to herself and what she had to express. She knew Katherine was not going to get up and walk away.

In fact, Kate found herself rigidly holding her cup and considered the fact that it was not in pieces on the floor a remarkable example of her self-possession. As she listened to the growing surety in Judy's voice, she put the cup aside and willed herself to relax, sit back, and hear the young woman out. She folded her arms loosely across herself, again all too aware of her rather intimate apparel. As Judy's focus softened and became more vague, she found herself flicking her own eyes over Judy, noting the long, graceful fingers gripping ample thighs, allowing herself to see for the first time, really, the full breasts, and thinking, *Yes, she is a young woman.*

Kate knew, within herself, that she had been attracted to this young woman from the first day she had set eyes on her, nearly a year ago. Judy Baltierra, second from the top on her alphabetical roster, had walked into Katherine's English 306 class, 20th-Century American Writers, and sat right in front of her. From then on Kate had had a growing struggle to dampen her awareness of Judy, to maintain the usual student-teacher relationship, to eventually hide her feelings from herself. For having Judy in her class that semester had been mixed agony and pleasure: Judy was an excellent student, incisive and creative, with a flare for language and literature—a delight to any teacher—and yet, as the weeks had gone by, Katherine's initial attraction had strengthened to where she had felt it necessary to suppress her excitement at seeing Judy on campus, at hearing her voice on the phone when she called with questions about assignments, at watching her walk through the door at the beginning of every class. All in all, it had been with relief when the end of the term had come and she had known she would not see Judy during the summer.

The long hot months had dragged by, and Kate had convinced herself that she had forgotten about the young woman with the auburn hair and slightly freckled nose, who was within a fraction of Kate's own height but of a heavier build. Not beautiful by today's standards, Kate had once thought, likening her to a Rubens painting, but very attractive, with thick lashes over hazel eyes, which seemed always to have the spark of mischief flickering in them, and that wonderful hearty laugh that could bring a smile and her own answering laughter to Kate. In Kate's eyes, Judy was beautiful, and Kate knew she was connected to her somewhere down around her navel.

Suddenly she was aware that Judy was speaking directly to her again, seeking her with her gold-flecked eyes. She pulled herself back to the present, to what Judy was saying.

"I thought, last spring, that when I was out of your class and wouldn't see you anymore, I would get over my feelings about you. And I did manage to engross myself in my summer internship.

"But when I returned to campus in August to register for fall classes, it all came back, stronger than ever, and I knew that somehow I had to deal with all of this, not run away—that I couldn't pretend to myself that I could get over you anymore." Her eyes were focused and intent again, and Kate hung now on Judy's every word, mesmerized. "I decided to start seeing a counselor and talk about all this—"

Kate gasped involuntarily.

"It's OK. I'm not seeing anyone connected with school," she hastened to assure.

Kate felt herself breathe again. *Thank God, thank God, she's mature enough to recognize what that could've meant!*

Judy went on. "You would have no reason to know this, Dr. Nikles, but I've known since I was about 12 or 13 that I'm gay. I just sort of worked it all out for myself. So that wasn't the issue—the issue was what I was going to do about my feelings for you." She paused again, picked up her cup, and drank the rest of what Kate thought must have been, by now, piss-cold tea. Then she shifted and sank down on the pillow again, somehow managing to scoot it closer to Katherine as she did.

Kate felt trapped—she could not shift or draw back any far-ther and did not know that she cared to hear any more about Judy's counseling, either. She gambled. "More tea?" she asked and stood up, feeling safer.

Judy looked up at her, reproach warring with sympathy on her face. Kate guessed Judy knew she was having her own struggles just now. Judy dropped her gaze after a moment, mumbling, "No, thank you," as Kate edged toward the door.

"I believe I will," she tossed over her shoulder, praying as she went that Judy wouldn't follow her. In the relative priva-cy of the kitchen, she allowed herself to experience her own agitation, leaning against the bar and putting her head down for a moment. She tried to breathe easily and relax while the water heated. Then she retreated to the bathroom. As she washed her hands she examined herself in the mirror, at-tempting to ascertain that what she was wearing was neither suggestive nor seductive. She debated changing, or raking her hair down, but knew that was just too absurd. *What has hap-pened has had nothing to do with nightclothes!* she told herself, gazing ruefully at her reflection.

When she returned she noticed Judy had moved back a lit-tle, but she contrived to sit sideways in the chair anyway, try-ing to put yet more space between them. She waited for Judy to begin again, knowing that she would take up the conver-sation unasked.

Judy toyed with a loose thread on the pillow before she began to speak, but when she did her full attention was centered on Katherine. Kate found it very disconcerting. "So I've spent the past 2½ months looking at my feelings about you and have come to some important awarenesses."

When she paused Katherine interjected a diverting question. "Who've you been seeing?" she flung over her coffee

Judy shot back a look that said, *I'm not falling for* that *one!* "Karen Wise," she replied sharply. Then, amending carelessly, "Know her?"

Kate fancied that she had paled noticeably. "Yes," she murmured, sipping her decaf. If Judy only knew what Kate knew! Kate and Karen had once been lovers—a long time ago, but still… She was relieved that Judy seemed to have paid very little attention to her reply—she was gathering herself to move on. *How intent she is!* Kate thought.

"Well, I found out that *some*"—she emphasized it heavily—"of my stuff about you has to do with my mother."

Kate flinched. *Her mother! Jesus Christ, her mother? We're only 15 years apart! What was a 15-year difference when I was Judy's age?* she asked herself and could not remember. She was amazed that she seemed to convey a sense of calmness to Judy when inwardly she was feeling as if she were losing it.

"But," Judy emphasized further, and then her voice softened again, "I also got it quite clear that I love you." That direct gaze—which Kate had found occasionally unnerving from the first row of a classroom was fixed on her again, and Kate felt compelled to respond.

"Judy," she broached, half expecting to be cut off again, "Judy, do you even *begin* to realize what you're saying?" She acknowledged the look on Judy's face with a change of direction. "All right, you do realize at least *some* of what you're saying? But, Judy, you hardly know me. How can you possibly think you're in love with me? Judy—" She broke off, at a loss for words in the face of the determined expression the other woman wore.

They sat and stared at one another for a moment—Judy with the coolness of clarity and resolve after puzzling through a confusion and Katherine with a blend of incredulity and pleading on her face and in her eyes. Abruptly, but not hurriedly, Judy got to her knees again, only this time she was inches away from where Katherine sat shrinking into her chair.

"Katherine," she said in a near whisper, "I want you. I love you and I want you and that is that." Her eyes bored into Katherine's, and Kate realized the pupil dilation she had observed earlier had nothing to do with drugs—it was quite simply caused by passion. She felt her heart leap into her throat and knew she must get away. But how? Judy's hands were on the arms of her chair, her body blocking escape.

She sat forward, intending to push past the other woman if necessary, but Judy gave way with one arm. Katherine struggled to her feet and turned to Judy, who remained half crouched in front of the chair. "Judy, please," she began again. "You can't possibly think that I could get involved with you—" She took another tack. "What does Karen think of all this?" She knew she was grabbing at straws, but she felt she had to try to regain her space and her composure. *How could I have let myself in for this?* she questioned silently.

Judy stood and faced her squarely from a foot away. "Karen thinks I need to work this out with you, on my own, and in person...which is why I'm here tonight," she added, moving a bit closer.

Kate found herself turning and stepping away, but as she did so she decided she was not going to give any further ground. She sighed and drew herself into her center "All right, Judy, what if I said I am not interested in you, not interested in being involved with you?"

Judy stepped toward her again but less aggressively. "I think it would be a lie, Katherine," she replied quietly, her voice holding a quality that was almost a sadness.

Katherine met her look, felt herself being searched, knew the truth lay just below the surface. "Judy, you are—I am—there are 15 *years* between us!" Judy made no reply, merely continued her unwavering appraisal. Katherine stepped toward her, but she gave no ground either.

"Judy, we can't—it just won't work. There are too many differences."

"How can you know that without trying?" came the even reply.

As Kate heard the response to her question, she found her hands resting on the other woman's shoulders and wondered how they got there, but she did not withdraw. Instead she gripped harder, as if by the pressure of her hands she could force some awareness—or acceptance. "What makes you think I could love you or want to be with you?" She tried to be gentle with her words. Nonetheless, she saw Judy flinch.

"You've loved other women," Judy said softly, neither a statement nor a question, but a tentative framing of reality.

Katherine nodded, having long ago given up any thought of pretense. "Yes, I have," she acknowledged quietly, "but that doesn't mean—" She broke off as Judy's hands found her shoulders, and Judy stepped forward so that they were nearly touching. Kate could feel the space between them reverberating. Her heart was pounding madly in her chest, and she heard a roaring in her ears. *Dear God,* she thought, *if she doesn't stop—*

Judy kissed her, and Kate's heart stopped. She sucked in air as Judy released her, her hands involuntarily tightening on the other's shoulders. "Oh, Judy," she rasped, her throat aching and throbbing with suppressed words and feelings. Again their eyes met, and this time their gazes never wavered as Judy leaned toward her until their lips joined in another kiss

Kate felt all the months of reserve and self-discipline melt away under Judy's onslaught. She knew that with one more kiss, she would give in to the wanting she had struggled to ignore for so long. Apparently, Judy knew it too, for as she moved to kiss her yet a third time, she closed that last inch and put her arms around the woman *she* had been wanting for very nearly as long as Katherine had wanted her. They stood together in deep embrace, and Katherine's breath grew short, the burning spreading from where Judy's lips were on hers down into her belly. She pulled away, eyeing Judy with a new expression: a grudging pleasure in being won over.

"Well," she remarked huskily, "are we just going to stand here?"

"No, we're not," Judy replied evenly. With her eyes, she gave the victory back. "Lead on."

Katherine took her hand, turning out lamps as they went, and led her into the bedroom. It, too, was simple, except for the bookcase in the corner, where Katherine's gay and lesbian books reposed, along with her *Star Trek* books, a plant, a small print of Maxfield Parrish's *Ecstasy,* and a picture of Wonder

Woman. Judy took them in at a glance, much more intent on the woman in front of her as she lit a candle by the bed and turned out the electric lamp.

Katherine pulled back the bedcovers and then turned to Judy, slipping the pins from her shoulder-length sandy blond hair and shaking it out in one deft movement. Judy sighed softly through her teeth and reached to touch the thick cascade. "It's beautiful," she whispered. "You're beautiful." *At last,* her eyes sang, *at last I can say it!* And Kate heard the song and knew her own lay within. She opened her robe, the last of her barriers, and stood before Judy, waiting for her to begin to undress. But Judy was suddenly shy again, so Kate unbuttoned the sweater and jeans and kissed her, whispering breathily, "Take them off."

She shed her robe and stood in her gown—dark blue, plain, elegant. When Judy remained in her underwear and socks, Kate chuckled softly, stepping behind her to undo the bra and help with the panties and socks. Naked, Judy turned to Kate and once again embraced her. It was fire, through the silky fabric, their nipples erect and brushing. Kate momentarily stayed the renewed heat: "Judy, are you sure?" she whispered.

In answer, Judy knelt and began to kiss and caress her through the gown, and Kate felt her knees grow weak. She sat on the bed, stroking the auburn head and the strong back as Judy began to become acquainted with Katherine's body. Kate felt the moisture between her legs soaking her gown before Judy's mouth ever found its way under the long skirt. She groaned in pleasure and lay back. Judy wrapped her arm around Katherine's hips and lifted her onto the bed, then was above her, her full breasts hanging, rubbing on Katherine's breasts, belly, and clitoris. She pushed the gown up, and Katherine raised herself and slipped it off. She felt Judy's wetness on her thighs and hips and belly. Judy was an expert lover, and she soon had Kate dangling on the edge of an orgasm. As if sensing this she slowed her motions and pulled away a little. Katherine opened her eyes to find the gold-flecked ones smiling at her.

"Oh, Judy, if you knew how long, how many times I tried *not* to think of this!" They laughed together, and Judy slid off Kate, pulling her over her.

"Make love to me," she invoked.

As she matched Judy's skill with her fingers, tongue, lips, and body, Kate found in herself an intensity she had thought no longer possible for her. Together they climbed, reaching one peak after another, yet saving the crashing descent until the last possible moment. And it came when Judy's eager mouth found Kate's breasts as she arched backward, her clitoris pressed against Judy's belly, her leg in Judy's crotch, her fingers milking Judy's nipple. "Oh, God!" Kate cried, finally giving herself to Judy as their orgasms seized them, carrying them on succeeding waves of pleasure until their spent bodies came to rest against one another and quiet settled over the room.

"Merry Christmas, Katherine," Judy murmured through a sleepy smile, planting a gentle good-night kiss against her cheek.

Kate lay holding her, their bodies entwined in total repose. *Well, it must be Christmas Eve by now,* she thought, and a glance at the clock told her it was so. There was a stillness in her she had not known for a long time. She recognized it as the stillness of completion and did not know how long it would last. But as she heard Judy's breathing slide into the rhythms of sleep, she thought, *Yes, sleep, love—your work here tonight is done, and you deserve to rest.*

She sighed, a soft sound in the silent room. *And my work has only begun.* Her mind drifted off to the previous late-summer day when she had seen Judy walking across campus—had picked her out of a crowd, from a block away—and felt her heart jump and her mind clamp down on it, denying herself the right to look with longing at the young woman whom she had not seen all summer. Because she had never really allowed herself to think she might become involved with Judy sexually, she had never thought ahead to this moment. Now she knew she must consider many things, and well.

Thank God she has only one more semester of school. At least, after that, if we're still seeing each other, there won't be that pressure on our relationship.

If we're still seeing each other, she said to herself. *Do I want to be?* she asked with her customary inner honesty. *Yes,* came the singing reply. *Oh, yes!*

Judy stirred in her sleep and snuggled closer. Kate looked at her and momentarily knew how young and fresh a thing she held in her arms, nuzzling near her breast. She felt a rush of tenderness wash over her, then another question: *Am I using her youth and her wanting of me to keep me from feeling old?* She absently stroked Judy's cheek, seeing her sleeping smile at the touch. *Oh, my dear, dear Judy!* Kate bathed in the tide of feelings again and hugged her closer. She knew right now she did not have the answer to her second question. She knew she felt and believed the 15-year age difference was signifi-cant, and yet, did age matter more than gender? She pondered

this, aware that she believed that gender was not the issue between lovers, but rather that they loved, truly, healthily. *Yes,*
she decided, *perhaps it does matter—in a different way. People
today are more accepting of same-sex relationships than they were
when I was Judy's age. But that only frees people to bond without
regard for gender. In this culture, in this day and time, 15 years,
when you're on the underside of 30, makes a big difference. There's
so much growing and changing to go through during those years between 12 and 30—I've already done all that. What if, as she grows
older and changes, she discovers she doesn't want me any more?
What if we didn't fit any more? What if at 30 she looks at a 45-
year-old woman and is repulsed?* Kate felt the hurt well up within her as she contemplated loss and rejection. She knew it was
one of her deepest wounds, that she had felt it at the outset of
her life, that being "different" had reinforced it, that her family had tried their best to mold her over. *And yet,* she told herself, *if this is what I really want, do I not treat myself the same way
I've been treated by denying myself what there may be in this for me
now?*

She considered the Judy who had come to her tonight and
found what she had always found: the clear, inquisitive, focused mind, seeking to apprehend the intangible, to grasp the
factual, to deal honestly with herself and the world around
her; a young adult with ideals that had taken some tarnishing
but to which she was still committed, which she still sought
to realize; the elf hiding within those mischievous eyes, with
that ready laughter and mocking humor, which, mostly, she
turned on herself; and, at the end of that last term, there had
been something more: a deference to her, Kate, on a level
that was unspoken in the student–teacher context. Could it

have been the awareness, then, of what she had come to mean to Judy? Kate supposed it could have been; she knew without question now that Judy was in love with her, and she had to acknowledge to herself tonight that there was much, much more in her than sexual desire for Judy.

She came back to the question: Could it last? And she did not know. *But,* she wondered, *does anyone know? Don't all people, gay or straight, take on faith that it will last and begin their lives together in that way? Marriage is no more than a legal institution today—and there are no guarantees.*

She untangled herself and turned on her side, Judy's arm still about her. She took Judy's hand and tucked it between her breasts, backing into Judy's belly, savoring the closeness. *Oh, woman,* she thought, squeezing that hand, *how I've loved you from afar. Can it possibly be what you want—what I want? Can I accept the "now," without jumping ahead into the future?*

Tomorrow, she thought. *Tomorrow we'll talk about this.* She snuggled deeper into the embrace, then realized she must extinguish the candle. As she leaned toward it one of the books on the *Star Trek* shelf caught her eye and she paused. She thought of Kirk and Spock and crew, and knew one reason she had made them all a part of her life was that they always tried—against all odds—to achieve their highest aspirations, while maintaining their deepest integrity. *All right, you guys,* she spoke to them mentally, *I'll try too!* Wonder Woman flashed a smile at her as she blew out the flame.

Tomorrow, she repeated as she sank back into Judy's sleeping embrace. *Tomorrow we'll talk.*

Shine

by Stephanie Rosenbaum

"The queen," Johnny says, turning over a card. "She's the one you gotta watch for, Mink. Bust your balls every time."

Johnny's trying to teach me to play poker, but so far she says I'm a slow learner. I'm a Libra, see, and we're not big on games of chance. We know too much about the trials of tempting fate.

Lately, though, I haven't been doing too much tempting—of fate or anything else. See, I'm not the kind of girl you'd picture to have a name like Mink. Johnny's girlfriend, Vikki—now that girl could be a Mink. Nails, lips, curves you could get shipwrecked on; Vikki doesn't walk so much as ooze. Her bones just get all liquidy, and she floats into a room like a smoke ring.

Me, I'm small and dark, with skinny wrists and a small, pointed cat's face. My real name's Delilah, and believe it or not my brother's name is Sam. Back in the early '70s when I was born, my parents were on a back-to-the-land trip, living in this Jewish commune in upstate New York. It was considered very righteous to give all the babies Hebrew names, but my parents just went biblical instead. Luckily, my last name is Minkowitz, so I've been called Mink as long as I can remember. I don't mind, actually; it saved me a lifetime of haircut jokes, and every once in a while I try to live up to it. But growing up with Sam, my Uncle Max who lived upstairs, and a mother whose idea of hell was having to get out of her gardening clothes, I'm not exactly up on the fine points of femininity. I'm not built to be looked at. That's a role for the Vikkis of the world, not me.

Johnny's built to be looked at but in a different way. She wears her coppery hair short on the sides and spiked up on top, although sometimes she doesn't bother to gel it stiff, and then her head looks close-cropped and velvety. She has that peachy skin that lucky Irish girls get, just this side of pink, with only a few freckles. But the best part about Johnny is her size. Johnny has some meat on her bones, and those bones are generous. She doesn't apologize for taking up space. In fact, she swaggers, especially when she's decked out in cowboy boots and the kind of pale blue ruffled tuxedo shirts popular with unsuccessful lounge singers in the mid '70s.

Right now she's wearing her favorite boots, black and shiny, with a hand of cards—hearts, naturally—fanned out in white and red leather across each side. She's drinking a beer and leaning across the kitchen table to riffle through the cards spread face up between us. I'm drinking iced tea and chewing on the ice. I usually drink bourbon, but I don't want to scare anyone. Outbutching her would be a bad idea, I think.

Johnny's crowd divides pretty evenly along butch/femme lines. Not that they all have always paired up with their opposite; there's always a couple who likes the boy-boy thing or the girlie girls who don't mind getting two shades of lipstick all mixed up. I like what I've seen of her friends: They have style, and although they take their identities to heart, they have a sense of humor about the whole thing. One girl even has a dog collar with a little bone hanging off it that reads BUTCH on one side and FEMME on the other. She flips it around depending on her mood.

But somehow I always feel like the kid sister around them, little Skipper to a roomful of Kens and Barbies. Like today, for example: I was wearing an old green schoolgirl kilt that was unraveling along the edge, a T-shirt that had shrunk, and a dark blue sweater that had stretched. And I don't go to Victoria's Secret, OK? I wear white cotton underpants, and I wear them till the elastic stretches out and I can't keep them up around my hips anymore. Vikki wears tiny black lace thongs, I'm sure of it.

But Vikki's not here and Johnny is. Or rather, I am, since we're in the kitchen of the home Johnny's house-sitting this week, taking care of the plants and the five-month-old puppy belonging to the two guys who run the landscaping business where she works.

In front of me Johnny's gathering up the cards. Her fingers wrap around the red-and-black pile and shuffle, cutting and recutting the deck better than any blackjack dealer. Johnny used to play blackjack—not professionally, she'll tell you, but for profit. The cards are snapping and riffling, and I can't seem to take my eyes off Johnny's hands. Her palms are wide, and her fingers are long, with nails cut short. There's a callus on each thumb from the yard work she does, and when I look at them my own hands seem to develop a mind of their own. But quickly I yank my hands back under the table, trapping them under my thighs before Johnny can notice anything.

"OK, we're gonna try five-card stud. That's the basic game. Now, the first rule of poker is: If you have nothing, fold. But if you have something—anything—then milk the other players for everything they're worth. Remember that. Don't bet unless you're willing to soak your partners for every penny they've got. If you can't take money from your friends, then don't play. Or just play for chips." She shrugs. "But chips are for pussies."

My hands are working their way up around my knees again. I slide my chair back to get some more ice. Yes, it's true: I have a big Vegas-size crush on Johnny. Every time she pins those turquoise eyes on me, my spine vibrates and I'm acutely aware of every inch of her. Especially her breasts. She carries them carelessly, not like she's shy but like she's just cool with them. Like, yeah, she has this gorgeous chest and she knows it, but she's not going to make any big deal about it. At least that's how I read her. Still, it's hopeless. She has Vikki, who looks like Rita Hayworth in thigh-high boots. Why would Johnny need to look at me?

The worst part about this crush is that I haven't got a clue about what to do. What will get her to treat me like anything besides a kid brother? I don't consider myself butch, exactly, but it seems like Johnny does, punching me on the arm like she does with her other butch buddies, advising me about boxer shorts and motorcycles, and even, like tonight, going out of her way to teach me things she thinks I ought to know.

That's what we're doing tonight: Johnny and five other women play a regular Thursday poker game, and I'm being groomed to join them. Like I said, I'm not much of a card player, and gambling is not my forte. Still, this is the first time Johnny has asked me over. She could be teaching me how to swallow fire or walk on a bed of nails; I don't care as long as we're alone together, in private. So far, being across Roy and Bob's kitchen table is much worse for my cool than seeing her and all her friends in a crowded bar. Every minute is like wobbling a loose tooth around with your tongue. It hurts, but you don't exactly want to quit, either.

I sit back down and start chewing on my straw. Johnny flips the cap off another beer. We've gone through the various merits of the royal flush, the royal straight, and both the inside and outside straight.

"See, here you've got a four, a five, a seven, and an eight. Alls you need is a six to make an inside straight, which is pretty good." Even though I've had nothing to do with picking the cards in my hand, I'm impressed with my luck. "Except there's only a 4-in-52 chance that a six is going to turn up in your hand when you draw again." Oh, I hadn't thought of it like that. "Now, if you were to do an outside straight, looking for a three as well as a six, then you'd double your chances." She's looking straight at me as she says this, and one hand is rubbing at a spot on her T-shirt, just at the place where the kitchen table meets her ribs.

"What about bluffing?" I ask her, looking right back. "Isn't that the big thing in poker?"

"The way you bluff depends on who you're playing with. Everyone's got their own way of protecting what they've got and letting slip just what they're really holding. You play long enough, you can read that easy. The rest you'll just have to pick up by doing it. So let's play." She shuffles the cards again, the red and black shuddering through her fingers with a snap. "Poker's not really good with just two, but you won't re-member any of this unless you play. Here, you deal. Re-member, dealer chooses the game." She slides the pack across the table.

OK, Mink, I say to myself. *Let's see if you can bluff through this one.* I push my glasses back up. I say out loud, "Seven-card stud. Three rounds." She nods and lifts her beer for another swallow. I deal. Three up, one down.

I glance through my hand. An ace down, a two, another two, and a ten up. "What are you betting?" I ask Johnny. There are no chips on the table. My pockets are empty. John-ny keeps her eyes on her cards, carefully rearranging her three cards, frowning, then moving one card carefully from one side to the other. "Got any money?" she asks, and for a sud-den moment I think she's going to offer to lend me a hand-ful of change. But Johnny's a gambler, and gamblers don't bet against their own cash.

I shake my head. There's a long pause. My fingers are un-raveling the edge of my skirt.

"Guess we'll just have to play for strip." For a second I don't think I've heard her right. Strip? Strip poker? It's so silly, so frat partyish. But then I catch her cool gaze and un-derstand about bluffing. *Is she testing me, seeing what I'll risk, what kind of guts I have? It can't be because maybe, just maybe, she wants to see me naked.* I don't want to think about that. Some-how, in all my fantasies about Johnny, my being naked—and looked at—is kind of glossed over. It's not that I want her to like me only for my mind or anything. It's just that scrutiny makes me nervous.

"Sure," I agree. "And the winner? What does she get?"

"Anything she wants," Johnny answers, fingering the queen of spades lying faceup in front of her.

"It's a deal." I look down at my ace of hearts, then over at her queen. Aces are higher than kings, or they can be lower than twos. It just depends on what you need in your hand.

"I win this round, you take off your sweater," she says. Easy. I look at my ace again, then back at her. "And if I win, you take off your shirt," I answer. She's wearing a faded blue work shirt with the sleeves cut off and pearl snaps that gap slightly in the middle. I deal. One up, one down. A king for me, a ten for her.

She takes another pull off her beer and glances over at the clock, looking rattled. This is a girl who's used to winning. But this betting was her idea, and she can't chicken out now without looking coy or, worse, a poor sport.

Toughness wins out, and she unsnaps the first little square white button, taking her own sweet time. Now I know why guys will spend their whole paycheck, dollar by dollar, just to see some woman take off her clothes. I've never watched any-thing so intensely in my life. When she gets to the last snap, I stop breathing. Underneath she's wearing a man's white ribbed undershirt, but no man, not even Marlon Brando in *A Streetcar Named Desire*, ever filled out an undershirt like she does. She's not wearing a bra. Mangos, melons, pomegranates: My mind is a cascading tumble of tropical fruits, and she is ripe for the pick-ing. I want to bounce their taut weight in my hands, feel her warmth, her heart beating faster, brush my lips against the apricot skin at the base of her rounded throat. I want to twist the thin fabric of that undershirt harder and harder, pulling it into a tight knot between her breasts, watching how her nipples prod through the stretched cloth. I want to yank that knot hard and slam her against me, my teeth against her lips, my hand gripping her back. I want to drive every thought of Vikki right out of her head, at least for as long as it takes.

Oblivious to the effects her magnificent butch breasts are having on me, Johnny bets again. "Your sweater—and your shirt." I raise one eyebrow. What cards is she holding? There's no way to tell; you can't count cards when you're only playing with two.

"Your belt," I counter. Now it's her turn to consider my motives. Her pants—black denim Ben Davises—aren't going to fall off if she unbuckles her belt. In fact, they won't budge. If I really wanted to get an up-close-and-personal view of her boxer shorts, getting that belt off won't do it, and she looks relieved. She won't be breaking her stone stance over a hand of cards, that's for sure.

What she doesn't know is that I have a terrible, terrible hand. A couple of twos, a seven, and a ten. Nothing matches; even the pair is practically worthless. But I've got a king down, and now I've got an ace down as well.

I deal Johnny her last card. She gets a six. I get a seven. She reaches for her belt. The kitchen is so quiet I can hear the space between the ticks of the clock. The leather slips against the denim, making a sound like water. She rolls the leather strap up in her hand and places it on the table between us. It's warm from her, so lately pressed up against her back, her stomach, the generous curve of her waist.

Last bet, but it's not for clothing this time. I'm still fully dressed. Johnny's breasts are rising and falling, a little faster than they were five minutes ago. A faint line of sweat beads her upper lip. One at a time I lay my cards down. A seven of clubs. A ten of hearts. A couple of twos. A four of clubs. The king of spades. The ace of hearts. Johnny rubs her hand across her mouth. She lays her cards down. A royal flush. The jack of hearts. The queen of spades. Johnny has beat me, but good.

She looks at my cards. She looks at her cards. I look into the dark hollow between her breasts across the table. Johnny gets up and puts her beer bottle on the counter. She puts my iced glass next to it. Then she walks back a few steps until she's leaning up against the stove. She crosses her arms over her chest. She looks at me. I stop breathing again. "Get up on the table," she says.

I don't make her ask me twice. I pull her chair out away from the table, pushing it off to the side. I hoist myself up on the edge of the table where her breasts had been resting just a minute ago and face her across the wide expanse of black and white floor tiles. White, black, white, black, white. Twice. She's ten tiles away. It feels very far. The clock ticks, then ticks again. My breath is still caught in my chest.

"Now," and her voice falls into the silence of the kitchen like a stone sunk into a still river, "spread your legs."

What game is this? Here is Johnny and here I am, but she isn't kissing me or wrapping me up in her arms or getting into any of the sweaty tangles I've been imagining in my teenage make-out fantasies. She isn't even near me. The only thing on me is the one thing I don't want: her eyes, running over me inch by inch. Is this some kind of poker game initiation? I can't quite imagine her telling Jesse or Lee or C.J. to spread their legs for her, though. They'd deck her first. I want to do something with Johnny—I want it desperately—but what I really need to know is just what she wants to do to me. *What does she want? A boy? A girl? Someone to flex her muscles over?*

There's only one way to find out. My knees open up a few inches. It's not enough. She keeps up that unsmiling stare until my knees are splayed open, pressed flat up against the edge of the table on both sides. She smiles at me then, just a flicker of teeth; then her eyes drop from my face to travel down my body to rest on the hem of my skirt hanging unevenly over my thighs. I hate her doing this, and she knows it. "Pull up your skirt," she says, and her voice is cool, even. She's in control. She doesn't really care; it's all one to her whether or not she gets to look up my skirt. But she's got her belt back in her hands, snapping it taut, then unrolling it again to dangle along her leg. I tuck the hem of my skirt into my waistband. Her eyes slip down to the triangle of white cotton between my legs, and she sucks her breath in sharply.

"Baby butch, my ass," she says. "That's what Vikki and all the girls say about you, you know. Cute little baby dyke. 'Teach her a few things for us, Johnny. Give her a little butch training, and we'll do the rest,'" she says, mocking the femmes of her group, who are always lamenting the lack of what they called "good" butches. "But I think that would be a waste of your talents. Talents you don't even know you have." Her eyes come up to my face again, and for a second her tough-girl stance drops completely. Her eyes blaze out blue as the pilot light burning in the stove behind her, and suddenly I get it: It's Christmas morning, and I'm the biggest box under the tree.

"Now, little girl," she says, and this time her voice is all butter and honey, the voice of a stranger who rolls down the window of his big air-conditioned car and holds out a handful of licorice and lollipops and all-day suckers. "Pull down your panties for me."

My cheeks burning, I lean down and pull the white panties down, letting them slide over one foot to lie in a heap in the center of a black tile, my knees still wide open to her steady gaze. The tip of her tongue flicks out, and she licks her lips, just a little. *Which of us is bluffing? Does she know what comes next? Do I? An ace, a queen, a ten. Her draw.*

"W-e-e-ell," and I can hear her Texas roots all of a sudden. "So pretty," she says, and I flush. I don't care if she's just playing out some fantasy script of her own; no one ever calls me pretty, and hearing her say it, especially in that drawl, hits me harder than a double shot of bourbon. My throat stings, and if my knees weren't already pressed against the edges of the table, I'd be clenching them together to keep my legs from shaking.

Johnny takes a step closer. "So pretty," she repeats, and I bite the inside of my lips.

Sucker, I tell myself furiously. *Don't be such a sap, Mink.* But it doesn't do a lick of good. "Might as well be hung for a sheep as for a lamb," my uncle used to say, just as he was about to do something bound to get him in hot water with my mom. If you're going to get yourself into trouble, he taught me, you might as well have as much fun as possible getting there.

I lean back on my hands and look Johnny deep into her baby blues. She holds my gaze for a second, then takes another step closer.

"Such a pretty little girl," her voice dropping to a breath. "With such a pretty little pussy. Why don't you show me what you've got there, baby?" Half commanding, half cajoling. The belt wriggles across her palm like a snake. "Let me see you touch yourself." My skin crawls around the back of my scalp. I have never done this for anyone, not in the heat of passion, not with anybody.

When I don't respond she takes another step. "Can't you do that for me, baby? No?" Her voice is still low. She folds her arms again. "Then I guess I'll have to do it myself." And in one swift step she is standing in front of me and the belt is wrapped around my wrists, tight, the buckle jabbing hard edges into my thin skin. Johnny's hand is grabbing my hair, yanking my head back. "Is that what you want, baby girl? 'Cause that's what you're gonna get."

My eyes are watering as she twists a handful of hair between her fingers, and I lean my head back into her hand, submitting not out of fear but desire.

Keeping her hand wrapped around my hair, she lets the other slide down the side of my cheek, across my lips, tracing the pointed edge of my jawline, sinking from just beneath my ear, down my neck, to rest on the damp skin stretched over the hollows of my collarbones. Then lower to unbutton my sweater.

I can see the reddish curve of her eyebrows, almost invisible against her flushed skin, the three silver rings encircling the curve of her ear. She is so close I smell the tobacco on her fingers, the honeysuckle in her shampoo.

Then finally, finally, she puts her hand on me. Or more accurately, her fingertips. The tips of her fingers brush up and along my leg, following the line of my thigh to pause just before the triangle of dark silky hair. She turns her hand so her knuckles brush so lightly against me. Then again, back and forth, soft as a handful of feathers. Her mouth is inches from mine, but she's not looking at me. My breath is coming choppy and faster, and every time she grazes my skin it's like a little electric shock, like the tiny crackle of static electricity that shoots up your arm when you go from touching a doorknob to someone's fuzzy sweater. Snap. Snap. I'm breathing so fast, the room is starting to go black and fuzzy at the edges, and finally I have to, I have to, and my voice tears out the back of my throat, and I say, "Johnny, kiss me." And she does.

She kisses me wet and sweet and sloppy, and I want to sink into it, to roll around in her kiss as if it were molasses. "Baby," she says, when I finally let her come up for air. "Baby," she says like a caress, but her eyes are wicked again. "Baby needs a little attention, doesn't she?" and she leans in to kiss me again, harder this time, pushing her tongue into my mouth.

Each movement of her tongue sends a quiver of heat down my body, a spark of heat down between my legs, and then her hand is slipping between my legs again, tracing the curve of my thigh, flickering at the edge of my pussy, beginning to stroke, gently at first, teasing at the opening, rubbing her knuckles to and fro while with her other hand she is pinching my nipple softly, twisting ever so slightly, then twisting a little harder, and with each twist my clit jumps under her hand.

She pulls up my shirt, ducking her head to take my whole breast into her mouth; she is sucking and licking, teasing my nipple with the edge of her teeth, pulling and sucking, while her fingers are still playing around the outside of my pussy, sliding up and down, easing between the lips.

"So wet," Johnny whispers, lifting her mouth from my breast. "Aching for it. Baby needs a good fuck, doesn't she." It's a statement she's making, not a question, but still she doesn't fuck me; she keeps touching me, my breasts, my thighs, my stomach, till just when I'm ready to blow her top cool, she slides two fingers into my cunt, smooth and easy but not slow. I don't want slow. I want fast, I want rough, I want a lot of attention. "Velvet," Johnny murmurs. "Silk," and she slides her hand back and then in deep, again and again. "More?" She breathes, and I breathe back, "More." I can't tell how many fingers she's got inside me now, just the rhythm, pushing down against her hand, the slippery filling and emptying.

But it isn't enough. I open my eyes and look up at her, at her arm pumping in and out, sweat beading again on her lip and around her hairline. "Please," I whisper, "please." It's like having to touch myself in front of her, only worse, because I can't do without it. "I want, I want, I want your whole hand inside me," I whisper, my eyes closed.

Then I feel her breath hot on my cheek and then her lips on mine, kissing me, flooding my heart. "Give it to me, baby girl. Give it up to me," she is saying, and I lie back feeling the weight of her body pushing against me, the whole power of her behind that solid arm, the burning flush of my cunt swelling around her hand as she rolls her fist around the mouth of my cunt, rolling it wet and slick as she slides inside and as I breathe, deep and deliberate, willing my body to open up for her, take her in, be filled.

A wincing shard of pain. I suck in a sharp breath and she stops, retreating. We hang there for a minute, joined, my feet pushing against the edge of the table. I breathe again, and there's a rush like water gushing down to fill a dry streambed after a summer of drought, and I reach down and feel her slippery wrist at the mouth of my cunt. Her whole hand is buried inside me, so deep, and I put my hand on my stomach to feel the lumpy shape of it down low. Slowly, she starts rocking her hand from side to side, just the smallest bit, and I feel waves rolling through my body, waves of heaviness and sensation. I am impaled, pinioned, my whole body wrapped around her fist.

"Oh, girl," she is moaning now, caught between wonder and amazement. "Delilah, what a girl you are," and I can't even think of answering because my head is floating somewhere up near the ceiling, up near the lazily turning fan and the dim glow of the yellow light making a sparkling copper halo around Johnny's head. With her other hand Johnny starts rubbing her thumb in circles over my clit. It's like being in a forest fire and a flood at the same time, and I think, *If I come like this, I'll die.* Which is, of course, just what Johnny wants, and she doesn't stop with either hand, and I can feel the flames of her fingers licking around my clit while her other hand sinks deep inside me, like metal, heavy and molten, until all the flames come together and I slam my hips up against her over and over until everything explodes. A volcano, a rocket. It's like that. There's no other way to describe it.

Later, much later, I turn over and look at Johnny. She is a hump of blankets next to me, deep in the sleep of the righteous and the just. Across the room daylight is glowing at the edges of the dark green shades. Softly, so as not to wake anyone, I slide out from under the sheet. Then, putting one bare foot lightly, carefully in front of the other, I walk down the hall and begin—with slow, tender strokes—to polish the table.

Picking Up Daddy

by Robin Sweeney

"You will know me, boy, by the way I cut through the crowd, like an animal tracking its prey, until I find you and make you mine."

That's what Griffin's latest E-mail said before she got on the plane in Philadelphia and came to claim me, a continent away, in San Francisco.

I stood waiting outside the gates of United Airlines. The collar she had sent me was in my right rear pocket, my boots polished, my jockstrap holding my packing dick in place, just like Daddy told me. My online daddy was coming to make me her boy, and I was going to pass out from anticipation.

Griffin had found me my first night online, and she spoiled me for all other cybersex and online cruising. Hell, she spoiled me for most in-person sex and cruising too.

It was a complete accident that she was able to find me. My first night wandering around the possibilities of America Online, barely computer literate, I found the gay message area. There I found the Leather Women board, and I had posted an ad:

> Jaded boy looking for other boys to play with, although her heart still would belong to Daddy, if she'd show up already. Not into fakes or pretending. Looking for a real connection. I'm a sick fuck into most kinks, who likes to pitch as well as catch, who is looking...

Turns out that *sick fuck* was a little too much for the family standards of AOL. (The pitching and catching part was apparently OK, though.) The online monitors who pull "objectionable" ads deleted my post, and I was certain no one would see it.

Griffin had seen it, though. In that window of opportunity between posting and pulling, Griffin read my ad and decided to respond.

"Fairly presumptuous, aren't you, boy?" her first subject line to me read.

Holy shit, I thought. *It worked.*

"You sound like the sort of lost boy who starts acting loud and tough to try to scare away the noises in the dark. You've probably started topping the girls in town, maybe even being someone's daddy, in an attempt to get your needs met. After all, if you can't get what you want, you might as well make someone else's fantasy come true, right? That's not working, or you wouldn't be putting personals online.

"I am willing to allow you to write me, if you lose the poor attitude and present yourself properly. If you are not capable of this, or are not interested, you need not respond. Otherwise you have 24 hours, boy. Yours truly—Griffin."

I was a newbie online, but I had been around the block as far as women go. I wanted a daddy, badly, but I hadn't found one. I dated a lot and had flings that I really enjoyed, but I always ended up topping my girlfriends. Griffin had pegged me right. I had been doing S/M for a while and had gotten a fair bit of experience. The type I like—women who look like 16-year-old boys—tend to be novices. I liked playing with them just fine, but having to explain to somebody how to tie my wrists to the bed just didn't inspire me to bottom.

Also, like most people I met, I was afraid of getting what I wanted. I didn't like to give it up to just anybody who asked. Daddies were supposed to know how to take a boy down. Most of the ones I had met weren't up to the follow-through I craved. I didn't want just to be submissive; I wanted to be told how to behave.

That's exactly what Griffin did. I checked her profile:

Griffin. Also known as Sir.

Female, Single.

Macintosh Powerbook 145.

Occupation: Student, cook, and daddy top.

Likes leather, dykes who are boys, and taming the untamable.

Quote: "Come closer. I won't bite…until you ask me nicely."

I wrote back. I had no idea of how she wanted me to present myself, much less how to do it in writing. If we were at a party, or a bar, I'd bring her a drink, be respectful, and call her Sir. How was I supposed to do that online?

"Good evening, Sir. I appreciate your letter to me and hope that you find my response timely. I am interested in learning more of what interests you in a boy. True, I haven't found many people I want to submit to, but I try to remain open to the possibilities.

"Sir, I apologize if my ad was too brazen. I never expected an answer, much less from someone who was going to give me an opportunity to present myself properly. Please, Sir, would you tell me exactly how you would have me present myself? Respectfully yours—Jay."

Twelve hours later my computer "said" to me, in a way that was grammatically incorrect but delightfully enthusiastic, "You've got mail."

"On your knees, boy," it started, "is how I would expect you to present yourself to me. On your knees, head up, and eyes forward, until I told you different. Arms behind your back, left hand holding right wrist. Legs spread, and don't let your ass touch the heels of your boots. Look me in the eye, boy. You're not a dog, and you're not a slave. You're a boy, and I expect you to do us both proud.

"Now tell me more about you, boy. What should I know? How would I tell who you are in a crowd if we were to meet at a bar?"

That was the start of almost endless letters back and forth. We didn't do what I later found out was typical in cyberspace. I didn't lie to Griffin, and she didn't tell me anything less than the truth. I explained my life in San Francisco, working at a retail store on Castro Street, living with a bunch of roommates, and playing with lots of women.

And looking for Daddy.

"My friends call me Jay, and my mother still calls me Janice. I prefer Jay, although I'm sure that's not a surprise. I'm not as tall as I act, Sir, which means I end up looking up at people more than I'm comfortable with. Five-two should be taller than it actually is, Sir. I'm a big boy, not fat, really, just solid. (I like to think that makes me more fun to hurt, but I'm not sure if that's out of line.) I'm pale, with light brown hair that I keep in a flattop. I wear jeans and T-shirts to work and dress shirts and ties to play parties. (It's that F. Scott Fitzgerald fetish, Sir.) I just turned 26 and have lived in San Francisco for three years.

"My eyes are blue when I'm calm and go green when I'm horny or sick and gray after I've been beaten. And, please, Sir, will you tell me about yourself?"

"A younger daddy," her next note said, "is what you're going to get with me. Are you a sick enough fuck to still treat me with the respect due Daddy? I turn 21 next month.

"I'm a student here in Philadelphia, although my family lives in New Hampshire. I miss that part of the country, but I don't miss my father and his homophobic bullshit. I came out my senior year of high school—which reminds me, boy: Tell me your coming-out story.

"I go to college at the University of Pennsylvania, which is exactly as uptight as it sounds. Full of frats and the boys who fill them, who aren't half as interesting as the boys I meet online. I'm out of place here and wouldn't have survived if it weren't for the people I meet online and the women in Dangerous Women, the S/M support group here.

"I work and study and read and write and terrify my dorm mates and cruise perverts, both live and online. I'm 5 foot 10, dark-haired, dark-eyed, part Irish, part German, and part Cherokee. I lift weights, cook professionally, and can't wait to be done with school.

"Now tell me what hankies you'd be wearing when you cruised me at the bar and how you would get my attention."

I did just that, spinning a fantasy about picking her up at the Eagle during a beer bust, in front of all the fags who don't understand why two women would be there, and going out into the alley and fucking like wild things, me on my hands and knees, getting ploughed by her from behind. She wrote back, adding flourishes like handcuffing me over a motorcycle and inviting other people to join her in fucking me.

I loved it.

With words she painted a picture I longed for. I tried to offer her as much from my writing as possible. We exchanged fantasies and conversations about our real lives. We gossiped about people we knew online and even managed to have arguments.

We wrote back and forth and sent pictures. At one point we exchanged phone numbers and started talking on the phone as well. We kept fairly different schedules, though, and I've never been that comfortable with phone sex. The phone didn't match the intimacy of our writing somehow. Early on I knew I wanted to meet her and be her boy FTF—face-to-face, in computerese. Griffin clinched my interest and made me want to really be her boy about two months after she first answered my ad.

One day there was a package on the kitchen table for me when I got home. I didn't recognize the address at first glance. Who did I know in Philadelphia? Then I realized. The package was from Griffin.

I was so excited I could barely open it. There was a note on top of the tissue paper that filled the small box.

"Boy," it said on the outside, and I unfolded it.

"I found this collar on one of my travels along I-95. In one of those little towns in New York, in a mom-and-pop store. I bought it that day and have kept it oiled and ready for the person I wanted to wear it. I didn't know who that would be, or when I would find them, but I knew I would someday have a boy who would deserve this.

"You must oil it once a week and wear it whenever you write to me or whenever you read your mail from me. You are also to wear my collar to the next leather event you attend where you are not otherwise engaged, and when you are asked whose collar you are wearing, tell them it's your daddy's. Much love—Daddy."

The collar was a plain black band of leather with a shiny chrome buckle. I held the collar up to my nose, and I smelled the oil she had rubbed into it and swore I could smell her too, even though she was thousands of miles away. I had never met her, but she had reached out, found me, and claimed me as her boy. I had never worn a collar before, even though I had wanted to and had told Griffin that when I was someone's boy, I wanted to wear a collar to mark me as belonging to Daddy.

I wore it that night when I wrote to her, on my knees in front of my computer.

"Daddy," I wrote, "thank you for the collar. i am wearing it now as i write to you. i can't begin to tell you how thrilled i am by having a collar from you, how much it makes me feel cared for and like i am your boy. i can't wait until i can actually see you, feel your touch, and be in your service. i treasure the token of your esteem that you have sent me. Thank you, Sir—your boy, jay."

We continued writing for several weeks, the collar never far from me. Griffin made me tell her all my fears and fantasies and would leave messages in E-mail telling me to put clothes-pins on my chest or ordering me to beat off while I read. I crafted long and complicated stories for her, involving more and more of my desires to please her and serve her as my daddy. I practiced polishing boots so I would be competent to take care of hers. I started wearing my keys on the right and telling people, "No, thank you, I'm taken."

Except snuggling up with a computer isn't easy, and the most delightful messages don't fill emotional needs after a while. Griffin realized this, of course. She was my daddy, and she was perceptive.

"Boy, I know it's hard being so far away, and I would un-derstand if you need to find a flesh-and-blood top to serve. However, you should not make plans with anyone for the week of March 2 through 10. Be at the airport to pick me up. Attached is my itinerary."

So here I stood, at the airport as instructed. Daddy's flight was announced, and passengers started filling up the gate area. I didn't see her in the first crush of people and worried, fleet-ingly, that she wasn't on the flight.

Then, just like that, there she was. The grin on her face I recognized from photos, but now she was real and in front of me. Her black leather jacket hugged her broad shoulders over a black turtleneck tucked into blue jeans. Her crotch bulged in a way that let me know that she was wearing a dick, and her boots glittered with their shine.

"Hello, boy," she said, as she dropped her carry-on bag and wrapped her arms around me.

Finally I was touching Daddy. Even better, Daddy was holding me. I put my head on her chest and tried to breath calmly. She smelled like sweat and leather and some sort of spicy scent, and it was intoxicating.

I felt her pull the collar out of my back pocket, and she put it around my neck. I watched her face as she buckled the collar on me. She looked at me and growled.

"Mine."

"Yes, Sir. Please."

She kissed me then, first soft and friendly and exploring. Then she grabbed me, hard, and pulled me against her, one hand reaching for the collar around my neck. Her mouth took over mine, the kiss becoming ferocious, and I melted into her arms. All my fantasies, all my desires, and all that E-mail were fulfilled with that one kiss.

She pushed me away and turned on her heel. She didn't look back to make sure I followed; she just assumed I would. That was a safe assumption too as I grabbed her bag and scurried to keep up with her long strides.

She headed into the women's room and moved to the far stall, one of the larger handicapped-accessible ones. She held the stall door open for me, and I blushed as I hurried past the lone woman at the sinks.

Daddy sat on the toilet, legs spread, playing with her bulge.

"Down, boy," she said, and I dropped to my knees. I couldn't believe she was doing this in the San Francisco airport, but I didn't want to stop.

"Take care of my boots, boy."

For a second I thought she wanted me to polish them, and I panicked. My boot polish kit was at home. Then I remembered one of her earlier E-mails to me, about a boy needing to love Daddy's boots with every part, including a boy's mouth. I leaned over and put my lips on Daddy's boots.

She groaned and shifted her weight and put her other foot on my back, pressing me onto the tile of the floor. I spread out, full-length, and tried to put my entire being into licking the boots of the woman I had just met and knew so well. I licked and kissed and moaned under her boot and thrust against the floor, rocking my hips. My packing dick pressed up against my cunt and drove me crazy, and I heard Daddy unbutton her jeans above me.

"Up, boy, and suck me off."

I scrambled to follow her instructions. Her dick hung out of her pants, and I dove for it. For so long I had beaten off at night, fantasizing about a daddy to service and please, a big daddy dick to fill my mouth. After Griffin started writing me, I created endless dreams about her, how she would take me and make me her boy, make me suck her big cock.

And there I was, forcing as much of Daddy's dick down my throat as I could. Daddy grabbed my head and groaned. I closed my eyes, rocking back and forth over her crotch. I opened up my throat and swallowed her as well as I could. Daddy was real, and her dick was too, at least as far as we cared.

Griffin pulled me off her dick, grabbed me by the collar, and pulled me closer. She started kissing me hard, harder than she had at the gate where I had waited for her. She undid my belt buckle and unbuttoned my jeans. I held on to her shoulders as she groped my packing dick, the pressure against my cunt almost overwhelming, my psychic attachment to my dick making me throb.

Daddy pushed her hand past my dick, past my dripping cunt, and, kicking my legs apart, started playing with my butt. It felt so good, I moaned in her mouth. She fingered me gently, and I could tell she had smoothed her manicure down to almost nothing for this. She pumped her fingers into my cunt once, twice, then pressed the moisture into my ass. My butt opened around her finger, and I let her inside me.

"Oh, please, Daddy," I whispered. "Please fuck me, Daddy. Please?"

Griffin nodded, and kissed me again.

"Yeah, boy. Daddy's going to fuck you. Take my dick in your ass and make me happy, boy. Yeah, I'm going to fuck you." While Daddy said this she pushed my jeans all the way down past my knees and turned me around. She pushed me over so that my nose almost touched the floor and I could see the pumps of the woman two stalls over. "Beat off, boy, and come for Daddy while I fuck you."

I felt lube trickle over my ass, and Griffin's fingers started spreading me open. I had practiced with butt plugs so I could take Daddy's dick like she had ordered me to in E-mail, but I was nervous. Griffin's dick wasn't the biggest strap-on I'd ever seen, but it was pretty hefty. I felt her press her dick against my ass. I started touching my clit, under my packing dick, breathing deep and trying to take her cock in my ass. Daddy pulled my hips closer to her, rocking me back toward her, and her dick started going inside me.

Then, so slowly I could barely tell she moved, her dick slid into my ass. Daddy pulled me back, and I moved against her, and her cock filled my ass completely. Just as slowly she pulled back out until her dick almost left my ass, and I heard myself whimper.

"Yeah, boy," she murmured above me. "Daddy's here. Fucking you. Making you mine. My boy."

She plunged back into me and started to move in a rhythm so sweet, I had to bite my wrist to not cry out. She grunted and moved inside me, and I rocked back in response. I beat off as Daddy hit her stride, pushing me on and off her dick. Soon, almost too soon, I came, with Daddy fucking my ass.

I lay there panting as Daddy pulled out. I felt her clean me off. I couldn't move, everything felt too good. Daddy buttoned her jeans and slapped my ass once to get my attention. I got up onto my knees and turned around.

"That's my good boy," she said. She wrapped her arms around me and hugged me close, like Daddy should.

"Let's get out of here," Griffin said. "Take me home with you, boy. I need to have you fuck me now, and if we wait much longer, it'll be here in the airport bathroom. And I don't come as quietly as you do."

I left the stall in front of Griffin. I walked proudly in front of my daddy and smiled at the woman doing her makeup at the sink as she looked quizzically at the two rumpled and grinning leatherdykes leaving a single airport bathroom stall.

Bitch

by Nicola Ginzler

So you lock yourself out of your apartment on the way to do a strip show at the local dyke sex club. The only other person with a set of your keys (natch) is your ex, Susan, whom you don't particularly want to ask for help. But you told her about the strip act in the hopes she'd show up and you could see whether she's been missing you. So maybe she'll be there.

The club will get raided and closed down by the police tonight, though—it's an election year, after all. The cops won't search anyone, fortunately, because you have a knife on you—a really nice folding one that's illegal to carry concealed. It's for performance mostly, but cops can't be expected to understand that.

You don't know any of this yet, of course. But on the way to the club you find yourself thinking that you're not really into doing this show; Corey, your latest butch lust object, can't make it. Her girlfriend—oh, sorry, *wife*—Trish, doesn't feel like going, and Corey's not allowed out by herself.

Corey's what you want, though, married woman or not. And married woman or not, she wants you too. She doesn't want to—doesn't want to want you; doesn't want to flirt with you, covertly, one eye on Trish's slow vicious temper; doesn't want to have to stop herself from touching you; doesn't want to be having an affair with you, the way she is, the way she does.

It started in the bathroom of another dark sleazy dyke club. Trish waited unknowingly for you back at the table. You pulled Corey into the stall with you, took her hands, put yourself between them. She jerked away from you as though the touch of you burned her skin. Breathing hard. Slid her hands back to you, tense, shaking, slid them up under your skirt, along your thighs, whispered, "Bitch. What do you want, Bitch?" You put your fingers lightly in the hollow of her throat, felt the blood hammering there. "I want to take you home," you said, sliding your hands to the back of her neck, and then I want you to fuck me—Daddy."

That was three months ago, and you've been her little girl since then. You'll call her at work. "Hi," you'll say and listen to the sharp intake of her breath, "I have some time tonight. How does 8 o'clock sound?" She may show up at 8, or it may be 7 or 9 or (once) 11—it depends on if and when and how she can get away from Trish. Most times you'll be there when she arrives, but sometimes you'll get tired of waiting and go out for the evening.

You must be worth it, though; she always comes back, materializes guilty and defiant at your door with a small tight smile and a long bulge down her left thigh. You let her in, unzip her jacket for her, and hang it up carefully. Then you walk back to her and stand close, take her hands, and put them around you. It seems like you always have to make the first move—she's not really cheating on her wife, you suppose, if you always make the first move.

That over with, she doesn't waste any time. She ties your hands behind you and pushes you down on her knees so she can shove that long cock down your throat. One of her hands is locked in your hair, the other cradles your face. She looks down at you and lets you take her dick into your mouth, lets you play with the head of it a little while with your lips and tongue. But soon she gets impatient and takes back control, pulls you deep into her piece, almost all the way off it, back on, faster and more brutal with each stroke. She's hitting the back of your throat. You're struggling to keep your gag reflex down, while tears spill out of the corners of your eyes. When she finally pulls out, your pulse is singing in your ears, and your cunt lips are swollen and wet. She looks down at you again, her smile relaxed now, possessive.

Later she'll fuck you. Then maybe she'll fist you hard, punch-fucking you until there's blood on her gloved hand. You'll strain to meet the thrusts of her arm, your head thrown back, wanting just to take it, to be taken. Listening for that particular groaning gasp that means she's gone over into animal, to where she can't help it, to where she can't stop it, to where she couldn't stop, wouldn't if Trish herself walked into the room just then.

If you've been really good, she might let you touch her after that, but sometimes you don't wait for her order, you just slide your hand around her cock and harness to where it's wet and slippery and soft, and laugh when she snarls at you. You know she's not going to make you move your hand away anytime soon no matter what she says. And sometimes when you have her like this, you'll make her say out loud how badly she wants you—enough to risk her marriage and her home and probably her whole life in this city.

But, no, you won't get to see Corey in the strip show audience tonight. You amuse yourself the rest of the way to the club thinking about her, about how she would've looked when you got onstage, displayed yourself of all those women—she'd be with Trish, of course, near the front but not too close, eyes riveted on you, your fists clenched at your sides but face carefully blank. Yeah, that would have been worth seeing.

You get to the club, finally, and Susan is there. You have a fight; she's telling you that every time she talks to you, you're so *negative,* and she's tired of hearing it, she wants to be friends but not if she's just a wailing wall for you. You never want to hear about *her* life, about how *she's* doing. What *do* you want anyway? You ignore the first part and just answer the last: "I want to stop being so desperate that I'd go to you for comfort." She glares at you and says, "If I thought you meant that, I'd leave right now." It's kind of a drag because you don't want her to leave. You're not done talking, but you couldn't have been more serious. "And if you didn't mean it," she goes on, "well, that was beautiful, that was so creative, that was perfect."

After a while of this you close down, just shut down and watch her mouth move and the words come out. You look at her, considering, then at a break in the flow you ask, "So…do you want to see me strip?" She meets your eyes for a split second, frozen, mouth open, then sighs and looks at the ground. "Of course," she says. "Always." You smile.

So you're changing into your strip clothes—the sequined dress, the long gloves, the black lace bra and G-string and garter belt—and that's when the police arrive. The DJ is arguing with the officer who is trying to confiscate the sound system. The boys in blue cast speculative glances at the crowd—

you wonder whose sensitive idea it was to send an all-male patrol to bust a dyke club. As you turn to leave, Susan in tow, you can feel the cops' eyes crawling up the seams in your stockings, over the curve of your ass.

You go to Susan's because you're still locked out, remember? Her lover, Stephen, is in her bed when you get there. He wakes up when you come in. Susan says almost unwillingly that you can spend the night if you want. It's too late for you to go home. You're not sure you want to stay, but it's late. And anyway you're still mad you didn't get to do your show, even if the audience you really wanted wasn't there. You're already in your strip outfit too, and that makes your decision.

So you ignore Stephen, even though the three of you used to share Susan's big bed every so often, when you and she were still together, and ask Susan again if she wants to see you strip. "Yes," she says, almost inaudibly. You know you could have just told her you were going to do it, without asking, but you wanted to hear her admit she wanted it—some things never change, you suppose.

You put the music on low because it's 4 in the morning now, slide the knife out of your stocking, flash it, put it back. The gloves come off first; they fall in delicate shivering piles on the hardwood floor. Unpacked cardboard boxes are scattered everywhere, and you have to watch your step. Stephen must have moved in with her, you realize. You try not to think about that as you pick your way through the maze, stopping to touch knife to tongue, to throat, to breasts, belly, thighs.

The dress is next, but you don't cut it off you as you'd planned for the club show—she's not worth replacing the whole front—you just unzip it down the back and tell her what she's missing. Then the dress is a discarded heap of pale shimmers next to the gloves.

Your hands are inside your G-string, and you're circling your clit with a wet, slippery finger. You're thinking about Corey again, about the feel of her eyes on you, the way her fingers would be tightening on the arms of her chair, how you could see her trying not to change position if it were her in front of you. You watch Susan's eyes flicker over you as you shift your weight slowly and deliberately and let your hands drift over your body.

You do use the knife on the cheap elastic of the bra and G-string and watch her jump as you slice through, snapping the blade shut afterward with a decisive click. You flip it out again, work the handle back and forth between your legs, feeling it slip easily between the slick folds of your cunt.

You hold the knife by the back of the blade and then you're fucking yourself with the handle, slowly—much more slowly than you know Susan wants you to, feeling the texture of the handle against your wet lips. The last song is almost over—abruptly you let the knife slide out of you.

As the music ends, you have brought the knife to your mouth; you're sucking your juices off the handle. Then you're on your knees, licking along the length of it like it's a cock, like it's your daddy's cock and you're between her legs and she's got you by the hair.

Your daddy isn't here, though. She's asleep next to Trish in the conjugal bed, no doubt. But Susan's right in front of you, looking like a rabbit caught in the headlights of a car. You smile to yourself, wondering what she'd do if you told her that.

"You're the most beautiful woman I've ever seen." She

says it without inflection, not a compliment but a statement of fact. Stephen chimes in, "Yeah, that was the sexiest strip ever." You'd forgotten about him. You swivel your head around to look at him and realize that he's the only man, the only straight man anyway, you'd have stripped in front of. You're not sure what that means about him...or about you.

Susan shakes herself all over like a dog and remarks, "Dunno if you'd win Miss Congeniality, though," and it catches you off-guard. You don't know what to do except laugh along with the two of them—just like you're all still friends.

But later when they're curled around each other under the covers next to you, you're staring at the ceiling in the dim light. Is that what it's about? Congeniality? Funny how you never figured that one out. And what it is about love, or sex anyway, that makes it so different from what you used to think it was. Is that all you do? Is that all anyone does? Use it like a weapon? You don't know. You're certain you don't want any new insights about yourself. "Self-knowledge is almost always bad news," the woman beside you in bed used to say with a smile. You turn over and listen to her breathing, deep and even, and try to sleep.

Le Main

by Julie Anne Gibeau

Le main. The French babe has this desperate, breathy way of saying it that makes me just crazy for her. She says it when I'm kissing on her for a while, on her face and her neck and down into her cleavage. *Le main*. And then she'll want me to put my hands on the down between her legs, where I can already feel the warmth and the wetness through her clothes.

Le main. The French babe told me it means "the hand" in French. When she says it she kind of swallows the end of the word up into her nose. They do that with a lot of words. It's like they don't really finish them, and you could wait forever just to hear the end of a word.

She's good with suspense. She knows how to make you wait. One time she called and asked me to come over to her place. When I got to her building, she jammed her head out the window and told me I would have to wait, so I stood outside and smoked cigarettes. It was a cold, damp day, and at about the second cigarette it started to drizzle. I was carrying a strap-on in a paper bag, and even though I put it under my sweatshirt, I got so drenched that the thing fell through the paper. I didn't even notice for a while, because somehow the harness got caught up on my pants and the damn dong was hanging at about knee level. I didn't notice until the school buses drove by, anyway.

When she finally let me in and saw the thing, she just shook her head. "No. *Le main*," she said. "*Le main*."

You'd know just by looking at her that she was foreign. She's so skinny she looks almost frail, and she wears these pants that fit her real tight around the butt and loose tops that hang real short. When she moves around they slide up so you can see the muscles in her stomach and the tops of her little pointy hipbones. Her hair is really short, and she combs it all down flat. I think she calls the color "chestnut."

Patty says she's delicate. That's what she said the first time I ever saw the French babe. It had been a rough day, so I went to the bar right after work to kind of chill. When I sat down by Patty, she put one hand on my shoulder and pointed toward the dance floor.

"Look what followed me home from school," she said. There's no dancing that early, so the dance floor wasn't even lit up yet. I could just see this woman out there dancing in and out of the shadows. It was a slow song, and she swayed back and forth and floated in big circles with her arms up in the air.

"Isn't she delicate?" Patty asked me. "She's new on campus. She's from France."

I couldn't take my eyes off her. She was like an angel out there, and I was afraid she might unfold her wings and fly away. I lit up a cigarette and took my beer over to a table near the dance floor where I could see her better. She saw me right away and came over to the table.

"A smoke for me?" she asked. Her accent put my head in some kind of cloud like I'd just walked into a smoky room. All I could see was the red of her lips and the shine of the sweat on her forehead. I was frozen.

"Please. A cigarette," she said.

I'd never been a slave to a woman, and I was proud of that. I'd sworn to never give up my bike, wait by the phone, or take down the car-chick posters in my bedroom. But here was this tiny thing in total control of me. My mind, body, and anything else she could have possibly wanted were hers. I lit a cigarette and handed it to her. She took a couple of long drags, staring into space, and sat down beside me. I was nervous as hell sitting there, and I'm not used to being nervous.

"I liked watching you dance," I said. She just sat and watched her smoke curling up toward the ceiling. I couldn't even tell if she heard me.

"Are you a student?" I asked her.

"Yes. I am new at the university," she said. She looked me right in the eye when she said it and held me in place as if that one little sentence were the most important thing happening on the planet. I had this total awareness of her body right then. I was aware of her tiny little waist and the dampness of her belly and the pounding of her heart. It was like I had my hands all over her, but I didn't.

"And you?" she asked. I just stared back at her. I was all flustered. "You are a student?"

"No," I said. I pointed to my uniform. "Groundskeeper on campus."

She frowned a little and made a crooked line between her eyebrows.

"I work outside on maintenance."

"Ah," she said. She pushed out the cigarette in an ashtray and stood up. "I thank you," she said. "What is your name?"

"Buster. My friends all call me Buster."

"I have never heard of that name," she said. "This is bust?" She took my hand and laid it right on her tit.

"No," I said, and I tried to pull it away, but she held it there. I glanced over to see if Patty or anybody was looking, but luckily nobody noticed my situation. The French babe was smiling a coy little smile at me. There was this heat in my face I remembered from my grade school days as a blush. I knew my hand shouldn't be there, but at the same time I was enjoying the warm round thing I was touching. I cupped my hand around it and squeezed as gently as I could.

"My name is really Sara Brown, but my friends call me Buster because there's a little character called Buster Brown."

"A character?' she asked.

"Yeah. He's like a little cartoon dude or something. Sara just doesn't fit me."

"I like Sara," she said. "You are a good Sara." She loosened up the grip she had on my hand, so I let go of her tit and picked up my beer. "I will see you sometime, Sara. Yes?" she asked.

I didn't want to seem too eager, so I shrugged and took a drink. "Maybe," I said. She went back out to the dance floor and started her dance again. The music was faster now, but she still danced in the same slow slinky rhythm. She reminded me of the way wheat moves in a field when the breeze blows.

I wanted the French babe's waist between my hands so bad, I couldn't take watching her very long. I downed the rest of my beer and took the empty up to the bar.

Patty winked at me. "What do you think, Buster?" she asked.

"I think you should keep an eye on her," I said. "This place is too rough for a girl like her."

"If she gets into trouble, you're the first one I'll call," Patty said. She laughed and slapped me on the ass. She's got a lot of energy, but she never can take things seriously. A lot of young ones are that way.

I left the bar and rode over to Sylvia's. She wasn't expecting me, but she was always in the mood for some, and the French babe had given my drive a little jolt. Sylvia must have been sleeping because she came to the door in her robe, and her bleached hair was flat in the back.

"Well, look at that," she said. "My dream came true."

I stepped inside, and she grabbed my ass. I was tired from digging up cable all day, but watching the French babe had done something to me. By the time I got over to Sylvia's house, my body was screaming all over to take someone, and fortunately Sylvia was always there for the taking. Her robe dropped around her feet.

I staggered back to look at her. Sylvia was a big, fleshy blond, and it took me a few seconds to take in all of her shining white skin.

"I'm not an art exhibit, slug. Let's get on with it," she said. She reached out and took my hand but let go suddenly. "You feel like a damn alligator," she said.

"I can't help it," I told her. "I work outside."

She took me by the sleeve and pulled me down the hallway and into the bedroom. She stood there naked, begging for it with those big cow eyes of hers. With a quick shove I knocked her onto the bed.

I'm not even sure how things ever got started with Sylvia. I guess I'd been alone for a while. I was worn out from having my heart broken over and over by a long line of nice girls. They really were nice girls, and I was missing the hell out of all of them when I met Sylvia. I was lonely, pissed, and drunk enough to be curious when she strolled up to me that Saturday night and shoved her hand down my pants. What Sylvia wanted doesn't begin with a formal introduction. After two years of going at it like cats in heat, we'd probably had all of about 20 minutes of real conversation.

"Did you have a good day?" I asked while I rooted through her toy chest.

"Shut up and fuck me," she said.

Sylvia liked it rough. Rough and rude. She pissed me off to make me meaner. Over the past two years she hadn't learned my middle name or my favorite color, but she'd become an expert at pissing me off. Besides, it's easy to be rough when sex is just sex.

I pulled on some fresh latex gloves from her stash in the drawer and grabbed some restraints. In a few seconds I had her spread-eagled on the bed. She struggled but only to make me flex a little. In the end she was always easy to subdue.

"You stupid ape," she taunted. "You're not woman enough to make me enjoy it."

My heart started racing, and I was more pissed off at myself than at her. She always got to me with that crap. It was just part of the game, but it made me want to do her like nobody else could ever do her. I wanted to be the only fuck she thought of, the only fuck she remembered, the fuck she felt when she touched herself. To be that it had to hurt, because to her that's all that really matters.

I yanked the restraints tight enough to make her squeal a little and slapped her meaty gut as hard as I could. She made another little sound.

"Shut up," I said and bit her inner thigh high up where it gets really sensitive. She moaned, but I liked that sound. I went back to the toy chest, pulled out an incredibly big dong, stretched a condom over it, and strapped it on. I heard the sound of her heavy breathing overlapping my own.

"Do you want to feel me?" I asked.

"I won't feel you no matter what you do," she said.

I jumped onto the bed and stood over her. "You won't say that after you choke on me, you bitch," I told her.

I knelt down and leaned forward and put the dick into her mouth. She moaned again, so I started humping fast and hard. I pumped so hard, I could feel the rub through my thick work pants. I took myself to the edge, then pulled out and slid down on her body. She was gasping. I started biting her tits while I reached down into the slimy abyss between her legs. She arched her back and let out this long, tortured moan. I slid down again, biting hard on her stomach. Then I crammed my hand into her.

Sylvia was about 15 years past being tight. It wasn't even hard to ball my hand into a fist and ram her for all I was worth. Meanwhile, my teeth returned to her inner thighs and worked their way up to her shaved mound. She came while I was biting there and twisting hard. I rode her jerking body like a wave, then fell back across her legs.

I just stayed there a few minutes, trying to catch my breath and forget the hot need I still had between my legs. Sometimes I got off with Sylvia. Sometimes I didn't. All I could count on was no special treatment for stragglers.

"Undo me," she said. "I'm cold."

I sat up and unstrapped her. She was wet with perspiration. I went back to the living room and got her robe off the floor.

"Thanks," she said when I came back and covered her with it. She rolled onto her side and faced away from me. "Help yourself to some food in the kitchen."

Sylvia's wet skin was glowing in the dim room like one of those albino cave fish. I stood staring at her, amazed that looking at the woman I had just fucked made me feel nothing. I had completely lost my appetite. For anything.

"What do you want?" she asked without bothering to look at me.

"Did I hurt you?" I asked.

"Yeah. Sure you hurt me," she said. She still didn't look at me. "Now let me sleep, Buster. I've got a date tonight."

It was still light out when I left the apartment. It was one of those nights when you just have to do something but can't think what it is. I had this itch way down inside me to ride on into the soft pink of the sunset just like I was riding into some babe's tender snatch, pressing with every inch of my body into the warm velvety cushions of her flesh. I pretended I wasn't thinking about the French babe the whole time.

I spent the next week doing a whole lot of pretending, but at night the lights would go out in that little movie theater in my head. I would lie alone in my wide bed replaying her damn dance about a thousand times. In the day I worked my ass off, trying to make my body ache enough to keep out the thoughts of her that crashed like waves inside my skull.

When Patty called on Friday and told me that the French babe had been asking about me, I realized I had two choices: swim or drown.

"So what did she say?" I asked.

"She wanted me to tell you she'd be at the bar tonight. She said she liked your eyes. They spoke to her."

I thought at first that Patty was pulling some idiot prank on me, but she never really went this far out of her way. A sick joke like this wouldn't have been Patty's style.

"I'm too old for her," I said. "There's almost 15 years' difference."

"I didn't say I understood it," she said. "I just wanted to let you know."

I had just gotten out of the shower that night when Sylvia called.

"I haven't heard from you," she said. She didn't wait for me to answer. "I have a couple of free hours. Come over."

I pictured her again the way she had looked the last time: a faceless wad of bitterness. I wondered what had come first, her being struck or striking back. Then I asked myself the same question.

"I don't think so," I said. There was a long pause, probably like the shocked silence just after an execution.

The corpse jerked just once. "Should I call again?" she asked.

"No," I said.

She hung up. No sign of life. No more fucks with my shoes on.

I dug around in my closet till I found a blue silk shirt I hadn't worn since way before Sylvia. People used to say it looked good with my eyes.

The bar was just starting to crowd up when I walked in. I found Patty on her usual stool at the bar.

"I had a feeling you'd be here," she said.

I ordered my drink and stood leaning against the bar. The dance floor was packed already, thick with coeds back for the fall. I couldn't have found the French babe out there if I'd had a crowbar. Patty took a drink of my beer and laughed.

"Nothing dresses up the old place like a whole herd of hot young things," she said. It was a good show but not the one I was there for. I took my beer and started walking around the place, squeezing tightly between women as I went. From the hungry looks I saw, I knew the action would be hot and heavy all night. I didn't know if I'd ever find the French babe.

It took me about 20 minutes to get back to the bar. I bought another beer and went to talk to Patty, but she'd already found another victim and closed in for the kill. She was a sporty little redheaded number who looked like she'd just stopped in from the tennis club. I watched Patty's eyes wandering, purposely obvious, up and down between the girl's tits and eyes. The girl chattered on and on. She looked excited and nervous, as if the attention of the lusty, drunk grad student was some prize she'd just won.

The redhead's tits were magnets for my eyes too, so I lit up a cigarette to distract myself. I smoked with my eyes closed. I could still see the light of the pulsing strobe through my eyelids. My whole body vibrated with the beat of the music and the tension of anticipation.

"A cigarette for me?" a voice said with an accent as dark and sweet as a chocolate bar. I opened my eyes to the French babe. She was standing beside me with a tiny smile on her perfect lips. I handed her a cigarette.

"*Merci,*" she said, brushing my hand gently as she took it. I lit it for her, and she took a long drag and looked out toward the dance floor. Then she looked up and watched the lazy trails of her rising smoke. She said something I couldn't hear, but I was sure I saw a familiar word roll off her lips. "Sara."

It was too loud to talk, even if I'd known what to say. I just stood and stared, but just looking at her made me crazy. I put down my beer and wrapped my hand around the side of her slender waist. She tilted her head back farther and closed her eyes. I could see her heartbeat in the blue veins of her neck. I rubbed the silky skin of her belly. My breath caught a little in my throat, and something quivered way down deep in my gut. Her lips made the word again. "Sara."

I could have been inside her right then for all I knew, but a slap on my ass jolted me back to the bar. I turned around to see Patty, grinning and holding the redhead's hand.

"My work here is done, Buster," she said. "Good luck."

"I'll see you later," I said. Patty disappeared into the crowd pulling the redhead behind her. The French babe was looking out toward the dance floor again. I leaned over and put my lips very close to her ear. Close enough to touch it with my tongue.

"Would you like to dance?" I asked her.

She shook her head and pushed her lips into a little pout.

"Would you like to go then?"

She put her hand on my shoulder, pulled me close to her, and said into my ear, "Not yet." She held me there with her warm, moist breath tickling my ear and the side of my neck. An old sensation cut between my legs, and I felt a tender fullness there. She slid her hand up to the back of my neck and took my earlobe in her teeth for just a second. "Soon," she said.

The French babe let go and kept smoking her cigarette while I steadied myself against the bar and drank my beer. I stared at her, watching the outline of her nipples move up and down as she breathed. She smoked like she was making love to her cigarette. Long hits, eyes half closed. By the time the French babe was done, I felt so swollen I could hardly walk.

She looked me square in the eyes. "Now," she said.

I took her hand and pulled her through the mass of bodies to the door. I must have nearly pulled her arm off trying to get her across that dark parking lot and into my car. I fought off the need to kiss her. Instead I drove like a maniac to get her back to my place, where I could kiss her long and deep. Where I could kiss her like a girl like her ought to be kissed.

We didn't talk, even when I got to my building and led her up the painfully long flight of stairs to my apartment. After I let her in, I meant to get her a drink and put on some music—seduction by the numbers—but all I could do was pull her close to me and slide my hands up under her shirt and bra.

"Sara, I want to be yours," she whispered.

The light from the street slashed through the darkness of the room straight into her eyes. They glowed blue with a burning that seemed to come from someplace inside her. I kissed her. Her lips felt steamy hot. My tongue wanted to feel everywhere on her satiny skin, so I traced a path down over her chin and into the hollow of her neck.

"*Le main*," she whispered. She took my right hand in both of hers and put my middle finger in her mouth. She sucked on it, moving it gently in and out. I slid my other hand down into her pants and played with her fluffy hair.

"You want to?" I asked.

She moaned quietly. I slipped my hand out of her mouth and led her to my bed. Laying her down on the edge, I pulled her shirt off and unhooked her black lace bra. Her breasts were full and round, with soft, pink, upturned nipples. I took one into my mouth and teased the nipple hard with my tongue. The French babe's skin was sweet, with a tang like warm spiced cider.

She sat up and unbuttoned my shirt while I slid off her boots and pants.

"You also, Sara," she said. She reached down and unzipped my jeans. With our eyes locked together, I stripped and stood naked in front of her. She took my hand and pulled me close. I knelt and kissed between her legs.

"*Le main,* Sara," she said. Slipping on a clean glove, I put two fingers inside her and thrust in and out slowly and gently while I massaged her clit hard with my tongue. I felt her shudder and lean back, steadying herself with the fingers she dug into my shoulders.

She leaned forward and rested her cheek on the top of my head.

"*Merci,*" she whispered. I stood up and helped her lie back on the bed.

"No," she said. "Now you."

"You can relax if you want," I told her. I ran my hand along her cheek, and she turned her head and kissed it. Then the French babe got out of bed. I panicked.

"I'm sorry, babe," I said. "Did I do something wrong?"

I started to stand up to grab her, but she reached out and pushed me back down. "You must wait, my Sara," she said. She was smiling that puzzling little Mona Lisa smile again. She made a quiet, breathy sound from deep in her throat and rocked her hips around in a slow, graceful circle. She raised her arms above her head and danced the way she had in the bar that first time I saw her, except this time she was naked. And this time I could be sure it was all for me.

My eyes had adjusted to the darkness, and I could have sworn my other senses were sharper too. She was on my lips and in my nose, and the sound of her soft humming filled my ears. She came back to the bed and touched me all over with the lightness of feathers before she finally let me kiss her again. Then she kissed my shoulders and my tits and my knees and wrists and any other part of me before that sweet kiss came to rest between my legs. All it took was a few quick strokes with her tongue and I surrendered to her body and heart.

We've stayed together, the French babe and I. Next month when her lease runs out, she's moving in with me. It's not that I own her. She always does her own dance to her own song. Maybe it's not owning her that's special. When we make love and I hold her in the dark, it's a strange heart I feel beating in my arms, but it's one she keeps bringing back to me.

She's different from all my nice girls. The nice girls just want to be nice, and everything they do is as much about them as it is about you. They don't have the guts to be anything but nice. Sometimes my French babe isn't nice at all. Sometimes she makes me wait so long, I feel like I could break into a million pieces that hit the wall at a million miles an hour. Then I'll feel her breath on my ear.

"*Le main*," she'll whisper just above the drumming of my pulse. "*Le main.*"

Riding the *Silver Meteor*

by Marcy Sheiner

I've been riding the *Silver Meteor* from New York to Miami once a year for the past decade. I get culture shock from airplanes that transport me too quickly from one climate to another; the 24-hour train ride gives me time to ease into the right attitude for the annual family reunion at my parents' home. The slow, relaxing journey enables me to shed the stress of my workday world, while the return trip gears me up to face it again.

Sometimes I think I was born into the wrong century, that I belong in a world without telephones, E-mail, and supersonic jets, a world where people still find romance in a place seemingly as mundane as a train. When I sit in the lounge car drinking a martini, speeding through the darkening landscape, I envision the poker games that were played here in the '20s and '30s, the glamorous people who gambled, fought, and loved on the railroad. There's something about a train that's inherently sexual—its strength, power, and speed; the vibrations caused by moving steel upon steel; the way the train bucks and rolls to a stop. Lying in my efficient little sleeping compartment, I fondle myself in the darkness, conjuring up the ghosts of all the railroad romances I imagine were consummated on my foldout bed.

About three years ago my cabin was situated across from a lesbian couple. I don't know if they were playing a game or if this was their ordinary demeanor, but they looked like they'd walked straight out of some '30s Parisian salon with their short sleek hairdos, satin blazers, and bejeweled pipes. They cut exotic figures, sipping brandy from snifters and gazing into one another's eyes. During the night I heard the sounds of their lovemaking—raw, ferocious growls of unbridled lust. Alone in my sleeper I masturbated to the sounds of their passion, while the motion of the train rocked me to a deliciously prolonged orgasm.

Even just moving around on a train is erotically charged. Maneuvering through the corridors requires cooperation among the passengers. Usually someone will duck into an empty room to avoid a collision, but when that's not possible, one of them has to flatten up against the wall while the other sidles past. I've often brushed against hard nipples or allowed my breasts to graze someone's chest or spine, then later used the memory of the encounter in my fantasies.

Every year I try to talk my lover, Donna, into joining me. But we both know it would be a disaster—she's too much of a type-A personality to endure the confinement. Most likely she'd end up pacing the corridors like a caged animal. But we do have a semi-open relationship, which means we occasionally dabble in extramarital affairs, and she's given me her blessing to seek out an erotic railroad adventure. The right someone just never materialized.

Until my last trip.

Maybe it was my own vibes: I'd decided to go all out, to dress the way the railroad makes me feel. Since padded shoulders and trashy jewelry were back in vogue, I had no trouble looking like a gun moll in a calf-length black dress with rhinestone buckle, fishnet stockings, spiked heels, and a floppy feathered hat. When I boarded I settled my luggage into my room as quickly as possible and headed for the club car, surreptitiously peeking into compartments along the way. Enviously I eyed an empty first-class car with its sofa-size seat and double foldout bed, imagining the scenarios that must have been played out there.

In the club car I drank a leisurely cup of coffee, then headed to the dining car for breakfast, then back again to the club car for more coffee. This frantic back-and-forth activity was carefully choreographed to provide me both optimum exposure and an opportunity to assess my traveling companions.

A family with six kids trouped past my table—yawn. A pair of newlyweds sat across the aisle. An old woman, assisted by a young porter, tottered in on a cane. A tall, elegant woman in a purple jumpsuit slithered through the door, and my heart fluttered: Sizing her up, I decided she was bisexual and eminently seducible. Just as I was contemplating how best to proceed, *she* appeared: my ultimate railroad fantasy.

She might have stepped out of a time machine, so much did she resemble a '30s Chicago gangster. She was tall and thin, wearing a double-breasted three-piece tweed suit and silk tie, a natty fedora pulled over one eye, her patent leather shoes spit-shine clean. She consulted an old-fashioned pocket watch as she stood in the entrance to the club car, a serious expression on her face. Her skin was chocolate brown and her features delicate: long nose, thin lips, sleek jawline. Her eyes roved the room, briefly pausing when she saw me. Casually she slid into the booth facing mine.

My initial reaction was to flee, so terrified was I to let this marvelous apparition see the naked lust that had crept into my eyes. But then I pulled myself together to present the composed, worldly woman who lives inside every seemingly fragile femme. Looking directly at her, I lifted my cup in salutation. An almost imperceptible smile played at the corners of her mouth as she nodded and raised a hand to tip her hat. This silent exchange, lasting perhaps ten seconds, conveyed a wealth of information. There was little doubt in my mind that at long last my fantasy would be fulfilled.

After several minutes of pointedly ignoring her, I slowly stood up, offering her a full view of my bod, and strode past her on my spiked heels, feeling her eyes observing every move I made. Back in my compartment I bided my time, imagining making love to the tall, dark stranger. When I felt the moment was right, I headed for the dining room, three cars ahead.

In the second car I saw her approaching. The blood sang in my veins, and my nerves tingled with anticipation. In the few seconds it took for us to meet—during which our eyes remained steadily fixed on one another—I tried to figure out the best course of action. *Should I flatten myself against the wall? Wait for her to do so? Sidle past frontward or backward?* There are some things our mothers simply failed to teach us.

As I should have expected, she took control of the situation. Flattening herself against the wall, she gallantly waved her arm for me to pass. I made a hasty decision to offer the feel of my ass rather than my breasts and turned my back to her. Despite her wool suit and my rayon dress, I distinctly felt something hard nudging the crack of my ass: My God, she was packing! Right here on the *Silver Meteor!* The woman had balls. It was all I could do not to totter on my heels as I kept on walking, feeling her eyes boring into my spine.

I sat in the dining car unable to eat my lunch, my panties getting wetter and wetter. Suddenly it occurred to me that I had no clue as to which compartment or even which car she was staying in. For all I knew she would disembark at the next stop. Near panic, I left the dining car and made my way through the sleepers, through first-class and the club car, even up and down the coaches. Not a sign, although she could have been behind any closed door. Defeated, I returned to my cubicle, where I spent the next few hours brooding that I might never see her again.

It was late afternoon when one of the porters appeared at my compartment bearing a glass of sherry on a tray along with a tiny envelope. Opening it, I found a note saying simply, "Dinner at 8." It was unsigned.

"Who," I asked the porter—although I knew very well who—"sent this?"

"The gentleman in the next car, madam. In Compartment B." I laughed at the porter, at his assumption that my beautiful butch apparition was a man. Baffled, he smiled politely.

Hastily I scribbled "Yes" on the note and gave it back to the porter with a hefty tip. Alone, I stared at the drink. I'd always thought sherry was for ladies with delicate sensibilities and had never even tasted the stuff. I downed it in one gulp, then sputtered as an intense heat spread across my chest, making my nipples tingle.

I spent the next few hours watching the landscape speed by through the twilight hours. I had no idea where we were—Virginia? Georgia? For all I cared we could have veered off into Tennessee. I felt suspended in time and space, in another world altogether. The little drama between me and my '30s gangster was a play I'd long wanted to star in, and in this atmosphere it was easy to pretend that it was real, that I was indeed a gun moll and she a mobster. I fantasized about becoming her steady girl, her "wife," spoiled with furs and jewels, living a dangerously thrilling life on the lam.

In this persona I changed into a low-cut red dress and gaudy rhinestone earrings and sashayed into the dining car, feeling people's stares—for the most part approving, though some were amused. She was waiting at a table that, unlike the others, had been adorned with real roses and a lace tablecloth. A bottle of French wine accompanied the standard railroad fare of greasy chicken and instant mashed potatoes.

As we sipped our wine and poked at our food, I followed her lead and hardly spoke. We didn't even exchange names but just gazed at one another, occasionally allowing our knees to touch beneath the table. Once or twice one of us remarked on the quality of the food or the service, but for the most part we simply allowed ourselves to experience the electricity crackling between us.

At the end of the meal, she paid the check, then rose and motioned for me to follow. She led me to her compartment—which, much to my delight, turned out to be the first-class cabin I'd admired earlier. The bed had been unfolded, the covers pulled back to reveal black satin sheets. Before I could laugh or make any comment, she had her mouth on mine, her hands roaming hungrily up and down my torso. She blew in my ear, kneading my breasts with such intensity, I felt faint. She reached behind and unzipped my dress, then stared at me appreciatively. Gently she pushed me onto the bed and proceeded to take off her clothes.

When I saw her naked body, I was momentarily taken aback—she was so skinny that every rib stood out. The dildo, harnessed around her bony hips, was enormous against her wiry form. She dropped to her knees and knelt before me, put her mouth on my crotch, and blew hot breath through my silk panties. She removed my underwear and kissed my belly, lightly circling my navel, then moved down and rained passionate kisses all over my mons. She bit and nipped at my inner thighs before turning her attention to my stiff, enlarged clit. With the tip of her long tongue, she licked around the outer edges, avoiding the sensitive head, until I clutched her hair and urged her to take my clitoris into her mouth. All the while the train was speeding through the night, its motions and vibrations intensifying our movements.

She worked her tongue deep inside me, moving it in and out with what seemed like superhuman force. I'd never felt anything like it. She continued tongue-fucking me while she pressed a finger to my clit until I came, thrashing and moaning and pressing her head against me. Laughing with pride, she climbed on top of me and thrust her dildo inside, pounding away until she too grunted in orgasm.

She was so light, I hardly felt her weight on me as we drifted into sleep. Eventually she rolled off, and we curled around each other. I wouldn't say it was a restful night, since every few hours one of us would wake up and paw at the other until we were fucking again.

Daylight found me on my knees, exploring her pussy with my tongue. As I was savoring the musky smell and taste, the train began to slow down until it was crawling along, stopping and starting, barely moving an inch a minute. From the corner of my eye, I saw that we had entered a freight yard where a crew of men were working. I moved to close the shade, but she grabbed my wrist. "Wait," she said, reaching for the dildo and harness. Quickly she put it on, then pulled on my hair, pushing my face between her legs.

"Suck it." I hesitated, glancing toward the window. Workmen were leaning on their shovels, watching the train go by, hoping no doubt for a scene such as ours. Supporting herself on her elbows, my gangster looked out the window, then at me.

"Come on, sweetheart," she coaxed. "You'll never see these guys again. Show them what you can do with a cock. Show them how good you suck girl cock."

A thrill danced up and down my spine. She was right: Why not use these guys in this already theatrical scenario? I pulled my long hair to one side to give my audience a full view and lapped hungrily at her long, sleek girl cock. I played the scene for all it was worth, excited by the workmen's imagined reactions. Would they realize that we were two women? Would this excite them? Outrage them? Briefly I noted that most of the men were white. We were not only two women but also two women, black and white, having sex in the Deep South. With renewed excitement and a feeling of delicious rebellion, I bobbed my head up and down on her cock.

"That's right, sweetheart, show the boys what you can do. Show 'em how good you suck girl cock. Yeah. Show 'em how much you love it."

Her words excited me even more. I fingered her clit furiously as I sucked, feeling her mounting excitement. Rubbing myself against her shin, I came just as she did, picturing dozens of hard cocks shooting come into their pants out in the freight yard. Then the train picked up speed again.

An hour outside of Miami, I gave my gangster lover a long juicy kiss and returned to my compartment, where I washed up and put on plain cotton slacks and a blouse. The porter carried my luggage to the end of the car, accepting my tip with a knowing twinkle in his eye.

My parents happily embraced their little girl, and I kissed the cheeks of a bevy of siblings and cousins—the whole damn family had come to meet me. As they urged me toward the car, I managed to peer through the circle to catch a glimpse of her. Briefly she turned and tipped her hat before striding off into eternity.

Me and My Appetite

by Lesléa Newman

I was sitting with Angie at Dunkin' Donuts taking my time, as
neither one of us was in a big hurry to get to work. Angie was
having black coffee and an old-fashioned, but I was going for
broke: a hot chocolate with whipped cream and two mocha-
frosteds. Gotta do something to spice up your day when all you
have to look forward to is eight hours of sitting in front of a
computer terminal with no one saying anything to you except
"Don't your eyes kill you, looking at that screen all day?" or "I
don't know how you do it with those nails of yours."

Angie and I don't talk much in the morning. It's bad
enough to have to be up and dressed before noon; at least
Angie understands it would be too much to expect me to be
civil about it. We just meet at some dive before work to for-
tify ourselves and give each other the once-over. You need a
girlfriend to tell you if your seams are straight, if your earrings
match, if your slip is showing.

We finished our doughnuts and whipped out our compacts and lipsticks in one smooth motion, like a dance. Angie

tends toward orange, which you can only get away with if you have beautiful bronze skin like she does. I go more for pinks and reds. We flipped open our compacts with our left hands and swiveled our lipsticks up with our right. As I was outlining my upper lip, I saw Angie's eyes leave her mirror for a split second to glance over my head and then return to her reflection.

She finished doing her mouth and, scraping at a smudge on her chin with her index finger, said, "Don't turn around, but we are being admired."

"By who?" I asked, moving my compact a little, like a rearview mirror that needed adjusting.

"By whom." Angie corrected me before rolling her lips inward and pressing them together to even out her lipstick. "By that young man at the counter." She pointed with her eyes.

I lifted my mirror for a better view. Crew cut, leather jacket, white T-shirt. "Christ, he looks all of 16," I muttered, patting a dab of powder on my nose. Angie put her works away and swiveled in her seat. "You ready?" she asked, lifting her jacket off the back of her chair.

"Yeah, yeah." I was still fiddling with my face when our not-so-secret admirer turned on his stool to reach for a napkin and there in his profile was just the faintest outline of breasts. I gave a little gasp. Our *he* was a *she*.

"Girl, what is so fascinating about your face this morning?" Angie was on her feet, one high heel tapping with impatience. "Are you coming or what?"

"Or what," I said, catching the little butch's eye in my tiny mirror. Her face was openly curious, and I gave her a little wink that said, *Hold your horses, baby, I'm coming.*

"Angie," I put my compact down. "Will you please tell Mr. Franklin I have car trouble and will be a little late?"

"What?" Angie looked at me and then over my head at the counter for a minute. Angie knows boys don't interest me in the least, so she must have seen what I saw because she sighed and shook her head. "That's the third time this month, Sally," she said, giving me one of her *tsk-tsk-tsks*. "What do you want to go playing with her for, when you got a good woman waiting for you at home? And besides, Sal, she's jailbait."

"I'll make sure she's of age," I said, like Angie was my mother. "And anyway, Angie, variety is the spice of life, and I can't help it if I have a hearty appetite." Angie has never understood this. Hell, a woman who always has a plain doughnut and black coffee for breakfast can't possibly understand the pleasures of jelly-filled, coconut-dipped, chocolate-frosted, or vanilla creams. Luckily Angie doesn't have to understand. The only one who has to understand is Bonnie, and she understands just fine. Bonnie is a dream come true. She doesn't mind sharing me as long as I follow the rules: not in our house, not in our car, no staying out all night, and no follow-up phone calls or love letters. And most important of all, Bonnie doesn't want to hear about it. Angie thinks we're nuts and she's always throwing me that Paul Newman crap—why go out for hamburger when you've got steak at home—but hey, it's worked for me and Bonnie for 13 years, so who is Angie to knock it?

"So what is it this time?" Angie picked her pocketbook up off the table. "Flat tire, muffler problems, fan belt, carburetor..." She counted off the possibilities on her long orange nails that glowed under the fluorescent lights.

"Um…let me think." I tried to remember what I had told Mr. Franklin last time. I really should write this stuff down.

"She's waiting," Angie said, tapping her foot again. "She just got a refill."

"Oh, just tell him I'm waiting for the auto club to come give me a jump-start. Everyone knows that can take all day."

"You won't have to wait all day to get jumped, believe me." Angie fluffed out her hair and gave me a little wave. "Don't do anything I wouldn't do."

"Oh, c'mon, Angie, I want to have some fun."

"Fuck you," Angie mouthed. Then she blew me a kiss and was gone.

I lifted my compact and opened it again to check out my affair du jour. I caught her reflection in my mirror and ran my tongue lightly over my lips. Her eyes widened. Then I snapped my compact shut and rose as if I planned to leave. I lifted my coat from the back of my chair and folded it over my arms, but instead of walking toward the door, I merely lowered my butt onto Angie's still-warm seat so that now, even though we were across the entire restaurant from each other, my girl and I were face-to-face.

"More coffee, ma'am?" A waitress appeared with a fresh pot.

"No thanks. I will have another doughnut though."

"What kind?"

I didn't hesitate. "Vanilla creme."

My baby butch was watching me for a sign, but I wasn't ready to give it to her yet. The waitress brought my doughnut over, and it looked luscious: two light brown golden cakes joined together with sugary white cream swirled inside and overflowing the top in a tantalizing peak. Even though

I'd already had two doughnuts, this was a challenge worth rising to the occasion for. And as I've already told you, I do not eat like a bird.

Without taking my eye off the girl in the wings, I darted my tongue out and licked the white cream once, and then once again. Through the din of coffee being poured, cash registers ringing and newspapers rattling, I could swear I heard that butch moan. I dabbed my middle finger into the cream and then put it into my mouth up to my first knuckle, sucking gently and rocking my finger in and out of my mouth ever so slightly. My girl slid off her stool a little and then regained her balance, propping herself up with her elbows on the counter and resting her helpless head in her hands.

I looked at my doughnut, licked my lips, and then, locking eyes with my baby butch, I brought that doughnut up to my mouth and proceeded to lick and suck the creamy filling out of that pastry with as much passion as I've ever felt in my entire life. My little dyke leaned forward wild-eyed, half rose out of her seat and practically did a somersault headfirst over the counter.

When I was done I patted my mouth delicately with a napkin, and without bothering to reapply my lipstick, I opened my purse for a cigarette, which I placed between my lips. At last my poor baby knew she was welcome. She bounded across that greasy floor in two seconds flat, flicking her Bic.

"Sit down," I said, accepting her light and gesturing to the empty seat across from me. We looked at each other for a minute. Her eyes were burning. "You look mighty hungry," I said, delighting in her blush. "What's your name, lover?" I asked, putting my hand on top of both of hers. She was hanging on to Angie's empty pink packet of Sweet 'n' Low for dear life.

"Sonny," she breathed, interlacing her fingers with mine.

"Sonny," I repeated, kicking off one shoe. "With an *o* or a *u*?"

"Oh," she moaned, as my bare foot rode up her leg underneath her jeans. I took off my other shoe and caressed her firm calves with my feet, silently thanking the goddess that I had worn slingbacks that morning. Some of my shoes have so many buckles, even Houdini would have a hard time getting out of them.

Sonny's calves felt firm, like she worked on her feet all day. "You want some of my doughnut, Sonny," I said, for it was a statement, not a question. The poor girl could only nod. "C'mon, then." I put my shoes back on and rose. Sonny was at my side in a second. Someone sure raised her right. She helped me on with my coat, standing behind me while I took my hair out of my collar and gently teased her face with it.

"Where we going?" Sonny asked, eager as a puppy, as we left Dunkin's.

"You got a car?" I asked.

"Yeah," she said, half turning, "but it's a few blocks back that way."

"Never mind," I said. I didn't need her car; I needed to know she was over 18, though to tell you the truth, I don't know if I could have turned back at this point. "You're old enough to drive?" I asked, putting my hand on her arm. "How do you keep looking so young and handsome like that? Your skin is soft as a baby's." I traced her blush with my index finger.

"I don't know," she mumbled. "Just lucky, I guess."

"Oh, you're lucky," I agreed, taking her arm again. "Real lucky. In fact," I purred, stroking her arm through the sleeve of her leather jacket, "you have no idea how lucky you are."

I steered her toward a door, which of course she pulled open for me. "The Easton Mall?" Sonny was puzzled.

"Do you care?" I asked, looking around. "I mean, are you in a hurry?"

"No," Sonny said, and I stopped walking to thrust my hands onto my hips, pretending to be insulted.

"I mean yes," she stammered, mortified at offending me. I shook my head and rolled my eyes as if I were disgusted that all she ever thought about was sex.

"Yes and no." Sonny was helpless, which is just the way I wanted her.

"Good." I stared walking again. "I didn't think you'd mind if I picked up a few things."

I steered her through the light crowd of young mothers pushing strollers, junior high kids cutting school, and bored housewives looking at dishtowels, until we came to Macy's. We passed housewares, juniors (where I paused briefly to admire a teal suede skirt), and sleepwear until we came to lingerie.

"Now, let's see." My hands swam through the racks, gliding over satins and silks. "What do you think of this?" I held a black long-sleeved button-down nightshirt, cut like a man's pajama top up to my chest.

"Oh, no," Sonny said. "That's all wrong for you."

"Really?" I pulled my hand away from my body to study the outfit at arm's length. "You pick something out, then," I said, pretending to be disappointed as I hung the monstrosity back on the rack.

"How about this?" Sonny lifted a hanger full of red lace and feathers and held it toward me. "I've got a charge card here," Sonny boasted. "I'll buy it for you."

"Silly girl." Butches don't know the first thing about shopping. "I have to try it on first."

"Oh." She looked disappointed, but her face lit up when I said, "Find a size 14, and I'll meet you in the dressing room."

I took off my coat and waited for Sonny. I didn't have to wait long.

"Here," she said, proud as anything. I took the negligee and pushed her gently, my hand against her chest. "Now you wait out there until I have it on and then you can tell me what you think."

I closed the curtain between us and called, "Now don't go 'way," as I let my skirt drop to the floor in a puddle at my feet. Sonny could only see me from the knees down, but I was sure her eyes were glued to the ground as I let blouse, bra, slip, stockings and panties pile up in a heap. I stepped back into my heels and slipped the teddy over my head. It fit perfectly: The lace cups lifted and squeezed my breasts to maximum cleavage, and the sheer material fell over my stomach in silky folds, ending in a hem of feathers dusting the tops of my thighs.

"Come in," I sang from behind the curtain.

Sonny stepped inside and slumped against the wall, her watery knees buckling.

"Do you like it?" I breathed, twirling around so the teddy flared out, giving Sonny a peek at my glorious bush and derriere.

"You look beautiful." Her voice cracked. "Shall we wrap it?"

"I'm not sure." I turned away from her to consult the mirror. Sonny stood behind me, her reflection drooling. "I'm not sure about this strap," I said, shrugging my shoulder a little, which caused the strap to slide down my arm. "Can you adjust it for me?"

Sonny stepped forward, and her trembling fingers touched my flesh at last. I caught her hand and moved it from my shoulder to my breast. She caught her breath in a loud gasp, and I had to shake my finger at her. "Sh," I whispered. "We don't want a flock of salesgirls in here asking us if we need any help, do we?"

"No, ma'am," Sonny whispered, starting to shrug off her leather jacket.

"Leave it on." I caught her to me in a full body hug and gently nudged her head down to the nape of my neck. She nibbled her way down to my nipple, spent some time there, and nibbled her way back up again in search for a kiss on the mouth. But I save these two lips for Bonnie, so I just lifted the naughty nightie up over Sonny's head, and from then on there were no complaints. Sonny licked and sucked my entire body until that creme-filled doughnut had nothing on me, let me tell you. I was just about to explode when we heard footsteps that stopped right outside our dressing room. The voice that belonged to those sensible shoes asked, "Are you finding everything you need?" to which Sonny replied, "Oh, yes," and proceeded to find them all over again.

Finally Sonny came up for air with a sticky grin. "Yum yum," she said, wiping her mouth on her sleeve. "Finest breakfast I ever had."

I laughed. "I like a woman with a big appetite," I said, watching the lust stream from her eyes.

"What are we having for lunch?" Sonny asked, imagining, I'm sure, spending the rest of the day, if not her life, with me.

"Well, let's see," I pretended to ponder. "Why don't you see if this outfit comes in powder-blue?"

"But red's definitely your color," Sonny said, a little whine creeping into her voice.

"Variety's the spice of life, sugar." I opened the curtain and shooed her out. "Light blue, baby. To match your eyes."

"OK." Sonny took off, and I quickly got dressed. I had already made sure the teddy came only in red and black, so I had a little time, because if I knew Sonny, she would rather die than come back to the dressing room empty-handed.

I straightened myself out and peeked out from behind my curtain. I could see Sonny with her back to me, shaking her head as some poor saleswoman held up a light blue full-length slip that was close but no cigar. Grabbing my chance and my purse, I slipped out of the fitting room out of the store and out of the mall and ran down the street toward the office, which is no small feat in three-inch heels.

I was only an hour and 20 minutes late for work, which wasn't too bad, considering. I passed Angie at her desk and hissed, "Meet me in the bathroom."

"Do I smell?" I asked when she came in.

"Pee-yew!" Angie wrinkled up her nose. "So tell."

I told, with Angie shaking her head and interjecting "uh-huhs" in all the right places. "So you left the poor girl all alone in a lingerie department with a salesgirl trying to make her quota?"

"Yeah." I filled a paper cup with water and took a long sip. "You know how heartless I am."

"So that's it for Dunkin' Donuts." Angie folded her arms. "You know Sonny'll be there watching for you every morning for at least a month."

"I know." I tried to do something with my hair, but my reflection said *freshly fucked* no matter how I combed it.

"And we can't go to Denny's anymore or the International House of Pancakes either." Angie shook her head. "Sally, what am I going to do with you?"

"Feed me toast and coffee in the car," I said.

Angie laughed. "That would be the only way to keep you out of trouble."

"Did Franklin say anything?" I touched up my lipstick.

"Nah, but we better get back to our desks." Angie looked at her watch. "Only an hour until lunch."

"Thank God. I'm starving."

"You and your appetite." Angie led the way out. "You want to grab some chow mein at that place on Fifth Street.?"

"I can't," I said as we walked toward our station. "Remember the redhead?"

"Oh, God, here we go." We stopped at Angie's desk. "What about the pizza place on the corner?"

"No good."

"The deli on Third?"

"Uh-uh."

"The Taco Villa on Forest?"

I shook my head.

"Sally!"

"What can I say?" I shrugged helplessly. "Me and my appetite."

"We better go to my house for leftovers," Angie said.

"Sounds good. What'cha got?"

"Sally, what do Berniece and I always eat on Wednesday nights?"

I didn't even have to think. "Spaghetti."

"So that's what we got."

"I'll take it." I'll never understand Angie and Berniece. Seven years together, and they eat the same thing every week: pot roast on Mondays, chicken on Tuesdays, spaghetti on Wednesdays... Don't they ever want anything different? There's no accounting for taste I guess. And anyway, who am I to judge? Besides, Angie makes the best spaghetti sauce this side of the Mississippi. I'd do anything for a serving of it. Even leave Angie's girlfriend, the beautiful buxom butch Berniece, in the capable hands of the chef.

Underneath

by Linnea Due

I'd already passed where the Berlin Wall used to be—where most of it still was—except now people were chipping away at its pitted concrete surface with mallets and chisels, trying to gouge out a piece decorated with red or blue graffiti. The people who weren't hacking at it were stamping their feet with cold or trying to chat with the Poles who were renting the chisels from makeshift portable tables.

Only a block farther east, six or seven Russian soldiers were huddling over a bonfire of broken-up chairs, beating their woolen-shirted arms against their chests. Two lucky ones still had their coats to sell, or their watches, or their souls, because they came drifting toward me like wraiths out of the warmth of their fire, muttering, *"Entschuldigung, mein Herr,"* in what even I recognized were bad German accents. I shook my head hard, and they jumped back as if I'd struck them. What could I say—they'd scared me worse than I'd scared them? I kept my mouth shut and moved on into the darkening evening, toward what someone in the blinking neon, in the bright lights of the West, had told me was the only dyke bar in East Berlin.

I kept trying to picture what this district had been like during the war. Linden trees. Banners. Black cars running to and fro like voracious animals that snatch people up, devour them, and then spit out the bones as they cruise through an intersection. No one watches the picked-clean skulls crazily rolling across the pavement until they fetch up with a faint clack against the gutter.

Not liking my imagination, I wandered near some workmen who were demolishing a building, wanting to be jolted by their jackhammers back to January 1990. I looked on as they removed sections of foundation to uncover piles of debris. Under the debris was more rubble—crumbled stone, brick, broken crockery, glass, even pieces of a child's doll: a leg, an arm.

It took me a moment before I figured it out. Bombs and shells had leveled this whole section of the city, so nothing had been left *but* rubble. What could they do but build on top? Every structure around me had its feet in despair.

Standing there 45 years afterward, atop acres of broken cement, seeing this battered gray building being destroyed so it could be replaced by another gray behemoth, the new one leading the way to capitalism with as much hope and trepidation as the other had ushered in communism, made me blink back tears so hot they scalded my cheeks. One of the workers looked at me in surprise. Then he leaned over gracefully, as if he were a ballet dancer, scooped the doll's leg off the ground, and held it out to me. I had to take it, although it nauseated me. I dropped it in my coat pocket and nodded at him gravely. Then, mutually embarrassed at being caught showing emotion, we dropped eyes and went back to no-feel/no-see, the art of avoiding connection that equals caution in the late 20th century.

I continued on my way, wondering how people can live with what they know is underneath. I'm an expert at underneath. I passed my hand over my smooth cheeks, scratched my upper lip to assure myself I was now me. Me didn't happen often, and hardly ever on these trips abroad, when I must chair international conferences. It's probably why I'd come to these gray streets where even the birds knew enough to stay away. The finest scientific minds of our generation would not be cavorting in a dumpy little lesbian bar in the Eastern sector.

The heavy wooden door was unmarked, but I could hear women laughing inside. I pushed it open and stood revealed by a naked bulb that swung merrily in a gust of wind. I swung the door shut, but the bulb continued to dance, casting wild shadows into every corner, revealing women here, there, all of them silent and looking at me. I pictured what they saw: too tall, too thin, a face both hard-edged and sleek, gray eyes, dark brows, a topcoat that was too fine. As the bulb ground down, they turned away, but I could feel them mark the place so they could return later. Why? Because I didn't look like them? As if I'd eaten cabbage all my life and smoked cigarettes when I had not even had a cabbage?

Only one woman continued to stare, and she too was different. I stepped to the bar, ordered a beer, and then nodded at her. The bartender sent a drink her way. She sipped it, watching me. I put my foot on the rail. Someone whispered something to her. She didn't respond. She kept looking.

She was blond and solid, the kind of woman who seems ordinary until you catch her eyes and realize how magical she is. She glanced down at the floor when I moved my foot from the rail. I liked that. When I smiled slightly she didn't, and I appreciated that too. She was wearing a cashmere coat, and her hair was professionally trimmed. She'd never eaten cabbage in her life.

After a very long half hour, she wrapped her scarf around her neck, opened her purse, and applied lipstick the exact color of her lips. I didn't move. The bartender, a big woman with a soup-bowl haircut, flashed me a sign that meant, "Beautiful people belong together." I ignored her, ignored the blond, even when she stopped by my table to softly murmur, "*Danke,*" in a low, quiet voice that sent an earthquake through me.

The bartender shook her head as the blond moved toward the door, as she hefted it open with difficulty and slipped out. The light did its erratic dance. I drank off my beer, shrugged on my coat, donned my cap. Then I winked at the bartender and made for the door.

She was half a block away, walking west fast. I stuck two fingers in my mouth and whistled. She stopped, then swiveled around on one heel as if she couldn't believe what she'd heard. When she saw it was me, she kept her foot poised for a beat while we both stared at each other. Then I crooked my finger and made her walk all the way back. When she stood in front of me, I caught the ends of her scarf and pulled her toward me. If she didn't want it rough, I didn't want it, and we might as well know the score now.

"*Nicht hier,*" she muttered, but she kept her hands at her sides, and her pale eyes suffused with something deep that tore at me as well, until I was shut up with the objections, instead beginning to swoon until I was afraid I'd have to scrape her off the pavement. "English?" I asked.

She shook her head regretfully. No more regretfully than I, who'd been told to take German by my advisors in undergraduate and graduate school. Nobody would dare to tell me to take it anymore—nobody would tell the great Dr. Brewer a damned thing—but I wished they'd told me why I might really want to learn German. *Someday you'll meet a woman...* But she was touching my elbow gently, coaxing me, begging me with her eyes to follow. I did.

She lived in a walk-up on the east side, in a building that no one else seemed to live in, or even near. Maybe she didn't live there either, because she had trouble fitting the key in the lock, and she studied the numbered apartments we passed as if she'd never seen them before. Finally she stopped before a door and used the same key. That worried me. Could anybody get into every room? It was pitch-black inside, and I didn't like that either. She sensed my anxiety and put her hand on my wrist, kissing it quickly, as if I were a colt she needed to gentle. Then she leaned over and lit a candle. She removed my cap with a quick apology, placed it almost reverently on a chair, then returned to smooth back a shock of my hair. My heart stopped thudding, or more precisely, it started thudding more pleasantly. I wanted her, and here would do as well as anywhere. At least it was warm. A radiator hissed somewhere in the shadows.

I could make out a mattress on the floor, covered with one of those big goose-down comforters Northern Europeans use as bedcovers. I made a twirling motion with my index finger, and she got the message, taking off her cashmere coat, placing it with my cap on the chair, and moving in a slow circle, her arms upraised, so I could see her. She kept her eyes on me as long as she could, then whipped her head around so she wouldn't miss anything. "*Bitte*," she murmured. "*Bitte, komm her*." But I didn't. I made her come to me. I made her kneel down. I made her take off her blouse button by button, and then her bra. Her breasts were as large as cantaloupes, and as weighty, and it was all I could do to keep my hands off them. But I stayed back. I made her undress all the way, on her knees, and enjoyed her struggle to stay upright as she pulled at her hose and her shoes. Then she wanted to touch me, but I wouldn't let her do that either.

I got down on my knees too, yanked her hands to her sides, and began kissing her, licking her closed eyes, which made her shudder, and plunging my tongue into her ear, which made her gasp. Then I kissed her very gently, slowing it down, letting her pick up the pace until she was heaving against me, rubbing like she was in heat, her heavy, firm breasts pressing into me like glory, like when you fall in the freshest-smelling, softest pile of grass or the coolest, silkiest pond on a hot day. I thought I'd waited all my life to feel those breasts against my chest, and then I told myself I was being a fool.

Because I was getting confused with all these bests and mosts, I wanted to do something I knew how to do, so I began touching her with my hands. It was quicker than I would have liked, but I couldn't bear this mushy feeling that kept welling up like hot candy that burns even as you gobble more and more of it. But touching her didn't help.

Instead there was a strange instant when I felt shocked and delighted all at once, as if a bird I hadn't seen had trilled right next to my ear. The world turned on its head, and I never wanted to leave. That's what happened just because I touched the skin on the inside of her arm.

I spent a worthless period wondering what it meant. Worthless because I already knew—I just wasn't ready to admit it yet. Suddenly I knew a lot of stuff all on top of each other, like why I couldn't put off touching her, why I hardly touched anyone, why I lived the reclusive way I did. And I understood that this woman whose name I didn't know, whose language I didn't speak, would never leave me again, at least not in her soul.

I don't like to act crazy, even with myself—maybe *especially* with myself—because my life is so very circumspect and controlled. So I stared at my hand, where it was still pressed against the pores of her skin that felt like salvation, and I wanted to shout with joy, but I also wanted to gnaw the goddamn thing off, like a fox will when it's caught in a trap, sacrifice that traitorous limb to save *me*. Yes, me. The remarkable Dr. Brewer, ice-cold and razor sharp. Right now I needed both those qualities.

Why this woman? I asked myself. But I had no explanations, only certainties. For a scientist, that's a very uncomfortable place to be. So just as I'd thought touching her would get me past the mushy stuff, I bowed my head to go after her nipples. I wanted the familiar. I wanted to dominate her, to overpower her, to control her. Not that it would help; I already knew that. But I had to try something.

She began moaning, and I really hoped we were the only ones in this strange building. Unlike the hot candy that backed up in my throat, her nipples were like jujubes that never get sucked away. I gnawed at the jutting head, where it's hard and rubbery, while my tongue worked over the sweet spot in the middle. She whimpered when I bit her, started panting when I tweaked her hard. Then I pulled off my shirt and made her suck me, twisting her hair whenever she got too rough, while

I continued to torment her nipples with my nails and the tips of my fingers. I could feel the whimpering come right out of my tit, hear the gasp when she couldn't keep sucking through the pain. I was so wet by the time I pulled her off that I was leaking all over my shorts. I passed a hand between her legs. She flooded the finger I trailed between her lips.

I pushed her on her butt. She managed to fall gracefully and sat with her legs apart, the way she'd landed. She was smiling at me. She knew too, knew I couldn't cut off my mouth like I could my hand, knew I couldn't cut out my cunt. I was lost. "Slut," I told her. She looked expectant, searching my face for clues to the meaning of this new word. "You'd go home with anybody who whistles at you. Spread your legs for strangers, wouldn't you?" We were long past being strangers, but not knowing English, she didn't get the joke.

I pulled my knife out of my boot and smiled, holding it up for her to see. Then I caught the nub of her nipple on its tip. She stopped breathing. I left it there until she took a very careful breath, and then I pulled it forward and up a hair. She stopped breathing again. I took away the blade, careful not to tear her skin. She was whimpering and grabbing at the hand that wasn't holding the knife, wanting me to fuck her, I shook my head. "You're getting too greedy," I said. "Entirely too greedy."

I unbuckled my belt and made her pull it out with her teeth. She was good at that; maybe she did it all the time. She offered it to me in her mouth, her eyes soft and sweet. I turned her over my knee and started out slow. She liked pain; she began plunging her hips up and down in rhythm with the strapping, and soon she was sighing in pleasure even as she was yelping from the blows. I kept bringing down the belt until she was hot all over her butt, until she started jerking away and crying out louder than I thought was wise. I stopped, grasped her hips, and wrestled her up on her knees with me behind her. It was at the time I was unbuttoning my jeans, about to put my prick into place, that I saw the woman in the corner.

I hadn't seen her before because my eyes hadn't adjusted to the dim light, and after they had, I'd been too busy and blown away to do anything but fend off the inevitable. Besides, she looked more like a fantasy than anything. Dressed entirely in black, her head encased in a discipline hood, she stood absolutely motionless, her arms invisible, breasts jutting forward. Her hands must have been tied behind her back, and her elbows as well, judging by the way her tits were presented, as if she were thrusting them at us.

I had been staring at her, but there was no reaction in those eyes I could, in any case, barely see. And because of the hood I had no other clue to her state of mind. I glanced at my blond, who was looking at me the corner of her mouth slightly uplifted. So my blond was a top, I surmised, switching in front of her girlfriend and forcing her to watch. What else could this kinky little scene be?

I looked at the blond, then at the hand I'd strapped her with. Did I still need to gnaw it off, or had I been freed from the trap by the presence of the hooded woman? But nothing had changed; I knew that just as I'd known everything all at once. The only difference was that now I was angry, realizing I was a mere design element in the blond's minor masterpiece. She'd shown up at the bar hoping to lure me. No, not me. Any top. Anyone who'd follow her to this spider's lair.

Except I didn't believe that. She had wanted me, Dr. Brewer, but that made no sense either. And what now? I wondered. I wasn't sure I cared for my walk-on role as the heavy; it made me feel used. When I feel used I get nasty, but that would feed right in to Ms. Top's script. I rocked on my heels, thinking about it. I could walk out of here, but what would that get me but a case of blue clit?

Then my blond leaned forward and stroked my cheek with the backs of her fingers. She brought her fingers to her lips, kissed them, and touched my cheek again, saying, "Shave?" in a tentative voice as she stroked down to my jaw. Then she traced a line across the slight rash on my upper lip. The woman in the corner never moved a muscle. And I decided, as I had about the dark room and the keys and the trap and even the certainties, that I didn't give a damn. I pulled her against me and we kissed. And wondered whether she'd said "slave" instead of "shave." It seemed like a funny word for her to know.

She rolled the condom down my prick with her mouth, and then she took the bulbous tip between her lips. I kept my hand on the back of her neck, but I hardly needed it. The girl was the original deep throat, and it took me only a couple minutes to come, then come again. The nice thing about being a dyke is I can shoot all I want and still have a load in my rifle. And right then I wanted to be inside her in the worst way. So I pulled her around and settled her down on the floor with her hips in the air. She laid her head on her scissored arms and got ready. I knelt behind her, shoved her hips down a trifle, and guided in my prick. She took it easy, and I whomped her butt, still hot from the strapping, back so it was jammed against me and her juice was dripping all over my thighs. As I pumped her, she started making weeping noises that got progressively lower and more guttural.

I looked up at the woman in black and saw that those eyes had come alive. They were piercing me like arrows, but they were neither murderous nor excited, and they sure weren't re-signed. As I kept watching her watching me, I started to get frightened. This was no slave forced to witness her owner twist-ing and screaming under the pounding of somebody else. And twist the blonde did, like a snake trying to keep down a rabbit that refuses to die. She wanted to stay impaled on my rod, but she also wanted to move, and she wanted me to move—I oblig-ed her even as I kept my eyes on the woman in the hood. I didn't know who she was, and I wanted to keep it that way.

But that didn't stop me from plowing her girlfriend. In fact, the fear made me exultant, like I'd just walked off a cliff and discov-ered that in death I was saved. Nothing else mattered, not at that moment. I was free and flying. I kept ramming my prick into her from behind, and she kept grunting like a miner carrying a heavy load up a long ladder until she suddenly shrieked and spread her arms, splaying out her fingers. I came too and collapsed over her back, slick with sweat. We rested there, exhausted, until I realized the woman in the corner was no longer in the corner, that she was, in fact, coming closer, and that the arms I'd assumed were tied behind her back were rising from her sides. She was wearing a cape, so those arms resembled bat wings, no doubt to match her mask, which had not been a hood at all but was more a hard leather shell, with flaring sides and a raptor's beak.

I didn't lose it, but I did pull out pretty fast, causing my blond, whose orations had plunged into baritone, to revert to soprano. I stuffed my prick unceremoniously into my pants, then got to my feet and backed off a step as the woman in black came another two steps closer. The blond was watching both of us like we were a fascinating TV show; I wanted to sock her and save her at the same time. As I was backing up I tripped over my shirt, and it just took an instant to pull it on. Nothing left but my coat.

I'd leave the belt and the cap.

By now those bat wings were parallel with the floor, and the woman had begun to make a hissing noise that sounded so much like the radiator that I began to wonder if I'd fantasized the heat too. I wanted this to be a nightmare, and even more, I wanted to wake up. That's when I found my coat and the door and scrambled out into the hall. And walked quickly down the dark, dingy staircase to stand outside and stare up at the building. To see nothing, no lights, no bats, no blonds. Most of the windows were broken or boarded up. The boards won't last, I thought as a few Russian soldiers scuttled by and glanced at me speculatively. I threw a few cigarettes on the pavement to distract them and then walked toward Kurfurstendamm, where lights still blazed and people talked and drank liquor and steaming hot coffee and no Russians crouched over burning chairs.

I woke in the night screaming, on my knees in the bed, grabbing at my shoulders as if I could tear them off. A giant hawk was digging its talons into my flesh, its wings beating at my sides, its triumphant cry shrieking in my ears. I lay back down, sweating like a pig in the freezing room, trying to ignore the discreet knock on the door: "Dr. Brewer? Are you all right?" Finally I had to drag myself up to murmur something reassuring when all I wanted to do was sob with terror. But when I woke again, my head was fuzzy and heavy, and I wondered if I'd made up the woman in the corner. And made up my certainty too. I'd never felt more uncertain in my life.

An hour later I was at the conference, among my colleagues and too many fawning acolytes. Today I liked the attention, and that bothered me. If I needed adulation, I was in worse shape than I'd realized. I had turned toward the men's room to try to pull myself together when I noticed the blond. I stood mesmerized as she swept past me. She wore a blue badge, which meant she was a presenter, and as I spotted her name I saw she was the author of the paper I had planned to hear next. So intent was she on reaching her session, scheduled to begin in two or three minutes, that she didn't notice me. But her partner did.

"Dr. Brewer," the woman said, nodding slightly. I do hope Lisette and I did not frighten you last night." She had a faint accent, Latvian, I decided. Trying to place it calmed me slightly. I glanced at her badge and was not surprised to see that she was from the Soviet delegation.

The woman reached out as Lisette had, touching my cheek with a single nail. I don't know why I didn't jump away, but I seemed paralyzed, my arms hanging uselessly at my sides. "Lisette was so fascinated that you shaved, but I told her those soft cheek hairs are a giveaway. I suggest you eliminate the mustache, though. You hardly need to establish your 'credentials' any longer, and that rash is not becoming."

It was absurd to ask who Lisette was or who the Latvian was. I knew perfectly well who they were, scientists like myself, and with less to hide than I.

"Exactly, Dr. Brewer," said my companion, as if I'd spoken. "The wonderful thing about Lisette is that she is like a

beautiful crystal-clear lake in which you can see all the lovely little fish and the sparkling pebbles. Whereas you and I are
like old muddy farm ponds, with so much muck in our souls
that we are choking on it. Wouldn't you really like to find
out what's underneath the brilliant Dr. Brewer, who never
could have achieved such fame had it been known that
Nicholas is really Nicola?"

She smiled, and I remembered the talons in my shoulders,
the claws digging into my flesh, going right for the bone,
where they'd find purchase, find something to hang onto...

"I'm sure you'll be going to Tokyo in April, Dr. Brewer.
Lisette and I shall be expecting you. Now, good day." She started down the hall, but then she halted and whirled on her high
heels. "Oh, Nick, I nearly forgot. Lisette thought it was so charming that you fancied she didn't know English. She asks that you
come prepared with an array of humiliating names she can pretend not to understand." She laughed lightly, like an antique glass
shattering, and I wished again that I had never seen those eyes.

"Lisette is like a child sometimes," she said with an indulgent
smile. "And you, I suspect, may not like being her plaything.
But you look so cute when you're angry." She planted her nail
against my eyebrow this time, and I heard conversations behind
me stop as people turned to look. "But don't worry. After
Lisette has had her fun, the two of us shall have plenty of time
for a tryst. We'll see whose mud we can sling, isn't that the expression?" Her shoulders were shaking in amusement as she
clicked off across the gray marble tiles. My face beet-red, I
plunged my hands into my coat pocket only to pull out that terrible doll's leg, and I knew nothing would ever be right again.

Amour, Amour

by Maureen Brady

I. First kiss

We walk the river park, gazing out, then back at each other, our eyes sparkling with blue, yours more like the water, glinting green. I want to hold your hand but hardly know you. Hardly know how to say why my heart keeps wanting to home in next to yours.

Your hands are busy, possibly nervous. You tell me how you embarked to see the world in youth, your European travels. The couple you stayed with in Germany who made love in front of you. I see your innocence standing side by side with your determination to escape the provinces you grew up in and become worldly. Remember my own rickety shuttle through youth: the man on the train who reached for my crotch behind the screen of his *New York Times,* the photographer who wanted to shoot a toothpaste commercial of my smile but said I'd need to expose my breasts as part of the audition. People do things like this, I thought but did not say, that same determination overriding my dismay.

The mention of sex from your lips makes me study them all the harder, and this only makes me want to hold your hand again. We are sitting on a step by then. I lean into your shoulder, press it for a second. You say you are moving to the other step because you need to smoke a cigarette, if I don't mind. I don't. I want to smoke now for the first time in more than a decade, watching your small ritual—your fingers holding the cigarette, your breath imbibing it, the smoke curling upward. I wonder if I am going to get myself in trouble if I draw up the courage to kiss you.

You more or less ask how lesbians decide to kiss each other, confessing that you've nearly always been with men. I relate my coming-out, the agony of the days I waited for the woman to seduce me before I realized she was patiently, respectfully awaiting me, since I'd declared myself straight.

All the way back up beside the river, I think about your hand, how nice it would be in mine, how awkward it feels to keep apart like friends, like strangers, like birds flitting from branch to branch but landing beside each other.

Later, after you feed me the delicious pasta sauce you've stirred all day, making it into an aphrodisiac, I bump your shoulder again—this time with my head—as if I am a lowing sheep, and you grab it with your arm and hold it for a moment. Then, before thought can come again, I hold your hand, and you hold mine, and who can say who made that happen? It doesn't matter. It makes me bold enough to lean across and kiss you.

Some days down the line you say, "You can tell if someone will be a good lover by the way they kiss, don't you think?"

"I could tell about you," I say, remembering your desire, how it captured my upper lip and pulled at me and made me want to go into your tide, utterly.

II. Possession

I think I am too tired to come. Maybe too tired to have sex. But then I think I'll let you do what you want to anyway. And you go exploring with your fingers. You rub my clit, which seems almost indifferent for a short time, though for all the past days our sex has never been ordinary.

You work at it. You don't give up. And then you go with your mouth licking me, and somewhere in there I feel your energy come into focus. Your power becomes the shape of a cone, as if you are a tornado touching down and I am the earth you want to ruffle.

My head falls back farther, my limbs go slack, my cunt goes open. You come back up and hold me, one arm surrounding me as if I were a baby. You lift me onto your leg and fuck me with your other hand and watch me swoon and come to you. And come some more. Circling high into the sky. Leaving this planet for the moment. Yet never leaving you behind. You take me everywhere I go. You take me.

III. Separation

You disappeared. How could you disappear so utterly when I thought you were right behind me? It's what I fear the worst, the most: complete desertion and disappearance. You told me we were close to danger, that I should back up. I thought you meant retrace our steps to the other subway line. I thought you were right behind me. I went single-mindedly, my head never turning around, trusting you were in my footsteps. When I turned around, you were nowhere. There was blank air. There were strangers. There was silence and frigid air.

I was lonely right away like I'd been before I met you, before you arrived in my life looking wholesome, possible, eager, lovely.

My heart fell down an elevator shaft into a bottomless hole. There was no landing. I peered at all the people, called your name, not out loud, which would make me seem crazy since you were not there, but silently I prayed your name. Retraced my steps, searching as one examines the weave of a fabric for a misstitch. How could the weave come apart when it had been coming together so exquisitely. When your head lying upon my shoulder had come to feel placed there by an angel. When your popping an apple slice into my mouth had come to be an anointing.

You have been gone one day and one night, and this is what I dream.

IV. Reunion

You fly home in bad weather. I don't want you flying in an ice storm, but I don't want you to be late either. I've borne our days apart with whole segments of myself submerged in a holding tank, and I don't know if I can bear another.

We undress each other slowly. Our bare chests touch tenderly, our breasts get kissed and greeted. My eyes search your face, roam your body, learning you all over again, while recruiting memory of the routes that have become familiar.

A pitch of fear mediated by desire into a high, thin note hangs in the air, vibrating. We dart from our memories of separation to our memories of union. We are new again, and yet your smell has gained a hold on me with ancient remnants to it. I fall headlong into your spell. Your mouth is so soft, I am amazed once more at the power it has to flood me.

Length to length, our pants kicked off, our hearts joined, our mounds shimmer a current from one to the other and back again. We create a sensation that both anticipates and quite possibly surpasses the pleasure of orgasm. I say, "Can I die now? Because I think I've gone to heaven."

And you say, "No, I want you right here, on Earth," and know you have me.

I lick you until enough light teems out of you to adorn the crown of my head, which makes me wonder how sex ever got associated with badness, when it is good enough to tell us we are home.

Life With B:
Erotica in G, Opus 33

by Lindsay Taylor

ADAGIO (slow tempo), with moments of RITENUTO (holding back):

March 4, 1992. Your office. Overlooking the Brooklyn Bridge. Six-thirty p.m. The other attorneys have gone home for the evening. I'm resolved to bring a sexual harassment suit against my supervisor. Your legal advice is business as usual. Seven months later you'll tell me how that night you had to fight the other feelings.

March 18. You phone me at my office to further clarify my options. You leave out the one I hoped you would include.

March 30. I learn from the mutual friend who referred you that you are an odd assortment. Your now-divorced parents brought you into this world as a red diaper baby and sang you to sleep with labor songs. You were bred in Berkeley, Calif., with all the makings of a lefty. In the late '60s you and your then-fiancée, a hippie trapped in a business suit, demonstrated at events history now calls the freedom of speech movement. Like so many of your fellow baby boomers, the '80s found you leaving the world of protest far behind. You became a lawyer and bought a Beamer.

You soon learn from the same mutual friend that my past began in New England—though many years later. You learn that I exude an upper-middle-class worldview but lived a life of impoverished gentry. You typecast me as the quintessential New York dyke who wears too much black, knows all the good Chinese restaurants from midtown to Hudson, recites the underground lesbian club scene from *a* to *z* and decorates her coffee table with *Out, Girlfriends,* and *Girljock.* You learn that in 1985 I fled from New England and planted my one suitcase in SoHo, sight unseen. You're impressed that I've moved up the ranks in the recording industry so quickly for someone in her 20s, though are quick to remember that with my pending sexual harassment suit, this soon may topple.

April 4. I confess to my lover of three years, who also wears too much black, that I have a crush on you. She accuses me of being infatuated with an authority figure. To console myself, I write:

I can't believe I've been thinking what I've been thinking. It started soon after I met you. It's only gotten worse-better. I think of how I would make love to you. About three times every hour. Thinking the thought. And making love. I imagine how you sound when you reach a climax inside yourself. I want to know how this sounds.

I hold my lips apart and imagine yours brushing over them. I picture myself slowly laying you down on your bed. You have fresh white cotton sheets. But not for long.

I descend upon your welcoming naked body. You take me in. I move slowly over you, touching you lightly. You move with me, guiding me. Your well-defined biceps lead me to believe that customarily you have to be coaxed into being a bottom.

I ask you how you like to be made love to and how you want me to begin touching you now. You playfully tell me that you want me to find out for myself.

We share eye contact that doesn't make us turn away. Your warm blue-gray eyes make my insides sink. I brush back your golden brown hair, revealing a hint of gray underneath, and lean on my elbows to look at you. You grin at me as you reach out to touch my light brown hair, remarking that my eyes seem to be growing greener. You let me into your mouth, deep. You murmur, and it seems to come from your whole body. You wrap your arms around me and pull me in. Our bodies become moist. I stay in your mouth.

With my thigh I make light circular motions over your clitoris. Your short, irregular breaths tell me that you like this. I give you one more deep kiss before descending on the inside of your legs. You spread them for me, telling me that I am well on my way to finding out what you like.

My tongue barely brushes inside you, the sensation of mango forming around my mouth, as your body jerks up and arcs like a small wave. You spread your fingers wide and flat before settling back onto the semi-fresh white cotton sheets. You pull on my shoulder and ask me to come up to your face. You whisper that you can have a second orgasm. I quickly cover your mouth with mine and insert two fingers. Caught by surprise, you inhale quickly. I place your middle finger on your clitoris and begin a soft circular motion. You flutter, unsure as to whether you should feel pleased by or exposed from touching yourself in front of me. I keep my mouth over yours.

Together, we move inside you. Within moments your body arcs again. You sigh inside my mouth. I do not take it away. Seconds pass. Suddenly, you roll us over and we flip positions. I can barely catch my breath as you straddle yourself over me. You turn me over on my stomach and press down hard on my upper arms. You begin to laugh mischievously. You take the back of my neck in your teeth and begin spreading my legs from behind.

I can't believe I've been thinking what I've been thinking. I can't believe I met you filing a sexual harassment suit.

May 26. At your suggestion, my lover, your on-again, off-again lover, you, and I have dinner at the Russian Tea Room before the one-night-only appearance of the San Francisco Gay and Lesbian Chorus. Your profile. Your smile. Your gestures. Your laugh. Do not go unnoticed. Part of me wants you to notice I am noticing.

June 1. Business as usual. The opposing counsel drags its feet responding to my claim. The subsequent days and weeks and months are spent responding to false counteraccusations and overcoming ploys to make me resign out of exhaustion. Your lawyerly persona is frustrating.

July 4. Independence Day. My lover and I call it quits, each of us knowing that a separation was coming for two years. Even though, I can't stop the tears in a crowded restaurant, but in the back of my mind I wonder if this new development will bring me closer to you.

July 25. The notion of "One must give up to get" is not playing itself out. To console myself, I write:

Pain, that place we find ourselves from time to time. We feel the gouge, and we must fill it. Somehow, and quickly.

My attorney has become this gouge: A long, steep series of stairs. Walls smeared brown-red. A room that has gone damp.

My attorney told me today she was on her way to beginning something with her, a new "her," in fact, someone with whom she'd been playing racquetball. The news about my lover and me had not made a difference. Her shift in energy made it painfully apparent that they had already made love. They also made plans to go to Nice in late summer.

I teetered above those long, steep stairs. A rusty piece of steel dragged up through my throat. I tried not to show any emotion. She had put the matter to bed, though differently than I would have. How strange it felt to have her leave me before she was ever there to let go. I hated her. Loved her. Wished her the best. Still wanted more.

I took the subway to my ex-lover's apartment to feel wanted, maybe even needed, yet knowing the truth about you both but still needing the fantasy from each of you.

I stood on the stoop. Was it my attorney who opened the door, light shining behind her? Was it she who invited me in, to enter that place of pain we find ourselves from time to time? To feel the gouge and fill it, somehow and quickly?

I greeted my ex-lover, thinking to myself that you will become a short story. I will relegate to fiction my unmet fantasies of you—especially the one on your kitchen floor minutes before your guests arrive along with the one in the stalled elevator—for safer keeping, but knowing all the while that you will never completely go away.

August 20. A bright blue postcard from Nice stuffed in between two bills. I'm relieved to hear from you. Behind your words *Nice is delightful,* I can tell that the itinerary is not going as planned. I can't help but pray it gets worse.

August 30. You're back in your office feeling like you never left. I try to offer solace for the fallout between you and "the her" but am painfully aware of my own agenda.

ADAGIETTO (tempo slightly faster):

September 1. Your phone message consists of inviting me to have dinner at Deco with several of your friends before *Mefistofele* at the Met and informing me that my employer not only wants to settle but also wants to extend my contract. My insides move up and down and sideways as I listen to your message. As I play it back several times, I can't decide which piece of information makes me more ecstatic. Your voice is lighter. I sense progress. To control myself, I write:

RealFantasy. I stretch out onto the sofa. It is warm and welcoming, having been in the afternoon sun for hours. I lay back my head and sink a few inches. I breathe in deeply, letting myself feel like liquid settling into place. I unbutton my white oxford shirt and pull it to each side. I snicker to myself, thinking how conservative I like to look. I spread my shirt wider, revealing my chest and breasts. Yours come into view.

As I touch myself I begin touching you. I make light strokes around your nipples. Mine become erect. Liquid emerges from between my legs. I remain still, my eyes closed tightly, making you last as long as I can.

October 2. A respectable dinner at Deco on Amsterdam. I'm the last one to arrive at our table of seven. Strangely, the seat next to you is vacant.

October 7. The one-year anniversary of the Anita Hill-Clarence Thomas hearings. My case officially settles. Undercurrents rise to the level where business as usual had been.

ACCELERANDO (speed quickening):

October 9. I convince you (and myself) that I can ride 100 miles on my bicycle. White lie number one. Convincing you (and myself) allows me to join you in Cape Cod for a weekend bike trip that you had planned with your now ex-her. I offer to make the hotel reservation.

October 16. When we arrive at our hotel room, I explain that they only had double beds available. White lie number two.

October 17. We manage 75 miles on the pavement and cover a seemingly equal amount of ground in our personal lives. At the finish line, eight hours later, I confess to you that I have never ridden a bike more than 20 miles in my life.

Later that night, back in New York, I confess again. This time it's that I want you to spend the night at my apartment. Nearly an hour goes by before you agree to come up. Your bicycle takes up half my living room.

You plunk down on the sofa and tell me that you have reservations about getting involved with me—to say nothing of letting me handle any future lodging needs—because you are my attorney and 12 years older. You think it's best we be just friends. I lower my eyes and remind you that you no longer are my attorney but concede to my inability to change my age. In your silence, and in the way you hold me, I sense progress.

We shower together. You attempt to set boundaries by soaping me from the waist up. We kiss on the lips. We hold each other's wet, warm skin. We volley thoughts and feelings about what this all means until 5 o'clock in the morning.

ALLEGRO (fast), with instances of ALLEGRETTO (moderate speed):

October 21. Your apartment. You smile playfully as you let the tie to your robe drop gently onto the bed.

October 22. I ask you to undress me and you comply. I ask you to hold me tight and you comply. I ask you to kiss me deeply and you comply. I ask you to lay me down slowly and you comply. I ask you to get on top of me and you comply.

I ask you to begin making love to me and you comply. With you, I unleash the unbearable power of passivity.

October 23. Out of the blue, I suggest we fly to Paris. Just drop everything and go. You think the Keys are better, explaining there's less pressure to sightsee and, therefore, ever leave the hotel room. We book a flight the next morning.

November 1. In 85-degree weather, we make love morning, noon, and night. By shimmering candlelight and the music of Vangelis, I confess again, knowing that three is a charm, that I could easily fall in love with you.

November 9. Your apartment. We speak *the three words* that had been on our lips in Florida but dared not speak. We exchange apartment keys. You give me a going steady ring that I have to wear on my index finger to keep it from falling off.

November 30. I'm alone in my apartment missing you. To console myself, I write:

What makes you erotic? When I find the back to your earring on my kitchen floor. When you turn your head sideways on my pillow, accentuating your neck muscles. When we first catch sight of each other in a public place and you half shut your eyes, look down, and grin. When you force yourself to gain composure when I say something suggestive to you over the telephone—when you're at the office and your assistants are hurrying in and out. When you walk with calm self-possession. When I discovered that you were a femme and a butch. When your lawyerly persona melts away.

When your soft, moist lips find mine. When your tongue scoops me up into you. When you lie on top of me. When you place my arms above my head—and hold them there. When I tell you that I can't wait any longer. When you tell me to get on my stomach and insert two fingers—but then remove them just as fast. When you're on top of me clothed—when I am not.

December 20. Holiday season. Time to meet the in-laws. I am not what your mother had in mind. In a roomful of family and extended family, including your ex-lover of ten years, your mother rushes past me to embrace your ex.

December 27. Sitting on your living room floor, a fire crackling beside us, I give you a tiny box containing a gold ring. It's the first time I see Ms. Calm, Cool, and Collected uncalm, uncool, and uncollected.

December 30. All I replay in my mind is you holding my arms down, my legs spread wide, neck straining, and me pleading with you not to stop.

January 3, 1993. Sunday evening. We make love before you have to go back to the office. In the midst of preparing for a trial, you're working seven days a week. I feel widowed. To console myself, I write:

Nothing feels as good as our gaining rhythm together, in sync. Nothing looks as good as your breasts illuminated by the streetlight outside my window, nor me sliding down the front of you and slowly spreading your legs. When you telephoned, moments after you left, I didn't know what to say. Writing about you and me and us will be my only salvation.

February 13. I'm unable to fully put into words, phrase, or sentence the impact you have on me. With you, I have begun to understand the unspoken sense of emotions speaking louder than words.

March 5. You, lying there, your arms encircling your head turned sideways, halo-like. I know better. Your changing expressions translate a fine line between Shakespeare's peaceful *Ophelia* and Edvard Munch's ecstatic *Madonna*. Stay open to me. Let me in further and further. Farther and farther. There must be a hundred ways to love you and please you. I want to know them all.

April 20. Touching your slightly clenched hand as you sleep, I look at your fingers and think of how they go inside me. Leaning toward you, I brush your soft hair and let it fall back onto my hand. May I always feel these things? May I always feel these things.

May 15. You have said from time to time that your most outlandish (or, in your lawyerly words, your occasional but most compelling) fantasy is to sexually dominate me. I have given you permission to do so, but who, then, is dominating whom?

May 23. We stand at the edge of the bed. You turn off the lamp, and the candles take effect. In the changing light all that can be heard is your pinkie ring circling to a halt on the table. I know what you have in mind.

May 30. We wake up and enter the world. Each of the three roses you gave me the night before—the red, yellow, and rose—has a different scent. You're smiling. Your eyes are warm and soft, open to me. You welcome me into you. I feel this instantly in my soul. We embrace, not uttering a word, yet the room is filled with voices. With you, I have begun to understand that feelings are words spoken.

June 15. A quiet weekend getaway on Fire Island. Except for us. The first evening, you found your way on top. I spread my legs wide. They ached. I wanted all of you. I got all of you.

The second evening, you found your way up there again. I felt several soft waves. Yours came harder. And again.

The third evening, I found my way on top and never wanted to leave. Our mouths buried themselves on each other's neck and around each other's tongue until we had to gasp for air. I cried out that I wanted all of you. The room disappeared. We were lost, never wanting to come back. Fire Island felt the same way about us.

June 21. Late Saturday evening. A dimly lit street on the outskirts of Brooklyn Heights. We leave the party and slowly make our way back to your car. As we lock the doors you tell me how uncomfortable you felt when he kept eyeing me over the hors d'oeuvres. You hesitated, explaining that you didn't want to seem protective, most of all, possessive. I clench the hair on the back of your head and make a fist. The magic word. I whisper that you have permission to possess me.

Silence.

You say my words cut deeply. You smother me with long, wet kisses, leaving me to take short, erratic breaths. You bury your tongue in my mouth and saddle yourself over me. I unzip my pants and unlatch my belt. You arch your head, take a long, deep breath, and hold me tight. I spread my legs for you to enter. You move forcefully inside. I spread my legs farther until my knees are pressing underneath the dashboard. I desperately maneuver my body between the seat, the steering wheel, and you.

You move in and out of me and tell me to be quiet. You kiss me deeply while keeping watch. I spread my legs farther, stretching my arms and pressing my hands across the upholstery. I plead with you not to stop. I kiss and breathe and moan into your mouth before settling back onto the seat. You hold me tight.

Later that night I play Liszt's *Sposalizio* for you. The frenetic pace of that piece tells it all.

July 7. We'd seen the advertisement for *The Portman Perfect Weekend* several weeks ago: A five-star hotel in midtown

Manhattan. So close to where we both live and work. So far from where we both live and work.

A Saturday afternoon. Destination unknown. We drive through the city streets, your sunroof open and music playing. The world is ours. You say you need a new suit, the upcoming trial and all, and I have no reason not to believe you.

But soon you move into the right lane when I know, and you know, that you need the left lane for a new suit. You veer into the Portman valet area, jerk the car into park, and say, "We're checking in."

Three o'clock on a sunny afternoon overlooking Manhattan and beyond from the 31st floor. So close to where we both live and work. So far from where we both live and work. We have three hours to make love before our dinner reservation at the Russian Tea Room—where it all began.

I whisper that I want to undress you. You let me, never uttering a word. The room is filled with warm light as you and I descend upon the bed and each other. From behind, I insert two fingers, then turn you over on your back and insert them again. My mouth and tongue join my fingers, knowing that this will put you over that edge we love to travel. Within moments those familiar short breaths come from your lips as I move faster inside. When you hold my shoulders, I know we are close. Your body stiffens and jerks before settling back into place. Stopping momentarily, I know, and you know, that we can go back to that place one more time. You hold me tightly as I begin. Within moments you surprise us both by jumping off that cliff twice more. We awaken ten minutes before our dinner reservation.

The Russian Tea Room, where we enjoyed dinner and undercurrents. I hardly remembered how to speak that night.

I studied you, taking you in, hoping you wouldn't notice. Hoping you would. That night I ordered the same dish that your then-lover ordered, knowing how much I wanted what she still had.

We return to the room. The sun is setting. You suggest a hot bath. You're already in the tub when I begin undressing in the candlelight. The sound of your swishing in the water brings me to my knees by the edge of the tub. I slip my left leg beside you and hold you tight. I immerse my body into the water and onto you.

My lips brush over a thin layer of water to caress your soft, wet skin. I run my hands down the length of you, feeling you move with me. I cup your breasts and slide down your legs—and to that wonderful place in between. Weightless, we take flight.

We towel-dry and put on fresh robes, only to have you immediately throw off yours by the side of the bed. You glide on top of me. I pull you in. You bring me to the edge of the bed and wrap my legs around your neck. You lap me up, bringing me to you as you always do. You lie on top of me and hold me tight. You lean over on one side and insert your fingers, moving hard and steady. My voice releases a groan when you enter so suddenly. You bury your mouth over mine. You hold me tighter, trying to contain my moans. You take me again, and completely by surprise. We fall asleep with the bed lamp growing hot and Chopin's *Etudes* filling the room.

Morning comes and so do you, with my mouth and fingers. I too, from behind, my face buried in the pillows. Late morning comes and goes and so does check-out time.

August 8. Sensations of you. On me. In me. Moving me. Holding me. You exhaling hard. Me gasping in. You tasting my nipples. Me capturing your tongue. In the morning the mango we share turns night and day into one and the same.

August 9. A dignified all-Brahms concert at St. Peters Episcopal on West 20th. Midway through the concert I discover dried lubrication in between my fingers. The scent takes me back to where you started in me from behind and finished me off on my back. I cried out your name, as soft, even ripples flowed up from my legs. When it came time to lay you down, I used my tongue to make soft, circular motions over and around your clitoris before slipping in one finger at a time. When you teetered over that edge, ready to jump off and take me with you, you begged me to move harder. You pulled tightly on my hair, bringing me up to your face. You grabbed my shoulders, my hand still inside you, and told me to look into your eyes and keep moving my hand. I bore into your eyes, the intimacy nearly too much. I thrust deeper and faster, making hard circular motions, your wetness trailing my every move. You inhaled a sliver of breath before clutching me tightly and remaining silent.

ANDANTE (smooth, moderate speed):

August 13. I know we are meant to be together when the absolute moment I climax, alone, thinking of you, the phone rings. Your upbeat, seductive voice permeates the receiver.

September 27. All I replay in my mind is you looking up from your stack of depositions, over the top of your lawyerly horn rims, and saying, "I love you intensely."

September 30. As we begin dinner you slide a tiny box containing a gold band toward my plate. I feel deep within me just how much I want to be with you.

October 1. Lying on our backs, trying to catch our breath, I think of how we each have just experienced every letter of the word *passion*. I replay our lovemaking in my mind for hours. But as time draws me further from these moments, I am led unwillingly from their view.

October 3. Sitting on your sofa eating Cajun chips makes the world seem mighty right. That is, until the video is over. Then the world becomes really right. I unbutton my shirt while you're still talking about the film. As always, you notice immediately and put your lips between my breasts. As the credits roll, your hand slips into my already-unzipped pants, as you guide my hand along the rough fabric of your jeans. Fortunately we had the foresight not to rent a second video.

October 5. You hold me tight, bite my nipple just hard enough, rub your finger tip around my dripping clitoris just fast enough, as I repeat your name over and over.

RONDO *(final movement)*, *with* REPRISE *(recapitulation):*

October 9. You tell me how attractive I am and that you've been attracted to me from the minute you laid eyes on me. I reach for your hand.

October 15. Almost a year, my love. I travel back in my mind to the Rainbow Room at Rockefeller Center where, last October, you told our waiter we were beginning a relationship. Onlookers were gracious. Back to Florida, where we lost any semblance of a tan. To Washington, D.C., where we marched with a million family members. And always, back to the first five minutes whenever we arrive at a hotel room.

Cactus Love

Lee Lynch

Until that night, I'd have bet my bottom dollar I was a washout. It'd been ten years since I touched my last woman in love. Too much like walking barefoot onto a sprawling prickly pear cactus in the dark. I just didn't have the energy for love.

Then Van came, with her youth and her brains. I hired her to run the retail end of my cactus ranch. That left me free to spend all my time on the growing, the watering, and—well, I ran out of things to do. I'd watch that young body run around, enjoying the heck out of life. Even after her breakup with Ivy, she was back in the saddle before you could say "Jack Rabbit."

That was October. I can see her standing in the bright sunlight, one foot on the metal step of my trailer, saying, "I'm going down to the bar tonight. Want to bet I find a lover before Christmas?" What'd she do then? Went out and got one. I confess that girl's been an inspiration to me. I went out and got one too.

Whoopee! I feel like dancing with my cacti.

Billie is older than I am by a couple of years, but she doesn't look like anybody's cute little grandma. Van called her the Matriarch, from the way the young ones at the bar would chew her ear.

I watched Billie.

I liked looking at her, sitting straight as a ruler's edge at the bar. She's part Irish, part Zuni Indian—tall, very skinny. Her bones are so broad and strong-looking you'd think she was some desert wild thing. Maybe that's what put me off at first. I'd always been one for your younger, femmier types. But Billie, she's not interested in all that. She's not butch, not femme. She's no garden-variety female at all. She's a monument. I could listen to her talk about her life all night...

But it wasn't listening I did that first night.

She had about as much stomach for that smoky, loud joint with its watered-down country jukebox as I did. She always left around 11 o'clock, just before it got really loud and wild. I'd decided after the first few times I saw her that I wanted at least to talk to her. The next time I went to the bar, though, I dithered and dithered. Before I knew it, it's 11 o'clock, she's leaving, and I can't think of a blamed thing to say to her anywhere as good as "Would you like to dance?" I'd missed my chance. So I let it go another week.

But you know, she started coming into my head a lot that week. When I was in bed at night, I'd imagine her, with that long, strong body next to me on the white sheets. I imagined the life story she'd tell. And I imagined her hands on me. I'd noticed them when I was next to her at the bar ordering drinks. Some arthritis, a little stiffness and knobbiness. Still, you got the feeling that bit of bother would be as likely to stop her as spines stop a wren from nesting in a cactus. I could feel the seasoned fingers on my hip, on the other parts of me that were never this cushiony for my earlier girlfriends. I kind of just ran her through my head, to see if I'd like it, or if I only wanted her because we were close in age. I'd get wiggly at the thought of Billie's touch. Not many women can seep into my head like she did, in the dark.

So the next Saturday night, that lulu of a night, I asked her to dance. She looked down at me and said nothing, nothing at all. But there was a little smile that puckered the corner of her mouth. And those brown eyes like polished jasper looked like they were laughing. Then she swept me out onto the dance floor. Swept me out there and danced me around those young couples like she'd put me on wheels. I never felt so light on my feet. That darned woman took my breath away. I never wanted the dance to end.

I asked her back to our table. Van was sweet-talking her new girl, so they didn't pay us much attention. Luckily it'd taken me till 10:30 to get up the nerve to buttonhole Billie. By this time it was getting on toward 11 o'clock and noisy in there. I told her about my business, asked her if she'd ever seen a cactus ranch by moonlight.

"Well, no," she said, laughing. "I can't say that I have—or heard such a barefaced line."

It turned out she lived near the bar and didn't have a vehicle. I drove her out here in Pickup Nellie, my old white Chevy. We parked behind one of the hothouses. Wonder of wonders, there was a moon shining down. Not quite full, but full enough. The moon looked like it was pounding up there in time to my heart. The night was pretty darned hot for November.

We walked out on the desert a ways without a flashlight. She was wordless, quiet-moving. I was just enjoying the company, come what may. Big patches of waning yellow desert broom like earth-moons glowed at our feet.

We didn't go too far so as not to disturb any critters.

On the way back she took my hand. I thought I'd melt right there at her feet, like some little teenage person.

"You want to come in?" I asked when we reached my trailer house.

"I didn't come all this way to turn around now," she replied, her teeth white against that sunburned skin. There was a dog tooth missing. I thought of her moist tongue seeking out the empty spot, all alone inside her mouth. Holy Toledo, I know I'm a goner when ideas like that creep up on me.

Billie squints when she talks, like she's measuring you. "I've been noticing you at the bar," she said, over some iced coffee I threw together. "You're not my type at all."

I had to grin. "You're not mine either."

She nodded. "If there's one thing I have learned in my life, it's that you have to take things as they come. It doesn't do to fight your spirit; it always gets its way. If it wants to go changing my tastes in women at the ripe old age of 69, well, then, I'm ready."

"Same here," I said. "I never wanted another girlfriend. All that heartache. But—" And I told her about Van's coming and about the blood that got stirred up in my veins. "I could take the lonesomes," I told her, "till I started wanting again."

"I hear you," she began. "I sit in my little cement block apartment and tell myself I'll stay home with the cat, read a good book, watch the TV. I don't need that bar. It's not the liquor that calls me—half the time I order milk, trying to put some flesh on these bones." She lifted her arm like I could see the scrawniness under her striped jersey. "Maybe I feel useful there. The kids come and pour their little hearts out to me. Sometimes they think they want to get me into bed, but to tell the truth, their energy drives me up a wall. I'd never get any peace."

She paused, setting down her glass. "I'm thinking, little Windy Sands, maybe I could stand a change of pace."

I told you the lady was big. Those arms were long. She reached clear across my narrow tabletop. Now her eyes were like some wise desert creature's looking into mine for, I don't know what, for some kind of sign, I suppose. Then she kissed me, a little shaky from that distance, her hands kneading my shoulders. And I kissed her back, giving her everything I had to let her know it wasn't just the kids who wanted her.

I stood. Led her to the bedroom, still with her hands on my shoulders, like she couldn't find her way without me.

"I guess we both know what comes next," I said, laughing. "But I'll keep the light out if you don't mind."

"Why? Because you've got an old body?" she asked. "Hell, it's not even as old as mine!"

"Yeah, but you're slender as the needles on a pinion pine."

"I'm scrawny, you mean. And I have scars."

She switched the light on. I saw the scars. An artery taken out of her legs for heart trouble. Gut trouble where she'd been sliced open a couple of times. That took my mind off me. I was whole, even with this body as round and pale as another earth-moon.

We lay full out against each other, like we were hungry. Like we were on fire, and by pressing ourselves together we could put it out. We held like that. We held like that for a long time. It felt good, but it didn't put out my fire. The longer we held, the hotter I felt. I wondered if the same thing was happening to Billie but knew I wouldn't find out till I reached between her legs, and it was too soon for that, old hands at this stuff or not.

After a while I started rubbing against her and rubbing against her, just the way we were, pressed together. She kissed me again, and I smelled the iced coffee and felt her sweat and the heat of our bodies in the trailer's hot air. Her skin felt slick and marked like the moon. We kissed and pressed into each other. Then, swift as a crafty old rock dweller looking for shade, she wriggled her arm between us. Oh, she found out I was raring to go. I heard her exhale. I don't know for sure that she was excited before then, but hot ziggety if that didn't do it for her.

She took her lips from mine and started kissing and licking my neck and my face, her tongue in my ear, in my mouth. I rode the heel of her hand like she was some fine horse taking me out across the desert under the blue, blue Arizona sky, taking me up a mountainside, green and lush like it gets over on the east end of Tucson. We rode so fast, I could hear the leaves stir from our passage until the sound of a rushing waterfall began to grow. She stopped so that I could see, so that I could feel, so that I was that water falling from the mountain. Falling down and down and down and...

Ten years of bottled up pleasure. Everything spilled out of me.

What I said after that was, "I'm too darned exhausted to turn over. Can we talk for a while?"

"Sure thing, Windy, if you have the breath to talk. Was that too much for you?"

"Not enough," I panted, "not hardly enough, Billie."

It was the first time I heard that laugh of hers. The mysterious-sounding, low, back-of-the-throat laugh that reminds me of Frank Sinatra singing about "come-hither looks" in my younger days.

She began telling me about the places she was raised in New Mexico. I tried to listen, but sleep came over me like a red-tailed hawk on a tasty pocket gopher. All I recall is that it got too cold, nights up there in the mountains for her. She migrated south in her truck and got factory work where she could. Now she's retired.

I was out long enough for the moon to follow us to my bedroom, right inside the trailer window. Billie was asleep too.

Oh, the moonlight on that body. Billie was less than slender; she was as bony as an ancient saguaro turned brown and ribby. Hips, shoulders, rib cage—all made her like a cradle I just fit into. My hand waltzed over the juts and hollows of her. I felt weak. From exertion? Lust? Maybe all I needed was a little snack.

No, I couldn't leave the sight before me, the white moonlight on the deep-toned body. She was as handsome as all get out. It didn't take long until one of my caresses woke her. She opened her eyes and her mouth and groaned for me. I just plunged in then, wondering if she'd ever had babies. She was so big. Plunged one finger, then two, then a third. She made herself smaller around me. I was too short to reach up and kiss her. She was too hot to bend down to me. I rested my cheek on her breast, plunged harder, deeper, softer, slower, quicker. She brought her hands flat across my shoulders and drummed and drummed and drummed as she came.

"If I smoked," she said after a while, "I'd say that calls for a cigarette."

"Cigarette, nothing! A ten-gun salute!"

We settled for my snack.

She sat up all grins, like a little kid going to a party. We padded to the kitchen bare-assed, dragged every darn thing out of that icebox we could find and had ourselves a feast.

Billie didn't stop beaming during the whole meal.

What am I talking about? Looking at the gap in her teeth, the mussed gray hair, at those brown eyes like mirrors full of desert roads and pickup trucks, honky-tonk gay bars and jukebox-dancing women, full of 69 years of love and disappointment and love again. Ah, jeez, I knew I'd found somebody who was going to make all the mess and bother of love worthwhile, and I'm still grinning right back at her to this day.

The Ladies' Room

by Judith Stelboum

I don't know about you, but I feel uncomfortable and out of place in the ladies' room, bathroom, rest room, *women, chicks, hers, setters*. I used to collect all the cute names, like some people collect matchbooks.

I don't know if I'm supposed to dress for the ladies' room. Maybe they should have some regulation ladies' outfit to slip over what you're wearing before you go in, just so you look like a "lady."

I always check the door twice to make sure I'm in the right room. I walk in, and these two women (ladies) are combing their hair in front of the mirror. They're both wearing these tight little miniskirts, heels, and stockings. I can't help looking at their legs first. Nice! Then my eyes move up their bodies, noticing the thin see-through blouse of one and the tight sweater of the other. Their outfits reveal high, full tits on the one with the sweater and hardened nipples on the one with the blouse. One of them has thick, long, wavy hair. Voguey. Hair you can really grab and hold, wrap around your hand.

They're putting on lipstick and checking out their eye makeup. I don't have to check the door again…no doubt about it. It's hard to believe…but…this is my room too.

And I think, *Well, we do this the same way, anyway. Don't we?* So they're talking, and I listen as I pee, because I'm beginning to doubt that I really am in the right room. Something about Timmy and Danny and restaurants and Chrissie's wedding, and I hear them giggling. Maybe I should check the door again?

Anyway, I come out of the stall, and they're looking at their nails…so I look too. Wow, it's enough to give you the chills. Those nails…like something out of a horror movie—long and red like some animal all bloodied from a recent kill. Except these ladies can't retract their claws. But they're admiring the nails. In fact, they're now talking about Patti or Sue or someone who does nails. I'm fascinated and hang around washing my face and hands just to hear the rest of it. I feel like I'm in some foreign country observing the local customs. So interesting!

One of them has permed red hair, which I think has to be dyed because her eyebrows don't match her hair and her skin is sort of an olive color. Redheads are always fair-skinned; at least, from my personal experience this has been true. Trust me on this one! I know what I'm talking about.

Anyway, the redhead begins to get nervous because she senses that I'm eavesdropping, and she pokes the other one. OK, so now they look at me. Believe me, you know I look nothing like those two. I'm wearing my uniform: black jeans, white shirt, black leather jacket, dark aviator glasses.

I can see the contemptuous look on their faces as we stare at each other in the mirrors over the sinks. So I want to whip it out and dangle it in front of them. You know…I want them to see something familiar. Something they both will recognize as part of their world. But the truth is, no matter how long I've been playing with it, how hard it's been sucked and pushed and pulled, it just ain't gonna get that long. And I'm not packing today anyhow, be-cause…who would have thought I needed to?

I walk over to the door, lock it, lean against it, and say, "Excuse me, this is the ladies' rest room, and would one of you ladies—*women*—like to rest here with me for a while? I see there's a chair over there. Would one of you like to sit on my thighs? Would anyone like to sit on my face? Would you like some fingers for an appetizer or more for a main course?

"Or if either of you ladies would like, I can just lay out my leather jacket on the floor, and we can do it there. Don't be bashful or shy, baby, speak up. Tell me what you want! Personally, I like to talk while we're doing it. Don't you? I think it adds to the excitement."

Their contempt has turned to fear. They're clutching each other, mouths open, shaking. I think they're about to scream. Well, one is, anyway. The one with the longest nails. Yup, it's the redhead.

So I continue, staring at the redhead. "Well, I can 'do you,' but you could never 'do me.' No, sir—oops, *madam*—not with those nails anyway. Next time you see Patti or Sue or whomever, tell her that those nails are just too long for real lovemaking."

I walk over to the redhead and stroke her cheek—palm first, then with the back of my hand. She recoils from my touch, her eyes wide, face turned away from mine. I have all I can do to keep from smacking her hard, leaving my hand and signet ring imprinted across her face. Well, Timmy or Danny would have done it better, I'm sure.

"Don't scream now!" (Isn't that what all the rapists say?) I place my finger against my lips. "Sh." I'm laughing as I move toward the door, turn the lock, and walk out.

Turtlehawk Dreams an Ocean Breathing

by Lynne Yamaguchi Fletcher

When did wanting to kiss her turn to certainty that I would? When I turned from an eight-foot-tall painting of purple coyotes dancing in a red-and-orange night to find her watching me, the flecks in her eyes flashing green across the gallery, the tip of her tongue seeking the corner of her half-smile like a shadow nudging light.

We had spent the day together, meeting at 8 o'clock in the parking lot at the base of Squaw Peak to make the climb before the heat became too intense. In another few weeks 8 o'clock would be a late start, but this early in May, the daily high hadn't yet broken 100 degrees, and we could count on getting up and back at a leisurely pace without frying.

We took our time hiking up, stepping aside to let by the backpackers-in-training and the runners, some on their second or third trip up or down. We talked as we walked, about everything under the sun: the chollas haloed in the morning light, the hummingbirds sipping the first waxy blooms of the saguaros, the city spreading its turquoise finery (backyard

pools) below us as we climbed higher and higher, her growing up in the desert, my hopscotch journey here, her pending
divorce, my editing, her teaching—one subject segueing into
the next like morning into day.

She fascinated me. It wasn't her looks, though she was
pretty enough, with a lively face under a cap of hair four
shades lighter than my near-black, lit with random strands that
shone golden in the sun. Rather, it was the conviction of her
charm that drew me, the aura she projected, at once naive and
seductive, of a child-woman certain of her allure. She didn't
need a model's physique to claim womanhood; her being
pale, petite, and succulent proclaimed it. Sex was an attitude
with her, an angle of eye, a line of throat, a language she
spoke with assurance and, one was sure, fluently, though she
dropped only a word or two, perfectly pronounced, here and
there into conversation.

Winded and exhilarated from the final, vertical climb, we
lingered an hour at the top of Squaw Peak, longer than we'd
planned, sprawled on a rock face, basking in our bodies, taking in the Sunday-blue sky with what we'd learned about
each other. We'd spanned a range of feeling in our conversation, shifting fluidly from solemnity to silliness to sadness and
onward. Now we were mostly silent as we shared an orange
and drank from our water bottles, careful to leave enough for
the hot trek down. She'd sweat in patches, I observed, whereas my T-shirt and shorts were uniformly darkened.

The film of dust that had settled over her pink skin gave her
the illusion of a tan. She was the palest desert dweller I'd seen,
but she seemed blithely unaware of her pallor in this city of
sun worshippers. In contrast, I looked like a native. When,

unconsciously, I reached one brown finger to trace a line of freckles down her arm, she only smiled.

The trip down was quick, hot, and breathless, as gravity outstripped the desire for conversation down the steep slope. I led the way to the shaded water fountain at the base where, having finished the last of our bottles, we doused ourselves before getting into our cars. We both were dry by the time we got to my house for a quick shower and change of clothes.

She insisted I go first, so I set her up at the kitchen table with the Sunday paper and a frothy mug of juice and seltzer and hopped into the shower to rinse the dust off. I was in and out in three minutes but took my time toweling off to give her— and me—some time to breathe and assess the morning. I didn't want the exhilaration of the climb to skew my expectations: I'd skinned both knees falling for straight women before, and the memory stung enough to keep me stepping carefully. It wasn't love I wanted now but romance: to indulge in the getting-to-know-you rapture of a burgeoning friendship without drowning in need to tube the rapids without swallowing the river.

I left a set of towels for her on the edge of the sink, called out to let her know the bathroom was free, and disappeared into my room to change.

She surprised me then, appearing 20 minutes later in a sassy white cotton dress and turning her back to me with a "Will you?" My hands went hot and clumsy on the zipper. The sprinkling of freckles stopped below her shoulder blades. My stomach stopped at my groin.

The *Cinco de Mayo* festivities were still warming up when we arrived at the Buttes in her car, just short of noon. She led the way in, producing two tickets—her treat, her invitation—from a pocket I didn't know she had. Hungry from the climb and from want of a real breakfast, we went first for the food, loading our plates with Indian fry bread, fresh blue-corn tortillas, salsa, beans, guacamole, mesquite-broiled *pollo*. Balancing a pitcher of water under my plate, I followed her to a ringside table under the slatted roof of the pavilion. We sat and proceeded to feast.

The first of the bands was setting up, and she watched the preparations eagerly while her fingers tucked bite after bite into a mouth as eager as her eyes. She loved dancing as much as I did—and a wider range of music. Half a song and she was out on the concrete, half a plate of food forgotten. We danced together, she danced alone, she danced with any man who asked, charming each for the span of a song or two, but clearly herself charmed by the music. Salsa, jazz, rock, reggae, country, swing, her energy never flagged. In between sets and changeovers we amused each other making up stories about members of the crowd.

She was a terrific flirt. She could have flirted in any language, conjuring response with mirrors, not words: catching the light in the lake of her eyes; tossing it back in a glint of lips, a gleam of shoulder. To be the focus of her attentions was electrifying. My palms and soles hummed.

A troupe of dancers performed, torsos thrusting, feet throbbing hypnotically to the beat of African and Caribbean drums. I knew one of the male dancers through the local food co-op and introduced her to him at her request. As I watched, she looked long at his bare chest and muscled calves, smiling, and touched her lip; I heard him swallow. She led him to the dance floor when the next band struck up, and I watched him whirl and counterstep before her, solar plexus high and forward, his eyes intent on hers.

She was back in three dances.

I told myself again, sternly, not to take her attentions personally. Already, the warning felt like hindsight.

I began to feel drugged, with that split consciousness that says at once, "Whoa, you're losing control" and "I'm flying, fly me higher." No; yes. Two letters versus three: I felt the slide of the scales like a ship listing hard starboard as my ribs rose skyward. The mystery here was not what her eyes and fingers and mouth were doing but how powerless I felt to resist them.

I was quiet on the drive to Scottsdale, where we were to meet some friends to attend a gallery opening. She still spilled over with energy, but I had danced hard to shake free of the spell I'd fallen under and, happy just to feel both feet again, was content for the moment to play appreciative audience.

Our friends couldn't keep the surprise from their faces when they saw us together. It wasn't the fact of our arriving together—we were expected—but her high color and my off-balance grin that surprised them. They knew us from different contexts—her, more or less professionally, through the university; me, socially—and apparently the borders hadn't crossed in their minds.

One—Ricki—took me aside as soon as she gracefully could. "I thought she was straight," she whispered.

"She is," I answered.

Ricki punched me in the arm. "Tomorrow," she said, wagging a finger at me. "I want the dirt."

I laughed and rejoined the entourage.

"Animal Dreams," the show was called. The animals here could not be found in any zoo. Cartoonlike creatures cavorted in big, brilliantly hued paintings; clothed clay beasts prowled the square tops of pedestals; humanlike faces gazed from masks of paint and bone and feathers and teeth and fur. Were these animal dreams of humans or human dreams of animals? I found the work and the theme bizarrely fitting: animal joy, animal hunger, animal mystery.

I quickly left the socializing to the others and wandered off by myself to look at the masks. Peering into the faces, shifting my angle of vision to catch their shifting expressions, I was suddenly struck by the familiarity of the movement. Mirrors, I thought. Here was the artist flirting with the viewer flirting with mystery, power, fear.

One mask stood out from the others. Relatively plain except for a sea-green opalescent finish, it featured half-lidded eye holes and a beaklike nose under a high brow ridge. Small feathers hung at its temples, and the upper lip overhung the lower. Where its wearer's throat would be, a winged vertebra dangled. The unexpected effect was of utter serenity. "Turtlehawk Dreams an Ocean Breathing," the card beside it said.

On impulse, I began experimenting, trying to mirror the mask's expression. How well I succeeded I don't know, but for a moment, before I grew too self-conscious to continue, a feeling rose in me of light, as if I stood in the copper flame of sunset with stars in my head. The pitching sea I'd been riding all day calmed. I wanted to kiss her, and the wanting suffused me with happiness.

Before I could savor the feeling, Ricki snagged me again and dragged me over to view the paintings. Now the work mirrored me: colors of elation, shapes of joy. I grinned and, at a prod from Ricki's elbow, turned. Across the room her eyes flashed "Go." A wave washed through me, leaving in joy's stead a feeling, cooler, metallic, tall. My hands jumped. My center of balance went south.

"Uh-huh," said Ricki.

We were both quiet as she was driving me home. We had each declined our friends' invitations to go for ice cream, but I, at least, wasn't ready for the day to end. On impulse, as she turned down the road that cut through the desert park near my house, I suggested a moonlight hike. She was more than agreeable.

The small lot near my favorite climb was empty—unusual except on a Sunday night. After we'd parked she pulled an old quilt from the trunk of her car, and we followed a vague trail up the small red sandstone mountain. Halfway up we spread her quilt, staking out a rounded ledge facing the city to our west, with a shallow cave scooped by hot winds at our backs and a screen of creosote bushes between us and the lot below.

The city lights spread before us; a sea of stars spread over us. Balmy, not even sweater cool, the night air enfolded us in the desert's perfume. Wrapped in this intoxication of sky and dust and creosote and millennia of light, we leaned back, near but not touching, and soaked it all in.

We sat without speaking for a long time, until the erratic flight of a bat caught our attention. We watched it avidly, speculating as to its food, its nesting habits, the reasons for people's fear. We went off on a long tangent then about pocket mice, king snakes, jackrabbits, coyotes.

At this, the moment in the gallery flooded back and I lapsed into silence. What was she remembering?

The quality of the silence had changed. Charged now, the night seemed to be waiting, and we with it.

A moment of laughter was all it took.

The bat came back, with a companion this time, and she made a crack about Dracula's bride. I countered with a slur on Batman and Robin.

"What about Batwoman?" she asked.

"If that's Batwoman," I said, "the other one's Catherine Deneuve."

She frowned at me, confounded, then her eyebrows lifted and her mouth opened and she laughed. "Aha," she said. "And where is Susan Sarandon this evening?"

I nudged her. She nudged me back. We sat for several minutes leaning up against each other, feeling the intersection of our bodies, shoulders, arms, thighs. Finally, I took her hand, brushing the fingertips with my own, tracing, lightly, the grooves of her palm. After a moment I raised her hand to my lips, kissed each fingertip slowly, touching the faint salt of each with my tongue. I kissed her palm, dragging my lip across the pad at the base of each finger. Where two fingers cleaved, I licked, softly.

I looked at her. Her eyes were closed, her head tipped back and turned slightly away, as if listening for her name. I pressed my face to her palm, closing my eyes, then wrapped my mouth full around her first finger and tugged, drawing the salt from her pores, drawing the blood to her skin, drawing a moan from her opening throat. I met and held her startled gaze as I moved to the next finger, sucking deep, pulling back to take both fingers in. Blood filled my limbs. My tongue swam around and between her fingers. The smell of sun on skin and a hint of sunscreen teased me from the back of her hand. As I breathed it in I could feel her in me already, how it would be to fill this wanting.

Hooking her thumb under my chin, she pulled my face toward her, hunger and something like danger darkening her eyes. I let her fingers slide from my mouth and waited. Her lips touched mine like smoke from the fire between my thighs, and the center of my chest caught flame. She pressed into me savagely; the world fell away. And came back in a slow kiss made slower by the racing of my pulse. Breathing deeply, I savored the silken rim of her sweetly clean mouth, small arc by small arc, welcoming her tongue—the satin underside, the softly nubbled surface—with mine.

How long we kissed I have no idea. Long enough to drown and be resuscitated. We kissed till we reached a clean, clear place in our kissing and found ourselves wrapped around each other like vines after an April rain, satiated, drunk on fullness. We lolled against each other, laughing. And rested, face against face, breathing the night air.

And then we kissed again, and the hunger rose like a tidal wave from a sea shaken at its floor.

Suddenly four hands weren't enough, and her underwear was in my hand, my pants were to my knees, and she was over me, pinning my wrists to the rock, our arms taut over my head, her face fierce a breath from mine.

Eyes locked on mine, she lowered herself onto me, hot wet scalding my exposed belly. Deliberately, never wavering her gaze, she began to rub, back and forth, up and down, down and around. I was drowning in sensation. Juices flowed from me like hot tears. Feeling her gyrations beginning to center on my bush, I stretched myself longer—longer to stretch her longer, to feel the length of her body rolling against mine.

She wriggled lower, pulling my wrists down to my shoulders, her mouth at my chest seeking skin but finding shirt. She sat up, releasing my arms, to concentrate instead on her movements. My hands found her under her dress and gripped, slipping over the slick muscles of her thighs and buttocks as she rode me. Her hands gripped my ribs, then my thighs as she leaned back, pressing up on me. My pelvis and neck arched hard as I angled for fuller contact. I closed my eyes to focus on the center of our juncture.

We were like two oppositely charged wires, the voltage jumping in each with each roll of our hips, the ends brushing closer and closer, tantalizingly close to contact. Small sounds fluttered from her throat; my breath soughed through narrowed lips. Heat engulfed my pubis as my whole being strained toward her. The ends of the wires moved closer and closer, millimeters apart now, current leaping the liquid between them.

And then they touched. A deep shudder shook us both. A wave of liquid heat swept the insides of my legs and rolled from my feet, and the backlash rippled audibly through my chest and neck. She remained arched back, breathing long, loose breaths like sighs.

Kicking my ankles finally free of my pants and unbuttoning my shirt with one hand, I stretched the other behind her and unzipped what I had zipped that morning. Easing the dress from her shoulders, then over her head, I pulled her to me. Breast to breast, mouth to liquid mouth, we steeped in our mingled sweat.

We ended up on our sides, murmuring together forehead to forehead, stroking the length of each other's body for a long spell. Then the sound of tires on blacktop and a sweep of headlights below us swung me upright. Through the web of creosote I watched a lone car pass through the park.

When I turned back she was smiling, her body a feast of cream in the starlight. Feeling a purr begin in my chest, I bent to the cream, lapping the bowl of her belly and ribs with long sweeps as she drew her fingers through my hair. I worked my way slowly up to her breasts, nuzzling and lapping each nipple till it stood, then painting broad wet circles around the near nipple with my tongue. Eyes closed, she kneaded the small of my back with one hand, tracing my face with the other. I twined one fingertip in her damp pubic curls, then shifted to straddle one leg.

Cupping in my hand the breast I'd been licking, I leaned over her and took into my mouth as much as I could of the other. I sucked slowly with my whole mouth, alternately flicking the round berry with the tip of my tongue. Her hands tangled in my hair, urging me to her. The other berry I brushed with my thumb till I could feel her begin to undulate beneath me.

Her grip on my head tightened, and when I raised my head to look at her, she seized me to her, mouth open, devouring mine, all teeth and jaw and tongue and need. She engulfed my chin, scraping my neck with her teeth, sliding her hot mouth over my larynx. I broke away, startled, stiff-arming the rock we lay on to hold myself above her. We stared at each other.

My arms bent. I devoured back, flattening myself against her as she gripped my buttocks and thrust her thigh between my legs. I bucked against her, smearing her thigh with my juices. Our nipples chafed together. I ground my hip into her and myself against hers.

My fingers found her vagina, and I thrust two in to the knuckles. She bucked and shuddered and broke from my mouth with a cry. I rolled to her side. Her hips began to rock and rotate; her hands clutched at the quilt. Whimpering gasps sprang from her chest. I began sliding my fingers in and out with a long twisting motion. Her vagina ballooned. My fingertips circled her cervix. Her cervix pushed back.

My thumb on her clit, fingers pressing upward against the washboard inside, I began moving my whole arm in circles, slowly at first, faster as her hips responded as if with a mind of their own. Knees bent, her feet pressed into the rock, she bore down on me, hips in the air, jerking up and down, side to side, circling with me and against me. I closed my eyes and labored to stay with her.

My own body was on the verge of orgasm, my genitals so engorged I could have come at a touch. My skin sang; a howl leapt within my throat. I held my thighs tightly closed.

Her cries filled my chest, high grunting moans that punctuated her quickening thrusts. A quick in-breath and suddenly she went silent, her hips suspended in motion. A low cry began in her belly then, rising in pitch and volume as her vagina convulsed around my fingers and her hips jerked and dropped and her hands seized my shoulders and held on.

We lay, spent, for several minutes. Then, my fingers still in her, I leaned over to taste her. She shivered. I knelt carefully between her legs and parted her hairs with my other hand. She groaned and reached for my head, then fell back. Stretching my legs out behind me, I folded my arm under my chest and bellied up, touched my lips to those lips, and exhaled hotly. She sighed. I touched my tongue to the underside of her clit. Her breath caught and resumed. Easing my fingers halfway out, I licked them, savoring the heady fragrance on my tongue. And continued my slow lick up to rub my nose in her wet curls.

She swept her feet up my sides, gripping my head a moment, then rested them on my shoulder blades, her knees flung wide.

I lapped the spill of cream from the satin grooves on both sides of her clitoris. Then, gently, slowly, as I enfolded her clit in my lips, I began wiggling my fingers alternately back and forth inside her. I made my tongue as soft and flat as possible, tracing small, gentle circles against her. When I felt that bud swell I began sucking softly and running my tongue up again and again from her innermost lips.

I let my fingers slip from her and my tongue take their place. A low "oh" escaped her, and she pressed against me, tightening her vagina as I reached deeply in, kissing me back as thoroughly as she had with her mouth.

I drank her in and in.

Slick-faced, I returned at last to her clit, breathing on it softly, circling it with the tip of my tongue. Her hips echoed the motion almost imperceptibly. I continued the circles, slowly increasing my pressure as her circles became more pronounced. Occasionally I let my tongue flicker across her, resuming the circling as she would stop hers and begin to moan. Finally, she began to squirm against my mouth with a low whimper.

I began flicking her clit in earnest and slipped my fingers back into her to resume my back-and-forth motion. She began rocking up and down, her whole body now, and her whimper took on the same quick rhythm.

With my free hand I pressed her mound, pushing the skin back to expose her further. My flicking became a vibration, a thrum humming all through me, electrifying my fingertips, toes, clit. I felt as though I were licking myself, each flicker of tongue on her bringing me closer to combustion. But it was her I wanted, on me and in me. The force of my wanting narrowed to twin points of flame on the tips of my tongue and clitoris.

Her clutching of my ribs with her feet urged me on. Faster and faster came her staccato song; faster and faster came my answer. Then, as her rocking became a pulse and the hum became a roar, she jerked—almost sitting up—and jerked, jerked, jerked, jerked, each spasm smaller, subsiding like a basketball's dribble to a state of rest.

When her walls had stopped fluttering and our breathing had slowed to normal and the evaporation of sweat was at last beginning to chill our skin, I eased my fingers from her and climbed up to her head. She looked at me. "Lover," she said.

I grinned hugely and flopped on my back next to her, one hand rubbing my still-wet belly.

She nuzzled her way into my armpit, and I wrapped her in skin.

I was in some other space, breathing night, lulled by star-song, when I became conscious of something sharp brushing my nipple. I opened my eyes to find her teasing her finger-nails across my breast. Seeing me looking, she sat up.

She looked at me then, at my body, running her hands along my skin as though her fingertips held another set of eyes. I wondered if she'd ever really looked at another woman's body before. She kept returning to my breasts, cupping their curve in her palms, rolling my pursed nipples under her thumbs, bending finally to touch her tongue to one. She closed her lips around it carefully, exploring its tip with her tongue, pressing into my breast when I drew a quick breath and held it. Heat was beginning again its spread from my center.

She laid her face against my belly for a moment, turning her head back and forth to feel the smoothness against each cheek. My ribs began to prickle; my breath, to quicken.

I felt a finger teasing my bush hairs and stifled a moan—a moan she dragged from me in the next moment, her fingernails leaving four hot trails down the inside of each thigh. I started to sit up; she pressed me back into the rock.

She pushed my legs open wider and knelt between them. I curved around to watch her.

As she leaned in to look, I could feel my juices begin their slow cascade from my vagina. Sure enough, a touch and she held up a finger: on its tip a dollop of cream. Watching me carefully, she painted her mouth with it. She licked. She smiled. My insides flipped. I closed my eyes as desire flooded my forearms and thighs.

At the touch of her thumb as it pulled back the hood of my clit, I looked again. She was peering closely through the dim light into my spread lips. Her lips pursed. She blew across me. My vagina contracted, releasing another daub. She touched me again and painted the smooth wetness along my ribs.

She seemed to make a decision then and surprised me by moving to my side. She bent to kiss me, a short, sweet kiss, in the middle of which something like fire, her fingertip, seared the underside of my clit. A jolt shot through me.

She moved her mouth to my breast again, tonguing and sucking and rubbing her whole face over me. That single point of heat stayed on my clitoris, even as I began to writhe under the intensity.

She stayed with me, breaking her touch only to dip again into the river of my juices. Was her finger moving, was I moving against her, was this heat pure energy and not friction at all?

I only knew that my skin was raging, that I wanted her wrapping me like a fresh dressing on a burn. Or was it a match I wanted, ready to immolate myself on her pyre? I heaved my hips at that point of fire, bracing my arms and shoulders against the rock like a sacrifice.

All my consciousness came to exist in that single point of contact as that hot coal grew hotter. All awareness of my body vanished, though I continued to thrash, that incendiary urge driving me toward combustion. But the higher the heat climbed, the higher my threshold for heat seemed to rise. Thrash as I might, I could come no closer to flame.

Finally, I no longer knew whether I was chasing flame or fleeing it. A groan tore my throat.

She dipped again but this time came back above my clit, stroking the stiff root above the hood. Something in me melted. My body came back. I could feel her length stretched along my leg now, her head resting on my hip, my hands, one lost in her hair, the other pressing my own mound, the pleasure flowing from my center with each rub of my root. A long "a-a-ah" rolled from my chest. I rode the pleasure as if floating in a tropical sea, saturated with sun and lazy with longing answered. Dipping and bobbing, I let the swells lift me like breath, deliver me like breath. Closer and closer to sky I rode, basking in the billowing flow till the ocean rose in me and flung its swollen waters on my shore.

I moaned.

She slipped over my chest to cover me like a wave. My mouth found hers and submerged. All was water. We twined together like anemones on the sea floor, wet on wet everywhere, swimming in each other, around each other, our mouths and limbs and fingers everywhere at once. Turning, diving, flipping, and sliding in an underwater dance, we skimmed bottom. We sang sea. We came up for air to find ourselves mirroring each other, sitting mouth to mouth, breasts to breasts, legs scissored around each other, one over, one under, our cunts open and joined.

That night I would dream of ocean, dream an ocean breathing.

The Common
Price of Passion

by Jess Wells

"My dearest," Meg's letter said, "someday you will get off the train, and I will take your hand as it hangs by your side, raise it to my lips to kiss the palm that has always only waved good-bye, kiss the hand that has daily held a pen but rarely held me. 'Mine, finally' is what my heart will say. Mine, finally. My lips into your palm, your tiny slip of fingers across my cheeks and nose. Do you know that the mention of a train brings me visions of your wrist and the way I will sleep with the tips of your fingers curled in trust under my chin, your arm in the space between my grateful breasts? Make plans to see me. Tell me you'll be here. It has been too many years of making do with words, and these letters are beginning to show a woman forging hope into desperation. We are the stuff of sex and passion, my darling. That is who we are and must be. Send me faint gesture of a train ticket, a glimmer of a plane reservation. I await your arrival. Be, finally, adventuring."

"My dearest," she wrote later that week, "as I walked through my restaurant, my dress played with my thighs and asked me where you were. Today I dreamed of the down on the nape of your neck that leads me to the silk of your hair, of my lips accepting the invitation to bring my tongue to your ear. In my mind your neck has turned to receive my lips a thousand times since I saw you last (two quick days to sustain us for six long months!). Across a thousand miles the shadow of your body presses into mine and tells me that we need to be together, not just in thoughts, in the fleeting moments when the memory of you and the languid sex we shared makes me forget that I am driving in traffic, determinedly foraging for okra worthy of my grandmother's gumbo; not just in midnight visions that are so sweet and tangled that I awake, certain you are bringing strawberries from the next room; not just in the sudden feel of your hands moving up my thighs, trembling with the need to pretend that they do not know where they're going and aren't in a hurry to get there.

"I write, daring to say: Be my lover. Let me see you in the morning, wrestling with dreams of bag ladies and your dead father. Let me catch you absently staring out the window, the light warming your skin when you are scowling and you don't notice your beauty, not then nor when you're ironing in your bra or driving. Surely there is a way to capture this passion we have, this desire that makes the paper in these envelopes crackle. Your letters are my bones—they hold me together. They are the strength I need. Your letters arrive, and, mere paper, they manage to be your hands gruffly clasping my face to draw me to your lips, forceful with their passion. How can you dominate me with paper? How can you make me yield, collapsing under the sweet drug of my submission, wanting nothing more than to lie down and receive your skill? I sleep with your letter clutched in my hand, as if it could approximate the warmth of flesh.

"The memory of our fiery times together has kept me alive for years: the rendezvous in midpoint cities, the hotels, the backs of cars, the charade of chance meetings in museums, fleeting, forbidden sex in public places, and then the recollection of those times, the descriptions and dissection. I used to litter my bed with your letters until it was more paper than sheet and rise in the morning singing over the wealth of our love, of the attention and climax each postmark signified. Showering, I was careful of the water, as if each inch of my skin were covered with precious ink that should never be blurred.

"But, my dearest, you have to know that something is different now. The fog has brought in a need for comfort. Oh, I know you think that is preposterous, but these are times that require shelter. So I ask you, what is the price of this passion? I look at our letters, and they seem so thin, not infused with the blood and heat of flesh. I am sad. There. I've said it. I ache. If I ask you to meet me, to make more memories, it simply postpones feeling this bruise that I know is there. Did you know I had a birthday? That we had an anniversary? I went to a party last week and was the only single woman there and thus subject of pity and cheap sexual jokes. I couldn't tell them about you, couldn't describe what we have. I don't just want you. I want us. I can hear what you say: The tension of our separation fuels our passion. Those who know the realities of butter knives and nasal sprays do not know the ecstasy of the flawless passion we have, you will claim. I can see you pacing through the bedroom, my pubic hairs clinging to unlikely spots on you. You pontificate: "Consensus is the death of seduction." "Would you prefer," you nearly shout, "a love scene that begins with the question, 'Shall we have sex now or after *Roseanne*?'" Your reasoning and the furious sex you give me later have kept me all these years.

"Is the price of our passion this paper-thin love? All these evenings standing alone in the movie line, taking a book to dinner? Is the distance really what makes the sex burn so bright? You must ask yourself, my darling, which is the fuel—the paper or the love? If it is the love, it would survive. If it is the paper, is it a price worth paying? Write to me, my darling, and as I always close with a plea to see you, I ask you to take me in your arms. Break the mold and come sooner. Plan to be here months early. I cannot wait this time. Feed your wild streak and simply knock down my door. Be, finally, here."

"My dearest," Meg wrote later that month, "you are coming, aren't you? I am standing in such infuriating passivity, as if at an elevator that will not arrive, toast that will not golden-brown. I stomp my foot, and the prep cook puts her head down, chops faster. What can I tell her: I'm anxious for the arrival of the one who makes the sweat slick my body, who cuts my breath into short bursts with a simple move of a hand? I am waiting, and the air crackles with the void. Your letters have stopped since I asked you to fly to me, and I'll say it: I am in pain. The cold air seems to be against my skin all day as if I were not clothed. Where are your words? The memory of your eyes? Even your neck, drinking in the luxury of turning for my lips, moving slowly in a dream every night since, your neck is no longer moving. I feel like an animal lost on a windy night.

"Tell me, my love, can we put this passion away in a drawer like a scarf that doesn't match this morning's suit? And if you would have me do that, then what do I tell the fire in my chest, so willing to send flames into my hands so they will reach out for you, touch you in my dreams, touch me in reply? Shall I pretend I can put out the fire? Stop thinking of your eyes, your smile? Pretend that I could possibly stop the plan to cup the exquisite smallness of your head, the obvious place where these hands were meant to live. You wouldn't ask me to, would you?

"You are arriving, aren't you? Be, finally, committed."

"My dearest," she wrote in the middle of the night, "I know you're not arriving, and so this will be my last letter. I wanted you to know there is beauty in the small kiss. It is a kiss given in passing, in public, in airports, before opening the door to my mother's house. It is dry-lipped, close-lipped. It is not gripping or sweaty. There are no flailing arms or tangled legs associated with this kiss. It is tender because it knows the simple pain and fear of everyday life, it knows the unspeakable sounds of early morning. To this tender kiss, laundry is loving. I can hear you shrieking. You consider all these things so pedestrian, but there is, in fact, love and sex in the cups/mops/plates of two lives entwined. Now I wonder, *Why can't you see this, my beloved?* These are not just legs tangled or fingers engrossed in a message but lives entwined. Admittedly, there are no delicious tastes or grateful sighs in picking linoleum, but afterward every step becomes something shared—a thanksgiving—and when every step is a prayer, every object imbued with conviction and appreciation, they each carry their own little moan.

"I have been hearing these moans lately. I thought myself impervious to these sounds, but I heard them in a Laundromat, a couple standing in each other's arms watching the tumble cycle, in the theater line when someone offered an umbrella. For the first time I wondered if you would do this for me, and it made me sad. Does our passion actually require so much isolated investment? Why is that we can seem to afford only one type of passion between us? These other lovers have been willing to pay the common price of passion—to watch their sheets grow slightly cold in return for a warm arm clutching an umbrella. Standing in the theater line, the fog dripping off the ends of my hair, I wondered about the price I was paying for the passion we have.

"I saw a couple in their 80s yesterday, and I stopped in the street to cry. They tottered on each other's arms, unable to walk apart any longer, and their clothing was indistinguishable. Every inch of the two of them had been tended a thousand times by the other. Can you even imagine a passion that could burn not that bright but that long? I need to totter along with someone, my love, to be offered things that are pedestrian like coffee that is just my setting, just my brand, more difficult to offer than lips on my breast.

"My darling explosion of heat, I thank you for the burst of light that you have been, and through the puff of your smoke, I reluctantly give you up. The wider world of juice containers and mortgage payments calls me, offering dry kisses, passionate with a long, quiet history. I say good-bye. Be, finally, alone."

Down at Shug's

by Catherine Lundoff

I was driving my rig down the interstate, you know, that real boring stretch up north. So I started spacing out a little, thinking about the new waitress down at Shug's, 'cause there wasn't much to look at. Shug's is that restaurant in Cramerville where I always stop at when I'm on long hauls. I pretty much just do short hauls, natural foods, rice cakes for yuppies, that kind of stuff. Every now and again I step in and do one of the longer routes 'cause someone's sick or on vacation or whatever. Started driving when I lost my job at the factory, and it's good work mostly.

Anyway, this new waitress was hot. Asian gal, name of Amy, with this long black hair that she puts up in one of those "French rolls," I think they're called, real pretty face and the most gorgeous bod I've seen in a long time. Believe me, I've seen a lot. After all, I've been out for about 20 years, and she's just as femme as I like 'em. Since my wife and I split a while back 'cause she...never mind.

Well, let's just say that it wasn't a pretty breakup. Nope. Hurt like hell. Still does. Still not really up for looking or meeting anyone new. Why the hell else'd I be sitting around this fleabag bar, telling you my latest road stories? That sound like a butch with better things to do? OK, then. You get the next round.

So what happened was this. No sooner did I start thinking about that gal than I just had to stop by Shug's and check her out again. Wasn't even sure if she was family or not but figured "What the hell?" No harm in looking. I'd talked to her a little last time I was in, and flirting with a pretty gal, even a straight one, is better than nothin'. Plus Shug's a good 'un, and I like talking to her too. Life on the road's kinda lonely, and I didn't have nothin' to return home to 'cept the cats.

I was on my return from my run, so I wasn't in a big hurry, not so long as I had the rig back by the next afternoon. Stopped off to help another trucker with rig trouble on the way. He about shit when I got out of the cab and he realized I wasn't a guy. Figured he'd take my help anyhow, seeing as how there wasn't much of a choice. The point is that I was late getting into Shug's, like after 11 or so.

Thought my luck would have run out on me and she wouldn't be working, what with the place closing around 3. But since I like Shug OK and she makes one hell of a pie, I figured it'd be worth it. Good woman to talk to. I know 'cause she always works late nights, and we talk a lot. Pity she's straight. Anyway, I pull the rig into the lot, look through the window, and damned if Amy wasn't working the night shift. I checked my hair quick in the mirror and reckoned I looked as sexy as I was gonna get, at that hour anyhow. Quit laughing.

Well, I went struttin' across the parking lot. Had on my shit kickers and that big old belt buckle and Levi's like I always wear.

Yeah, I know I look like one of them Western wear ads—so what? Can I get on with the story? Least I don't chew.

I saw Shug working the counter, serving the couple of good old boys and whatnot that're hanging around at that hour. She gave me a big grin when I came in.

"Hey, Pepper! Long time no see. Want some joe?"

So I said "hey" and sat down at the counter to start shooting the breeze with my pal. The rednecks were giving me the eye, but then a few of them remembered me from other runs and nodded to me. Not like some places where I'd have a hell of a time getting served, let alone leavin' in one piece.

Got to be careful on the road. I carry a blade, but I don't carry it into diners and such as a rule, 'less I think I need it. Plus I trust Shug. She told me one time that her sister was a dyke. Got thrown out of the house when she was just a kid, and they ain't seen hide nor hair of her since. Shug figures she might still be around, so she's nice to any dykes she meets, 'cause she figured her parents fucked up once and she ain't gonna do it again. 'Sides, one of them might be her sister. So we know each other five, six years now, since I been driving, and I know from past experience that anyone at that stop who messes with me messes with her.

I had my eye on Amy, who was waiting tables, so I figured I was in for some time before she could sit down. No big deal, though. As long as I crashed by 3 or so, I could make it home pretty easy, and I had a sleeping bag in the truck so I could catch a few winks locked in the cab. Cramerville ain't big on hotels.

I am getting on with it. What's your rush? Got a hot date or somethin'? No? All right then. Half an hour or so goes by. It'd been a few months since I was through this way, so Shug hadn't heard about me and the wife.

"Oh, honey, I'm sorry. She couldn't have been any good for you. You gotta find you someone steady, like my Fred." Fred's her boyfriend, the one she won't marry 'cause she's got no use for marrying. Always says, "You done it twice, you done it a thousand times. Why throw good years after bad?" So she said this, then followed my eyes. "And she ain't it! What'cha want with a young 'un like her? She's OK, mind you, in spite of what folks around here say about her. Kinda wild, used to run with a bad crowd, but smart, you know? I gave her a chance 'cause she's cleaning up her act. But she ain't gonna be around here long. No, ma'am. Cramerville ain't big enough for a smart one like her. She'll be somethin' big-time. Hell, this is her last night working here 'cause she's taking off for college next week."

Shug's warning was fallin' on closed ears, 'cause if there's anything I like, it's a gal who's been around a little.

Amy swung by after the place started to clear out and sat up at the counter with me and Shug. She was even cuter up close and relaxed. So I asked her how she ended up in Cramerville, and she started talkin', telling me about how her family moved here from the Philippines 'cause her dad organized students at the university and the government didn't like it, so he had to leave in a hurry. Her uncle ran a store in a town nearby, so they worked there and saved up money to start their own place in Podunkville.

She told me about college and how happy she was to be gettin' out of this one-horse town. "If one more yahoo tells me how goddamn exotic I am and how he hears Oriental gals make fine wives who know their place, I'll shoot him," she said. Then she looked me dead in the eye and said, "You don't have any ideas 'long those lines, do ya, Pepper?"

Ya ever snort coffee out yer nose? I don't recommend it. I sat and thought for a minute, 'cause a question like that deserves a good answer.

"I don't think yer cute just 'cause yer Oriental or 'cause I think we're gonna get married and yer gonna play housewife for me. Can't say I don't notice you here more because of it, 'cause it's pretty damn clear that there ain't too many other folks like you around here."

"That's for damn sure," she said and laughed, kinda sarcastic.

I went on, pretty slow. "Plus you remind me of my ex about ten years or so back. And that's meant as a compliment, 'cause I think yer real pretty. I'm just kinda lonely since my wife and I parted ways last month. I didn't mean nothin' by checkin' you out, didn't want to offend you or nothin'. I'm real sorry if I upset you."

She just looked at me, like she's thinkin' on it; then she had to go wait on a table. So she came back after that and said, "I guess I'm not too offended, just so long as you're not a full-time rice queen. I hate someone makin' me feel like I'm interchangeable with any other Asian chick they could pick up or hittin' on me just because I'm Asian. Not like pickings aren't a little slim around here, if that's your thing." So I shook my head and tried to look innocent and sincere. She laughed and said, "You look like a basset hound. Give it up!"

So she started tellin' me about life in Cramerville, in between waitin' on the last few tables. She used to run with the wild kids, drinkin', drugs, the whole deal, 'cause it was a way to get out of meetin' everybody's expectations, and she wanted to fit in. Last couple of years, ex-boyfriend went to jail, friends got into harder drugs, got killed in accidents, that kind of stuff, so she got sober 'cause she didn't want to go out that way. By then, of course, she had a rep around town that wasn't too pretty, and she was sick of it. Plus a big break with her family 'cause of it all. She was figuring on moving to the city where there'd be more of a community for her, and she could start over, do somethin' with herself.

To lighten up the mood a little, I sorta leered at her and asked how come she's so comfy chattin' up an old war-horse like me.

She shrugged and said, "Well, my cousin used to live here, but she moved to San Francisco. You know, bright lights, big city, Sodom by the Bay. Went there a few times to visit and meet her friends. Some of them are even butch. I ain't your average hick, ya know." And she kinda tossed her head back, goofylike, just to show how cool she was, and laughed. "Plus I like butch girls. I think they're hot. And Shug vouches for you, says you're as close to a real gentleman as you can find these days." She winked at me, and I could see she was feelin' better, so I relaxed a little too, but I wasn't takin' any hints, even the ones you could see a mile away like those. I liked this girl. Didn't want her thinkin' I was another yahoo, and, hell, now I had a rep to live up to.

She went off and picked up the last of the dishes, 'cause the place had cleared out. Shug was finishing up with the last of the counter customers and shakin' her head at me. But she was smilin', so I figured she didn't mind too bad. Amy came back by and tossed me a rag.

"Why don'tcha help me wipe down some tables. I'll get done faster that way."

And she grinned back over her shoulder at me, makin' my stomach do flip-flops. I was a goner and I knew it. Just tryin'

to salvage the last of my cool for the night by then, but I
didn't want to leave just yet, ya know?

So I started wiping down tables. Amy and Shug talked for
a couple of minutes, too quiet for me to hear; then Shug
threw up her hands and headed for the kitchen. I wondered
what was up but didn't hurt myself worrying, if ya know what
I mean. Amy walked by, smacked my butt, and grinned at me
when I looked surprised.

"Good work. Maybe you can start moonlightin' here. I
wouldn't mind watching your butt for a while."

Shucks.

The coffee hit home after a couple of cups, so I put down my
rag and headed for the john. I heard the door open while I was
in there, but I didn't think nothin' of it. I finished up and stepped
out. There was Amy, looking in the mirror, watching me watch
her with a little smile on her face. Quick, I figured to act like I
wasn't drooling and swaggered over to the sink. She sat on the
edge of the counter, and I couldn't help noticing that the dress
of her uniform slid way up when she did that. Nice thighs in
black hose. Hmm. She let down that gorgeous hair and started
brushing it and kept looking at me. I hate when my ears start
blushing, but I ain't used to pretty young things in rest rooms
checking me out. Usually they think I'm a guy and they freak.

Well, this one wasn't freaking. She knew she was getting to
me, and she looked like a cat about to catch somethin'.

"Shug went home. She said good night and not to be such
a stranger. You gonna be a stranger tonight, Pepper?"

I was still gaping when she stood up and held the brush out
to me and said, "Would you like to brush my hair? I like having it brushed for me, and I bet you've had lots of practice."

Never one to turn down a lady's request and blushin' like nobody's business, I picked up that brush and went to. Her hair was all the way down to her very cute butt, and I was going for long, steady strokes. Let me tell you, it felt as good as it looked. Hell, I figured the odds on a gorgeous woman—straight, lesbian, whatever—asking me to play hairdresser were pretty damn long, so I might as well go with it.

So I was working away on brushing her hair when I glanced up in the mirror and caught her eye.

She said, "You know, I like you, Pepper. You got a nice honest face and the sexiest hands. I like butch girls. Not like I see many around here."

Then she looked kinda thoughtful for a minute and smiled and then, I swear to God this is true, reached up to the top button on her dress and undid it. She moved on to the second one, and by now I was breathing a little heavy.

"Interested? Unless you just like to watch…" she laughed a little, seeing the look on my face. Hell, I could see it myself in the mirror over her shoulder.

Needless to say, I turned her face around to kiss her before she could change her mind. She had the sweetest lips…and neck…and shoulders. I slid my hand along her thigh, up those nice silky stockings. There's something about hearing a real femme moan when you're gettin' to her. God, I love that sound! I was licking my way down her neck 'fore I remembered the restaurant and the fact that we were in the women's john.

"I locked the door. Shug doesn't mind too much, and she locked the place up. I promised to clean up. She didn't like my last boyfriend too much anyhow!" She laughed one of those deep throaty laughs—made me quiver in my boots.

Almost enough to make me ignore that one word.

"Boyfriend?" I whispered as I removed my tongue from her earlobe.

She just grinned at me.

"Don't worry. He's out of the picture, and we always did safe sex. It was the one thing I made sure I didn't fuck up, back in my wild youth."

Then she reached over to a bag on the counter, one I'd missed 'cause it was behind her, and I sure wasn't seeing past her right now. Damned if she didn't pull out some of those gloves and latex and stuff. "I come prepared."

I must have started to back off a little.

"Not interested, Pepper? Or afraid of a little ol' bisexual like me?"

She flipped her hair back and licked her lips. Right then, I wasn't afraid of nothin'.

"I ain't scared. Just never done it like that before, that's all. My wife and I were together about ten years. Didn't see the need. Bi, huh?" I was stuttering, I was talking so fast.

She grinned at me. Her hand went up to the top button on my shirt.

"We'll do it the safe way, I promise. That is, if you're still interested." Her palm grazed my nipple through my shirt, making me groan. "I'll take that as a yes."

Her shirt was unbuttoned so far, I could see the black lace bra she wore underneath. I'm a sucker for black lace. She sat up on the counter again, put her hands on my collar, and tugged me forward so I was between her legs. Then she started kissin' me, slow and careful-like, her tongue running around the inside of my mouth. I put my hands up to those top buttons on her dress. Man, more than anything, I wanted my hands on her black lace–covered breasts. Shit, I'm getting hot talking about it!

So I got her dress unbuttoned down to her waist, and I ran my tongue down to her boobs. You ever run your tongue over a nipple covered in black lace? Hmm. She was having my favorite reaction, arching her back and moaning, running her fingers through my hair.

I got my teeth on her nipple and started nibbling, just a little.

"Oh, yes! Just a little harder," she groaned.

Hadn't had an effect like that on anybody in a while. My one hand was around her back, so I started to run my other one up her thigh.

Damned if she wasn't wearing garters! No stocking on the upper thigh, just nice, smooth, silky skin. *Rrowrh!* My hand got a little higher, and she stopped it.

"Gloves first, honey."

"Oh, I don't need—" I started to whine.

"You aren't sure of that, and neither am I."

She looked determined. I picked up the glove and pulled it on with a snap, trying to look like I went to a safe-sex-for-women workshop some time in the last decade.

Back I went to that pretty mouth. Made me glad I don't smoke anymore. Woman tastes so much better without all that old ash—nothin' personal, mind you. And her kiss, mmm, sent hot flashes through me, and I ain't at that certain age yet, you know. Right about then I was wetter than I thought I could get, and it felt damn good. I figured I've got the stupid glove on, might as well use it as intended. Plus, no bullshitting around, I couldn't wait to get inside her. So I went back to

licking my way down her neck, and the way she was breathing and moaning, I knew I had her full attention again.

Real slowly I started moving my hand up her leg again.
Her pubes were soft through the glove and probably nice and
silky like the rest of her hair. She groaned and spread her legs
a little farther apart. Never one to refuse an invitation, I
slipped one finger into her crack. 'Course I couldn't feel how
wet she is really, but the glove got all slippery, so I knew I was
on the right track. I was sliding my fingers around her crack;
then I slipped one up inside her. She started riding it, so I
went for two, then three. Then I went for it, one finger up
her ass and my thumb on her clit, and I had all I could do to
hold her up with the other arm and keep driving. Ooh, that
girl, mmm, mmm.

She started coming with a yell. I got her nipple between
my teeth again, and she was holding my head so hard, it hurt.
She came again, two, three times, then again, soaking the
glove and edge of my sleeve.

"Damn, you're good," she whispered, and she kissed me
hard again, just to prove it. Well, I was feeling pretty good
myself right then. Lot of times I just get off getting them
off anyway, but I got the feeling this one was going to be
different.

Amy looked up at me under those long dark lashes, then
pulled me close as she slid off the counter.

"Now, what can I do for you?"

I started to tell her she didn't need to do anything. She put
her hand on her hip and looked at me like she don't believe me.

"Yeah?" she said and started unbuttoning my shirt and kissing my neck. "Think you're about to get flipped, hon."

She started leaving a line of little hickeys down my breast-bone to the edge of my bra, then slipped the shirt off my shoulders. She ran her tongue over the edge of the bra, then scooped out my tit. I groaned. So much for the tough butch act.

"Like that, honey? Me too."

She scooped the other tit out over the top of the bra and started licking and biting her way around. Whooey! I've had breast exams that were less thorough, and I was lovin' every minute of it.

I was leaning against the wall by this point, 'cause it was gettin' hard to think about standing. She slid my bra off over my head and then started undoing my belt buckle. Her dress was still unbuttoned, so I reached out and started playing with her nipple while she slid the belt out of my pants, real nice and slow. Once she got it out she moved the belt slowly against my skin up to my nipples, then slid the leather over them. Never felt anything like that before, and believe me, this was wilder at this point than anything I've done in a long time! Standing kept getting harder 'cause my pants were soaked.

She reached up and unzipped them slowly, kissing me the whole time. I reached back to cup her ass and pulled her against me for a smooch. She spread her dress open so those nice lacy nips were rubbing against my bare chest, and I was gone. Right then, if she said she wanted to do stuff with razor blades, I probably would have gone for it. My pants were getting dropped down to my boots, so she pushed me up onto the countertop and bunched everything up around my ankles so I couldn't move my feet.

Somehow I missed the part where she got the gloves on, but she was wearing 'em. Plus she had this piece of rubber, plastic, somethin', I don't know, in her hand.

"Wha's that?" asked the duke of smooth.

"It's a dental dam. It's so I can do this."

Then she planted it over my crack and started running her tongue over it till she found my clit.

"Oh, OK," I went between gasps. Didn't know a little piece of rubber could feel that good, let alone smell like bubble gum. She kept licking, and I started coming, and I never came like that before. It started deep in my crotch and just took over. This gal was the best.

"Where'd you learn to do that?" I managed to get out.

"Here and there. I wanna get you nice and wet for what I've got planned." She went back to work, and I came again, 'cause you know it gets easier after the first one. Then she pulled something else outta the bag, something that looked like a dildo, and stuck a condom on it.

"I don't know about that..." I started chickening out.

"You wanna try it? I'll stop if you don't like it."

I looked at this beautiful young gal, who wanted to fuck me, of all people, in a public john, and I was gonna say no? Not likely. To hell with my image.

So she slipped her fingers inside me to get me warmed up, not like it took much. Her fingers started driving in, couldn't tell how many, and I just hauled out the welcome wagon. Then came the dildo. Hurt just a bit at first, then damn, it felt good. She drove it in and out slow and steady, like the way she was kissing me. It was like gettin' filled up, pretty wild if you never used one. My hips were moving along it like they belonged to someone else, Elvis maybe. I gotta get me one of these things!

I came so hard, I was seeing lights. Hope Shug had gone home by this point, 'cause my yell was pretty damn loud.

Amy rubbed me and licked me some more for a while; then we just held each other for a little bit. Sure has sucked not having someone to be close to, after all this time.

She gave me this real sweet kiss and said, "You're the best, Pepper. Thanks for being with me tonight. I've been pretty lonely here, and I really wanted to be with someone tonight."

Anytime, lady, anytime.

So I stayed and helped her clean up, get the dishes into the washer, do the floors and all. Figure it's the least I could do after the night of my life. Couldn't go back to her place 'cause she lived with her parents, and my place here was the truck cab, so I offered to walk her home, and she said yes. Let me kiss her good night in front of the house, just like in the movies.

I was practically doing a jig back to the truck. Couldn't sleep, so I drove some more and got most of the way home before I needed a nap.

You know, I don't feel so bad about the wife now. Maybe the world's just full of beautiful young things dying to hop into bed with me. Well, OK, probably not. But one was, and I figure that'll have to last me awhile. Hell, I got jill-off material for at least a month out of a couple of hours.

Do I think I'll ever see her again? I wish. When my ex dumped me for her guru, teacher, whatever the hell she calls her, she said I wasn't flexible enough, too boring, too dull. And maybe I am. But for one night I was wild and crazy, cute even, and a hot lover, and it was helluva lot of fun. Maybe I'll even try it again some time.

Maggie's Hands

by J.M. Redmann

When the train entered the tunnel, Eleanor paused in her reading. In that dark, unexpected moment when daylight was swallowed by an underground passage, Maggie's hands would have…would have gone to unexpected places. Even after all their years together, Eleanor still hadn't known where to expect Maggie's hands to travel. Her breasts, between her legs, sometimes her thigh, down her back, under her ass.

"Touch should occasionally be unexpected," Maggie would say as her hands caressed Eleanor. And with Maggie it sometimes deliciously was.

The train left the dark tunnel, the bright sunlight suddenly blinding off the snowbanks. Eleanor was on the train from Boston to New York. Another academic conference. A paper to present. *We all must have our passions*, she thought, *whether it is the 19th-century novel or the local football team*. Her fellow academics would look askance at her if she voiced such a thought. A cause should elicit the passion; passion shouldn't be searching for a cause to attach itself to. Maggie had talked of the courage to follow your passions, adding, "I'm not talking about sex now, you know." Maggie's passion was photography, the play of light and dark, captured images of people in the daily routines that made up a life. For Eleanor it was the words on a page written long ago. She wanted to talk across those centuries, to reach into lives long gone.

Eleanor remembered how dislocated her life had become when Maggie entered it. That first night, when the only passion between them was sex. Eleanor's first one-night stand.

It had been an ill-fated hiking trip, organized by some women Eleanor barely knew. Three cars and one van of nature-loving lesbians transformed into two cars and one van of cold, wet, and tired women who wanted to get home. One car had been lost to an arguing pair of lovers (ex-lovers by the next weekend, she later learned). Eleanor was one of the displaced. Three women stared at the two remaining seats in the van. Maggie had solved the problem by turning to Eleanor and saying, "You're too tall to sit in my lap, so I guess I get to sit in yours." They had crammed themselves into the backseat of the van, sharing it with the piled-high hiking gear.

At first Eleanor had felt stiff and awkward; she wasn't used to women she barely knew sitting in her lap. She was unsure of where to place her hands. She wondered if Maggie would think she was trying something if she opened her legs a bit? Eleanor thought of herself as the shy, gawky bookworm, one of life's observers. She was 5 feet 9½ inches tall and had worn glasses since she was five years old. Maggie was shorter, her hair a mass of golden-brown curls, in contrast to Eleanor's straight dark hair. Maggie had been the one telling the jokes the other women had laughed at, taking pictures, cajoling them into revealing unexpected, intimate pieces of themselves. She was a professional photographer, had already had an exhibit of her work in some downtown gallery.

If Maggie felt uncomfortable about sitting in Eleanor's lap, she didn't show it. Eleanor had once asked about it later. Maggie had replied, "Stiff? No, of course not. I couldn't wait to be sitting on top of you. You were one of the quiet ones, a challenge. By the time the rain started, I knew I wanted to bed you." Eleanor wasn't sure if she really thought that or if she was just playing out the myth of Maggie as the great adventuress.

That night Maggie's hands had traveled. Eleanor would have never dared. She was both taken aback and pleased when Maggie put a hand on her breast. Just like that. It was only a few inches—what worlds can be traveled in a few inches! Maggie's hand on Eleanor's breast changed them from two strangers shoved together to potential lovers.

The train entered another tunnel, and with her face dark and unobservable, Eleanor allowed herself the luxury of fondling the memory, letting her mind linger on that first rush when the warmth of Maggie's hand had encompassed her breast. At first that was all, her hand on the breast, as if asking, "Is this all right?" Then Maggie's fingers began slowly moving, circling closer and closer. By the time her fingers finally reached Eleanor's nipple, it was hard and erect. As Maggie said later, "Of course, I didn't stop. That nipple of yours was waving a bright red flag in invitation."

No, Maggie didn't stop, but she moved slowly, almost teasingly. From one breast to another. Then away to Eleanor's neck or jaw, then back, her fingers hovering inside Eleanor's shirt, resting at that place where the breast begins to rise from the chest.

But the train left the tunnel, exposing Eleanor to the sunlight. Those memories created in the night—it felt unseemly to subject them to this glaring daylight. Eleanor was abashed to notice that her breasts had responded to the memory, her nipples erect and straining against her bra.

She remembered the harsh sunlight in the doctor's office. Cancer. A harsh word in the harsh light. That night she and Maggie had made love in a frenzy, clinging to touch, the physical. Six years together, and that one word reminded them of how quickly things changed, how mortal they were. Touch could not be held on to. It would leave. So that night they grasped it as tightly as they could. Maggie's hands traveled over Eleanor's body, touching, probing, as if trying to reach some essence of her, to mold a memory that would endure.

The chemo took away Maggie's brown curls, still not a gray hair in them. It came back white, all white, rushing her into a future that Eleanor thought they would share together, but Maggie aged quickly, leaving Eleanor still in her prime.

She fought that memory: Maggie withered, her head surrounded by tufts of white so fine it could hardly be called hair. She preferred the Maggie from the first six years, the real Maggie, as Eleanor thought of her. *Let the sunlight expose my breasts,* she thought as it glittered off the snow. *Let me remember Maggie and the heat that had been between us.* Defying the conductor, who almost walked close enough to catch any glimmer of her emotions, Eleanor remembered that first night.

Maggie's simple "Come to my place" after they were left off. Odd how Eleanor had never thought to say no. Resisting Maggie didn't seem possible. It was four blocks to Maggie's apartment. She had taken Eleanor's hand to lead her around a corner, then didn't release it until they were at her door and Maggie was taking out her keys.

Her memory was clear, pristine up until that point. She could remember all the details, the name of the corner store, Maggie's hand in hers, even the precise color of the leaves in the trees they passed. But once they were inside, images started cascading, one atop another. Her jacket came off. She couldn't remember Maggie taking hers off, but, of course, she did. They were in each other's arms. Kissing.

"I knew you weren't quite as shy as you seemed when you put your tongue in my mouth first," Maggie had said later. Eleanor had denied it. Maggie was the bold one. It didn't make sense that she, the shy, quiet one, would be the first to touch so deeply. But she wasn't sure, couldn't chase down the halls of her memory to find exactly what had happened. "I almost came right then and there," Maggie had added. Eleanor had still shaken her head in denial, but she rather liked the idea that she had a daring, sensual streak and could get lost in passion.

One clear image that surfaced was of them standing together, fiercely kissing, tongues thrusting back and forth as if vying to see who could press deeper, holding each other tightly, all hesitation long gone. She felt Maggie's arms letting go of her, her hands searching for Eleanor's breasts. This time they hadn't stopped at her shirt, at first pushing the cloth aside, then pulling her shirt off, tossing it quickly away. In the morning Maggie had apologized for the wrinkled mess when Eleanor had nothing else to wear. But in the night, in that moment of passion, it hadn't mattered.

Eleanor usually worried about things like that, took care of things. Remembered to turn off the stove and turn down the thermostat. Matched the socks into pairs. But that night all she wanted was Maggie's hands on her breasts.

"Get on the floor. I want to get on top of you." Another clear moment. Maggie's command, the coolness of the floor on her bare back. The sudden warmth and weight as Maggie let herself down onto Eleanor. The erotic shock of their bare breasts touching for the first time. Then the visions overlapped each other, fierce kissing, all the places that became wet: her breasts from Maggie's licking and sucking, the creeping wetness between her legs, from between Maggie's legs, their fingers immersed in that wetness, trailing it across thighs and stomachs. The release of orgasm over and over again. She couldn't clearly remember the first time she came; before the night was over, she came again and again. Eleanor wanted to remember that Maggie had called out her name for the first time, but it could have been the second time. Maggie had called out Eleanor's name sometime in the night. Perhaps that was what really counted: her name, the harsh, possessive way Maggie had said it.

"Five times," Maggie recounted the next morning as they sat for breakfast at an hour better suited to lunch. "I made you come five times."

"I didn't count. I don't count things like that," Eleanor had responded somewhat defensively. She couldn't be sure of the number and was a bit abashed that Maggie knew so well what they had done. "I came, you came. Are you complaining?"

"No, I came six times. No complaints, ma'am, not a one."

Sometime later, after they had moved in together, they tried to puzzle out the sexual charge between them.

"I always wanted to fuck a virgin," Maggie had said.

"I'm not a virgin. And wasn't when you met me."

"Oh, I know. Not a literal virgin. You were the reserved, quiet type. Glasses, always carrying a book. A coolness and restraint about you. I wanted to push that aside, to find the passion in you. Take you to erotic places you'd never been before. I imagined it would take weeks to seduce you."

"Instead of mere hours? You were the popular girl, the one the others wanted to be near, the kind who never paid attention to serious women with glasses who always carried a book."

Was that it, the sum of their desire? Opposites attracted? *No, it went beyond that,* Eleanor thought. Maggie had opened up something in her, gave her permission to be sexual in a way that her previous timid lovers with their shy hands never had. It had been OK to sweat and groan with Maggie, to be dripping wet and mess up the last set of clean sheets, to beg and curse and demand more. She opened a door that Eleanor had wanted to enter. Maggie liked playing her role—teacher to the younger, shier woman, a provocateur who made suggestions at the edge of shocking.

She remembered the time in the crowded elevator, Maggie behind her. Maggie had put her hand between Eleanor's legs. Eleanor remembered being astonished that she would dare. And nonplussed that there was nothing she could do to remove Maggie's hand that wouldn't bring attention to what was happening. The door had opened, and Eleanor had hurried out of the elevator, sure everyone knew. She said nothing as they walked down the hall. It was her first job teaching; they were going to her office.

Once there, with the door shut, she had turned to Maggie. "When's your next appointment?" Maggie had cut her off.

"Next…?" She obediently glanced at her schedule. "Not until after lunch."

Maggie locked the door.

"I can't do this here," Eleanor had protested. "And that stunt in the elevator—"

"No one saw a thing. You know I don't mind shocking you, but I won't embarrass you."

Eleanor realized it was true. Maggie played at limits but didn't violate them. There was that trust between them, the covenant that proclaimed, "I will not knowingly hurt you." It had built slowly in the three years they had been together then. But in that moment in her office, Eleanor saw it clearly, how sturdy that protective wall of trust had become. It wasn't just sex but encompassed everything, from helping her get up in the morning for that 8:30 class to holding her late in the night when tension or vague fears wouldn't let her sleep. Eleanor marked it, that epiphany produced by Maggie's hand in a crowded elevator, like a plaque recounting the history of a place that might seem inconsequential.

Maggie circled her to close the blinds at the window.

"What if the chairman of the department knocks on my door?" Eleanor asked.

"Don't open it." Maggie now stood next to her, close enough for Eleanor to feel the heat of her skin, smell a faint waft of her perfume.

"But what if he hears something?" Eleanor only made the protest because she wanted to keep alive the tension that she might say no.

"We'll be quiet."

"Seduce me." And Maggie had, her hands traveling slowly down Eleanor's neck to her cleavage, a tease and a promise.

Then her hand went back to where it had started, between Eleanor's legs, pushing and insistent, rubbing hard against the seam of her denim jeans.

Eleanor closed her eyes, shutting out the mundane world of an office painted beige, piles of the usual books. She let Maggie's hand become her only focus. First the pushing and rubbing through her jeans, then the slow unzipping of her zipper. Maggie quickly pushed aside the barrier of Eleanor's underwear.

"I love you," Eleanor murmured as Maggie's hand touched her directly. She had said it before, many times, but she still marveled at how the meaning changed, all the faces and levels of love. That it could be so alive here, in this quick sex in an office.

"And I love you," Maggie answered. Then she kissed Eleanor as her hand entered her.

Eleanor remembered clearly how Maggie's hand thrust into her. Other details blurred. They had been standing but ended up sitting on the ragtag couch that Eleanor had inherited from the previous occupant of that office. She couldn't remember moving, only Maggie's hand inside her, touching a piece of her soul. And Maggie kept that touch alive, as if she sensed that something had changed. Her hand slowed, keeping Eleanor at a plateau, prolonging the moment. Then long, deep thrusts, physical touching that echoed the emotional reach of their lovemaking. Eleanor remembered how vulnerable she allowed Maggie to make her, spread across that tattered couch, her pants shoved down around her ankles, face flushed, only a door between that and her professional life.

The train slowed as it came into New Haven. The change in motion interrupted Eleanor's memories. Maggie would never ride a train beside her again. Was there any point in remembering what had been?

After Maggie's death her mother had invaded their apartment. To her, Eleanor was nothing more than a lover, but she was the mother. Of course, she hadn't been rude, asking very nicely if Eleanor minded if Maggie's brother could have her Leica, daring Eleanor to place a greater claim on the left-behind pieces of Maggie's life than the family that had birthed and bred her. Not married, no children, two women: It didn't count with Maggie's mother.

Eleanor had retreated to the kitchen, claiming the cups and bowls that they had shared and eaten from. A turn to take a dish from the sink had revealed Maggie's mother going through the box of their photos. Eleanor took a step to stop her: These weren't Maggie's professional work; they were the record of their life together. It incensed her that Maggie's mother (her name was Jill, but Eleanor rarely called her that, just as she usually referred to Eleanor as "Maggie's friend") felt she could look behind any door in her daughter's life. But Eleanor had turned back to the sink. Maggie would get her final revenge for all those years that she had struggled to get her mother to accept Eleanor as more than just a friend. Her mother had refused to see it. Now she would. She would see the photos Maggie had taken while they made love. She would see her daughter in heat and passion with another woman. No, not just friends. If she wanted to look in that box, let her find what was there.

Maggie had needed a picture of two women kissing. She had offered to take some pictures for a writer friend, and that was one of them.

"Why not us?" she had asked Eleanor. "It'll be artsy, back-lit, no one will recognize us." She knew Eleanor would be shy about such a public display.

Safely assured of being only a blur and a shadow, Eleanor had agreed. The picture had been hard to set up, with Maggie running back and forth between the camera, Eleanor holding a pillow stand-in for a while so Maggie could play with lights and exposure. But the picture that resulted was quite good. Eleanor knew, given that she was in the photograph, that she couldn't really judge it against Maggie's other work, but it was one of her favorites. Maggie had given her an enlarged copy, framed, for her birthday. On the back it said, "To Eleanor. Love always, Maggie." The picture still hung over her bed. Love always. Eleanor thought of those words. But it hadn't been love always. Love had gone. No, that wasn't true. Love was still here; she still loved Maggie. But it had become immobile, only memory, no forward motion possible. Like that picture.

It had been interesting and mildly erotic to see that image of themselves, their lips barely touching but mouths open, waiting, sunlight streaming through the window they stood before, turning them into silhouettes of passion. She remembered how pleased Maggie was with herself for so clearly catching their desire. And Eleanor had to admit she enjoyed seeing it so distinctly captured. She remembered the look they had exchanged and how easy it was to go from that look to Maggie's suggestion that she could take some more pictures only for them.

Eleanor had agreed. At first she was awkward in front of the camera, too concerned about how she looked. But slowly desire took over. Maggie was too used to cameras to let one, even in this intimate a place, intimidate her. She worked Eleanor, her hands slow and relentless, relaxing her and exciting her both. She lingered on Eleanor's breasts, keeping her touch light, kisses soft, until Eleanor had to thrust forward for Maggie's mouth. The camera caught that moment of passion, caught all those moments of passion: Maggie's hand as her fingers slowly separated Eleanor's slick hairs, Maggie between her legs, the arch and stretch as Eleanor came, a quiet moment as they lay in each other's arms, then Eleanor as she traveled the same path down Maggie's body, the sucking and the probing, a cry that still almost seemed to echo from the silent picture. Those pictures they kept in a private place, hidden in an envelope in the bottom of the box.

Eleanor remembered the anticipation as Maggie developed the pictures, both of them standing close in the red light of the darkroom. Slowly a record of their love and desire emerged from the pans of chemicals. After hanging up the pictures to dry, they had made love again, goaded into desire by the images of themselves and their desire just past.

Sometimes Maggie would leave one or two pictures out, a signal for Eleanor. One day she had come home from teaching to find a trail of those pictures leading to the bedroom, with Maggie waiting naked under the sheets.

As she stood in the kitchen listening to Maggie's mother in the living room, Eleanor had again turned to cross that distance and take the box from her. But a startled gasp told Eleanor that it was already too late. Maggie's mother had left shortly after that, and she had not asked again about taking Maggie's best camera for her brother. Whatever guilt Eleanor may have felt was assuaged by this victory. And by realizing that she knew Maggie well enough to know how she would have reacted. Eleanor could almost hear Maggie's voice saying, "I bet now she regrets giving me that first camera when I was ten. Not to mention pawing through my stuff."

After Maggie's mother had left, Eleanor had sat and looked through the pictures, reclaiming them from those prying eyes. She remembered all the tears the images had brought forth, sobbing and crying as she held the picture of Maggie, naked, her hands clutching Eleanor to her breast. How could Maggie be gone but that ghost of a photograph still be here?

The New Haven passengers were boarding. Eleanor shook her head, physically dislodging the memory. It had been almost a year now. Maggie was gone. She picked up her book and started to read again, hoping that her disinterest would keep anyone from taking the seat next to her.

She had spent that last year in libraries, doing research, taking her passion to the words written a few lifetimes ago, trying to find solace in books that somehow managed to live beyond their authors.

The train began to slowly pull away from the station. No one had seated themselves next to Eleanor. She was relieved to be given the private space.

It was so mundane and so profound, this train ride. It was the first time Eleanor had taken the short, boring train ride from Boston to New York without Maggie beside her or waiting for her return. Perhaps that was why the memories crowded in. They needed to fill this empty space.

Eleanor remembered Maggie in the darkroom, outlined in that faint red light. She often sat on a stool in the corner and talked or listened as Maggie developed her photos. Only later did Eleanor realize what a measure of their partnership that was. Maggie trusted her to watch the pictures come forth, and sometimes a roll of film yielded only one good shot. At first Maggie had asked for only minimal approval from Eleanor ("This is the best shot, don't you think?"), but the years had slowly changed that ("Take a look at these. What do you think?"), and Eleanor's judgment had become almost equal to Maggie's.

At times Eleanor desperately missed those quiet times in that dim light. But even in the moments when she still had them, thought that those evenings with Maggie could go on without end, she knew the import of them, the quiet moments that make up a love and a life.

One night they were quiet, not talking. Eleanor was watching Maggie, the sure way she developed the negatives, taking them from one tray to another. She found herself watching Maggie's face, noting the lines that were now faintly etched at her eyes, the familiar way her brow furrowed as she concentrated, the curl that would not stay with the others but insisted on falling over her forehead.

Suddenly Eleanor wanted Maggie. Her desire was usually more decorous than that, waiting for bedtime or after a romantic dinner or when Maggie summoned it with a look or a word. She got off the stool, standing next to Maggie, close enough to almost touch. Eleanor pretended to look at what Maggie was doing, but her concentration was on Maggie, who seemed oblivious to Eleanor's desire, though Eleanor thought that it must be palpable, so strong as to send off visible sparks. Her hand rested on Maggie's shoulder, but that was not where she wanted her hand to be. Could she just change this evening, insert sex into it all on her own, with no sign or signal from Maggie? Maggie could, of course, but...Maggie was Maggie.

Eleanor remembered her hesitation, that even after all these years together she hesitated to be the one to push for sex. Usually she didn't need to. Maggie offered or suggested or hinted. What was she so afraid of? Rejection? Or was she really afraid of change, creating a new path, one that she was responsible for?

Eleanor let her arm drift from Maggie's shoulder down to her hip, her breast just brushing against Maggie's shoulder. Maggie remained intent on her pictures. Maybe she should just sit back down on the stool, Eleanor thought. Feeling the warmth of Maggie's hip under her hand didn't do much to lessen her desire. Then it came, the thought that preceded a change, like a door opening into a new room: Eleanor, five years younger than Maggie, usually let her lead. That had been the pattern in their relationship. Why, Eleanor wondered, why not change? They'd been together long enough for her to acquire some of Maggie's boldness. Why not add a few more possibilities to who and what Eleanor could be?

Instead of retreating to the stool, Eleanor moved directly behind Maggie, her breasts touching Maggie's shoulders, her hands on Maggie's hips. Maggie leaned slightly into Eleanor but only with the familiarity of touch, not with passion. Eleanor slowly but firmly tugged Maggie's hips, pulling her against Eleanor's crotch.

"These chemicals turning you on?" Maggie asked, but she didn't move away from Eleanor.

"No, you are." Eleanor let her hands travel, slowly sliding them around Maggie's hips, stopping just short of the place where her flesh rose between her legs.

"I've got to finish these."

"Am I stopping you?" One hand went to the top of Maggie's zipper. Very slowly she began unzipping it. The years they had been together had sharpened their communications to nuance and bare gesture. There were many ways Maggie could have said stop. She used none of them. Eleanor didn't stop. Her hand slipped through the open zipper.

"No, you're not stopping me. But you're proving to be...quite a distraction." Maggie pushed her hips into Eleanor, inviting her hand to go farther. Eleanor remained slow and deliberate, her hand tracing Maggie's hair through her panties. For the moment she didn't go beyond them.

Maggie finished whatever she was doing with the negatives and after rinsing her hands started to turn to face Eleanor.

But Eleanor held her in place, wouldn't let her turn around. One pattern was broken; she wanted to break a few more. Her hand was no longer languid. It slid beneath Maggie's underwear, finding her hair, dividing it, going deeper.

A fierce possessiveness overtook Eleanor. Maggie was hers, had given her the gift of touch and desire. She could stroke Maggie's hot secret places, explore them at will. They were the only two travelers on this journey of love and desire. She shoved Maggie's pants down, got them to her knees with her hands, then used her foot to take them down to Maggie's ankles.

Who else could she do this with? Who else had ever given her this power? Only the woman in front of her, with her pubic hair and tops of her thighs already slick and wet. Eleanor ran her hands over Maggie, touching the power and desire.

"What are you going to do to me?" Maggie gasped.

"Whatever I want," was Eleanor's answer. "Bend over," she said. She twirled Maggie away from the counter of chemicals, then leaned her over the stool. Maggie obeyed the commands of Eleanor's hands.

Eleanor's fingers easily entered Maggie. She thrust in, unrestrained, physical sex. Maggie rode her hand, thrusting her hips back, grunting and moaning in response.

It was quick, but at times profound things are. Maggie came with a gush of wetness that soaked Eleanor's arm to the elbow and a loud cry that subsided into harsh, gulping breaths. Eleanor draped herself over Maggie, one hand cupping a breast, the other still inside her. For the first time, Maggie had given all the power and control to Eleanor. Or was it that for the first time Eleanor had taken it?

When Maggie's breathing had returned to its usual rhythm, Eleanor had simply said, "Get on your knees."

Maggie had obeyed, not even bothering to pull up her pants. Eleanor had unzipped her jeans and then let Maggie spread her legs. She knew what Eleanor wanted, where to put her tongue and lips. Eleanor sat back on the stool and watched Maggie with her tongue pressed between her legs, Maggie's curls damp with sweat. Eleanor tried to hold off, prolong the moment, but her desire, building for so long, demanded release. She came and, unusual for her, came again.

She and Maggie didn't talk much about what happened in those few minutes (only half an hour had passed, they later realized). What was there to say? Was it just Eleanor's sexual peak, her mid 30s? Perhaps that was part of it, Eleanor admitted, but she felt it was more, that it was an understanding and owning of her power, not just in sex but in how she could influence the world. It was a lesson that Maggie had taught her.

A year—one brief year—later Maggie had gone to the doctor's office. And Eleanor has used that lesson, had fought for Maggie when the drugs and the cancer weakened her, pushed the doctors for better answers and, in the end, for relief from pain. She had cared for Maggie, carried her shit from the portable toilet in the bedroom and flushed it away, held her hand in the night when pain and nausea ruled Maggie's world. It was a brutal way to die, a slow creeping inch by inch away from life.

That was another lesson that Maggie had taught her: the despair of having a future taken from you. What might have been and now would not be. Eleanor was 36, single, and riding a train by herself. Caring for Maggie had so consumed her life that when Maggie died she felt lost and confused, barely able to stumble through the routines of her days. Maggie was also teaching her the lessons of grief and letting go. Slowly, so slowly, she was learning them.

The train again slowed, pulling into Stamford, Conn. Eleanor resigned herself to a passenger in the next seat; the train was too crowded for her to hope otherwise. A young college boy with a well-fed arrogance started to sit, then he spotted something better—something younger and blonder, Eleanor suspected. Several other people passed Eleanor by with the foolish optimism that the next car would be less crowded. She wondered which of them would come back this way to reclaim her empty seat on the rebound.

Then a woman stopped beside her and asked, "Is this taken?" At least she was polite enough to ask, unlike the rude college boy who thought the world owed him a train seat.

"No, it's not." At first glance the woman looked like another college student, but a second glance told Eleanor that she was older, mid to late 20s. She stretched to put her suitcase in the overhead rack. The sight of her breasts with the cloth of her shirt pulled tightly over them stirred something in Eleanor. *Nice*, Eleanor thought before turning her head back to her book. That's what she got from thinking about sex from Boston to New York. Now she was staring at some strange woman's breasts with what could only be called lust. Eleanor resolutely opened her book.

But the bundles' being placed in the seat next to her and the woman's jockeying and jostling to get settled, drew Eleanor's attention. The woman bent down to pick up a briefcase, revealing her cleavage. Eleanor didn't turn so quickly back to her book. The woman had attractive breasts, soft and rounded. Her skin hadn't spent too many summers in the sun, and they still promised to be soft to the touch.

Eleanor looked back down at her book, not to read but to shade her face while she thought of the feel of a warm breast against her hand, the comfort and thrill of that touch.

The woman gave Eleanor a smile and a nod as she sat, then opened up a laptop computer. She didn't seem inclined to talk, so Eleanor left her gazing at her screen. Eleanor felt faintly chagrined by her moment of lust. She read books; she didn't stare at the breasts of strange women on trains.

Eleanor tried to read again, but the glare of the sun broken by flashes of telephone poles and buildings made the pages too bright. She closed the book.

For the last year she had paid no attention to women, not sexual attention. Maggie's death was an end, and Eleanor had spent the year living in the wake of that ending place, numb to a future that didn't include Maggie. But she was here, in the future, and Maggie was not a part of it.

Eleanor didn't look at the woman but called back the image of her bending over, the inviting depth of her cleavage. She realized it was the first time she had thought of another woman, imagined herself touching another woman. Some faint beginning beckoned. Perhaps she could find touch and even love again.

Maggie had gone quickly, too soon, too young. But age would consume Eleanor too. It was inexorable; this journey would not stop. At her age, if fate was kind, she had a few decades left. But only that, a few decades. Sometimes a year, two years, ten seemed such a short time.

The train entered the tunnel for the last time, leaving the glinting daylight, the final minutes before they arrived at Penn Station and her destination. Another memory of Maggie's hands came to her, not the rushed grope for fun and titillation in the dark but from the last time they had ridden this train together. Another visit to another doctor, one last chance. Maggie had held her hand as they had traveled under Manhattan. They had said little, just that touch of their hands.

In the dark, by herself, Eleanor let go of Maggie's hands. They were only memory now.

The woman next to her clicked off her laptop computer. She stood up to retrieve her things from the overhead rack. Eleanor allowed herself to look at the woman's breasts again, their swell against the cloth.

Yes, she would find other women whose breasts she could cup her hand around; one to love and hold, if she was lucky.

Eleanor knew there were no guarantees. Love came as a grace, ephemeral, and it could go so quickly.

The light changed from the dim flashes of the tunnel to the flat fluorescence of the station. Eleanor gathered her things, putting the unread book back in her briefcase. Her overnight bag was up on the rack, but she was in no hurry. She thought of saying something to the woman but could think of nothing. She couldn't very well thank her for letting Eleanor fantasize about her breasts. They were only strangers on a train.

The motion of the train stopped. They had arrived. The woman got up with another smile and nod at Eleanor, and she made her slow way up the aisle.

Eleanor remained in her seat, letting the milling passengers elbow themselves and their luggage off the train. A few minutes of waiting would make it much easier to disembark. But she no longer merely watched the people with the detachment of numbness and grief; instead she saw hints of possibility. She looked at women, their hair, their eyes—were they confident or timid? Oh, yes, and their breasts. She let her glance linger on the women who looked smart and confident and who had nice breasts.

The train ride had not been long, but the most profound journeys involve more than just distance.

With the aisles now clear, Eleanor gathered up her things and got off the train.

Ruby Red

by Lisa Ginsburg

Ruby made sure her tits were tucked evenly into her new lace corset before she zipped up her leather jacket. She knew she would soon be unzipping the jacket for the crowd and wanted her nipples to push out into the pointiest part of the bodice.

Her housemate stepped into the room and let out a low whistle. "Ruby Red, you've gone and outdone yourself this time. Where *did* you get that red leather miniskirt?"

"Isn't it purr-fect?" Ruby asked, rolling the word off her tongue like a cat and running her hands over her ass. "Charlene lent it to me. She's marching this year, didn't want to wear heels."

"Damn, I hope this blind date mama of yours measures up to you. What did you say her name was?"

"*Sa*-sha," Ruby said with an exotic flourish and a lift of her eyebrows. She stepped into her black spiked heels. "Don't worry—she'll be hot. I can tell all by voices, and she sounded like a tiger in heat over the phone."

Ruby took her silver snake from the scarves it was nesting in on top of her bureau. For the finishing touch she put her hand through the middle of the spiraling silver. The snake coiled around her upper arm, its red rhinestone eyes peering behind her and its little forked tongue out tasting the air.

Ruby was late by the time she made it to 18th and Collingwood. Most of the dykes were already on their motorcycles waiting for the signal to line up. A few had started their bikes in anticipation, and the gunning of motors charged the air with expectancy.

All Sasha had told Ruby to look for was her Harley and an S studded on the back of her biker jacket. Damn, there were a lot of bikes. Tough and flashy women in high spirits lined the streets before their joy ride. Eyes were on Ruby Red as she made her way up the aisle of motorcycles. Ruby tried to glance on either side of her casually, as if she knew exactly where she was going.

One dyke with spiked hair and a leather harness over bare tits called out, "Hey, you looking for a solo?" and beckoned Ruby over to her bike. Ruby tossed her head. "Sorry, maybe next year." The dyke shrugged like it was Ruby's loss. Ruby smiled to herself, thinking here was her backup in case Sasha was nowhere to be found.

Halfway up the first block of bikes, Ruby was suddenly walking in the sun, out of the cool shade of buildings. She put her sunglasses on and feasted on the sight of dykes lounging around with their jackets off, baring the fine curves of muscle, triumphantly naked breasts, elaborate tattoos, or pierced nipples.

Ruby almost forgot to look for Sasha. Then up ahead she saw the biggest, baddest Harley around. She knew it was the one even before she noticed the jacket hanging from the handlebars with a big gleaming *S* to flag her down. The size of the bike thrilled her. It dwarfed the bikes on either side, making the 250s look like toys. The black and chrome were polished to a gleam and there was a rainbow flag flying from the top of the rearview mirrors.

The bike so demanded Ruby's attention that it was a while before she shifted her focus to the woman leaning on the seat of the Harley, her back to Ruby and an arm draped casually over one of the handlebars. This tall dyke with the powerful broad shoulders had to be Sasha. She and the bike were obviously a team. Sasha was talking to a couple of friends. As Ruby approached Sasha from behind, she savored this first view. Sasha had black hair cut short like a boy's, baring her muscular neck and shoulders. She wore a red tank top that showed off the cut of her biceps and the rolling movement of her shoulder blades as she laughed and gestured to her friends. Her jeans were ripped and faded, and a red handkerchief poked out of the left back pocket. *Mmm...* Ruby thought to herself, *I like what I'm seeing.*

Sasha's friends saw Ruby approach and nodded in her direction so that Sasha stopped in midsentence and turned around. She broke into a big grin at the sight of Ruby.

"So this must be Ruby Red." Sasha held out her hand and looked Ruby up and down.

Ruby took hold of Sasha's hand and held it still. Ruby felt Sasha's strong grip more than returning her pressure. Sasha's black leather biking glove had a well-worn softness that caressed the palm of Ruby's hand. "How'd you guess?" Ruby asked, smiling.

"Well, I can't decide whether it was that flame-red hair or those lips or even that skirt you have on. I know you didn't get that name for no ruby-red Dorothy slippers."

"But I can *still* get us to Oz," Ruby said, letting go of Sasha's hand.

"Hey, don't forget, baby, I'm doing the getting. You're along for the ride."

"So that's how it's going to be," Ruby said, but didn't argue. Sasha's friends laughed. One winked and nudged Sasha and another told them to enjoy their ride. They headed off to their own bikes, leaving Sasha alone with Ruby Red.

Sasha was about to say something, but there was a loud commotion of bikes starting up and heading into the middle of the street to get into parade formation. "Time for the show," Sasha said, grabbing her jacket off the handlebars and whipping it on. As Sasha swung her leg over the seat, the spur on her boot flashed, and Ruby saw that it was a pinwheel of labyrises. Sasha stood over the bike, gripped hard onto the handlebars and with all her weight bore down on the starter. A few more tries, and there was an explosion of noise and exhaust. The roar overpowered all the neighboring bikes. Ruby felt the pavement vibrating with the engine. Sasha gunned the motor. "Hop on—she's getting impatient."

Ruby waited until Sasha was facing the front of the Harley before she swung her leg up to mount the bike behind her. Her miniskirt was so short, Sasha would have been able to see Ruby's little surprise had she been looking, but it was too soon for that. Ruby had on a pair of crotchless lace underwear she had bought for this occasion. The rhythm of the bike danced between her legs as soon as she sat on the seat behind Sasha. She hugged Sasha's hips tightly with her legs.

"Hey," Sasha said, "no need to grab on just yet. We haven't even started moving. And knowing this parade, we won't make it over five miles per hour anyway."

"Just practicing," Ruby said relaxing her legs a little bit, only to squeeze tight again, release and squeeze, release…

"Whoa, Ruby, you better save that. I have to concentrate on getting this bike in line." Ruby relaxed, content to feel the heat of Sasha's jeans on the insides of her thighs and the expectant heat of her pussy so close to Sasha's ass. Ruby entwined her fingers in the leather laces of Sasha's jacket as Sasha kicked into first and swung into line.

They had to wait on an uphill slope before making the turn that would put them on Market Street at the head of the parade. They didn't speak, surrounded by the noise of engines, blasts of horns, and excited yells from the dykes on the threshold of leading the Freedom Day Parade. Ruby wasn't even looking around her. She was concentrating on the more immediate thrill of leaning her chest into the back of Sasha's jacket. Ruby unzipped her own jacket so her skin could feel the warm, rough leather and the sharp biting-in heat of the metal studs forming the *S*, which had started baking in the sun.

When Sasha felt the pressure of Ruby's breasts on her back she reached behind her and slid her hand underneath Ruby's thigh. Ruby couldn't take her eyes off that hand, how strong it was, the knuckles jutting out from the fingerless biker glove. Ruby leaned against Sasha's shoulder, her head swimming, lost in the feeling of her cunt opening up with that ache of wanting to be filled.

Sasha's hand left Ruby's thigh suddenly, before Ruby could figure out why, and with a sudden pop into gear, the Harley shot forward. Ruby sat up and hung on. The bikes ahead of them were roaring around the curve, and they soon followed. Once around the corner the scene opened up, with masses of people on either side of the wide street as far as they could see.

The crowds were already cheering and waving to the bikes ahead of them. Ruby was dazed from the dreamy sensations of her body. But cheers of admiration soon had her smiling and raising both fists to the crowd. She saw women nudging their friends and pointing to her and Sasha. All along the way people ran out in front of them to snap pictures.

"I guess we're a hit," Sasha said after a whole group of dykes gave them the thumbs up and yelled in appreciation.

"Mmm…" Ruby loved the deep huskiness of Sasha's voice. Now she pressed her pussy right against the heat of Sasha's jeans. When the bike sped up, Ruby's clit came down hard on the frayed seam running between Sasha's back pockets. Ruby let out a cry, arched up against Sasha's back, and wrapped her arms tighter around her waist.

"You sure like to ride close, don't you?"

"It's the only way to ride."

The parade moved forward slowly, with a lot of stopping and going, and often the bikes stood still for minutes. During one long wait, Sasha reached back to caress Ruby's hair. Ruby caught hold of Sasha's hand and put it to her mouth, nibbling on the fingertips and running her tongue around them. Then, suddenly, she pushed Sasha's fingers deep in her mouth and sucked on them.

Sasha exhaled softly, and Ruby felt her rock her hips slowly back and forth. Sasha reached back with her other hand to grab on to Ruby's thigh. Ruby took her hand and guided it up under her miniskirt. Sasha's hand quickly discovered her surprise; her fingers slid right into the warm, creamy wetness of Ruby's pussy.

Sasha moaned and looked back at Ruby to find a playful smile and eyes glittering with desire. "I think we should find an alternate route," Sasha said as she brought her hands back to her bike and swung it out of the parade. Ruby hugged Sasha close, pressing her cheek to her shoulder, breathing in the heat and warm leather. Sasha gunned the motor, waiting until spectators opened a path for them so they could take off up a side street and leave the crowd behind. Ruby kept her eyes closed, giving herself entirely over to anticipation.

The Festival Virgin

by Bonnie J. Morris

On the fourth day of Ceci Blum's first camp-out at a women's music festival, someone on her work shift called her a sheltered Jewish princess. This, on top of discovering live mold growing inside her sleeping bag, sent Ceci stomping out into the rainy night.

Fierce downpours had canceled the nighttime stage concerts, so the rain crew moved a few comedians into the dining hall instead for an abbreviated, cozy show. Ceci heard laughter and cowgirl whoops as she trudged toward the cedar-scented light and warmth emanating from the camp lodge. *Saturday night, and I ain't got nobody,* she thought bitterly, blowing her nose. Her fingers itching from mosquito bites, she finally managed to open the heavy doors and poke her head inside.

The crowded dining hall bulged with womankind. At one end countless pairs of wet socks dangled over the blazing stone fireplace. Food tables had been shoved back to accommodate rows of wooden folding chairs. It might have been any Camp

Fire Girls leadership council or folk festival milieu in America except that naked breasts predominated in glorious variety. There were white-haired women with creased faces and strong hands, toddling girl children beaming through face paint, women of fine bulk and women of thin sinew, deaf women and interpreters signing their conversations with urgent grace. Ceci saw black, brown, tan, golden, red, pink, and creamy white skin glistening in folds and ripples, the sheen of skin spiraling outward from the central configuration of breasts and bellies. Enormous breasts like full and intricate baggage; smaller breasts erect and goose-bumped by the outside chill; breasts scarred or missing from cancer surgeries; breasts stretched from lactation and some now swollen with milk for the nourishment of a dangling babe in arms. Muscles and veins ran beneath the rolling flesh. Here and there were sunburned white women ruefully atoning for yesterday's nudity, women rubbing lotion onto one another's chests with glad palms.

The smell of 200 body oils, anointments, and perfumes as well as healthy body sweat filled Ceci's nostrils, congesting her head further, yet conveying a subtler message of adult female sensuality that was pleasing to heart and mind. Well-trained in chemical analysis from her graduate school studies at MIT, Ceci quickly identified musk oil, patchouli, eucalyptus, Eternity, Jontue, Cachet, orange blossom, White Shoulders, rose water, Millionaire, Love's Baby Soft, Chanel, Youth Dew, and Arpege, as well as a secondary wave of Hawaiian Tropic, Coppertone, Nivea, baby powder, lanolin, Noxzema, and swirls of marijuana smoke. Struggling to breathe, Ceci peered through the sea of multicolor breasts and interesting haircuts, hoping in vain to find a seat.

Two lesbian comedians, perched on stools at the front of the hall, teased and sassed their captive rain-damp audience. "What's the real reason lesbians have short fingernails?" asked performer number one.

"Whee!" shouted the crowd.

"Because no one has any fingernails left after pulling open those discreetly stapled issues of *Lesbian Connection*," answered performer number two.

Ceci tried not to look too longingly at women kissing, women touching one another's bare limbs, women wringing out wet shirts and applauding the entertainment with bare-assed, unself-conscious approval. Steam rose in a cloud from the toasting socks, the drying hair of 200 heads, the bodies pressed close together in patchouli harmony. *Am I the only one here without a date?* Ceci thought miserably, sitting cross-legged atop a fruit crate. She fished through her knapsack for an aspirin and caught sight of the physics textbook she'd inadvertently brought with her to the festival. Hypnotized by reading matter under any circumstances, Ceci opened the book and began studying for the class she'd have when she returned to MIT the following Tuesday.

"Don't tell me you're reading a *book* here," laughed the woman nearest to Ceci. All she wore, Ceci couldn't help noticing, were high-tops and a tool belt. "Live a little, girl-friend!"

"But I love reading," Ceci replied, feeling defensive.

"I love women," Tool Belt tossed back, returning her gaze to the two comic performers. "Only live once, kid!"

Ceci scrambled to her feet, splintering the fruit crate into 15 pieces. *That's it—I'm out of here,* she thought grimly, her wet feet slapping flipperlike toward the exit. *I don't fit in. Nobody thinks I'm a real lesbian.*

Half running and half walking, she plunged out of the dining hall and down the hill toward the circle of workers' cabins.

I'll just sit here for a moment and bawl, Ceci told herself, ducking into the shelter of a wooden porch. She sat down with a defeated shiver, letting the familiar player piano of self-pity roll out its song inside her head.

The 25-year-old daughter of Holocaust survivors, Ceci had grown up well aware of her family's experience in wartime Europe, listening to adult discussions about oppression and persecution from the time she could first comprehend words. Ceci, raised in America, with her good grades and her accentless English—she was the one who could succeed, her parents believed, and they had encouraged her every academic triumph in school, urging her on from high school to college to the Ph.D. program she soon hoped to complete. When schoolmates and other children called her "egghead," "teacher's pet," or "geek," Ceci's parents reminded her that it was no shame to be a bookworm, that they of all people understood the name-calling that came with being "different." But when Ceci showed no interest in dating or marrying a nice Jewish boy, expressing instead a timid interest in the nice Jewish girl next door, her parents were thunderstruck. "*Schanda fur leiten!*" they cried—a scandal for the neighbors!

Ceci had discreetly withdrawn from their cries of shame, moving to an apartment in Boston and burying herself in her studies. Occasionally she made the trip by subway to Am Tikva, Boston's gay and lesbian synagogue, trying to weave together the parted strands of her own life. Then, one afternoon last spring while browsing in a women's bookstore for histories of women in science, Ceci had noticed a flier for the women's music festival and thought such a getaway might allow her to meet other young lesbians in a setting far removed from her parents or the university halls.

But she hadn't counted on meeting so many lesbians who laughed at her for being, as they put it, a "festie virgin," unfamiliar with camping, with festival weather, with S/M workshops, and with tofu surprise.

She sat on the cabin porch, mulling over all the new ways she failed to fit in.

One: I'm skinny and pale, burn easily in the sun, carry around an inhaler, have no athletic muscles to speak of, no softball history. I don't shoot pool, don't lift weights, can't seem to learn the two-step.

Two: I would rather study my schoolbooks than go to a female ejaculation workshop.

Three: I have no sexual experience beyond my fantasies, have never kissed another woman, never even made the first move. I lack the romantic and physical frame of reference these veterans take for granted. I'm a nerd in Jewish culture because I'm an unmarried woman, but I see that I'm also a nerd in lesbian culture because I'm a grad student. Where is the woman who will love me for myself? Why is it a crime to like reading?

Ceci's frustrated sniffles had alerted someone inside the cabin. The screen door opened, and a woman's voice called out, "Hey. Who's there? What are you doing sitting wet and alone in the cold night air?"

It was a worker named Trudy. Ceci had met her at the gathering for Jewish lesbians Friday night, had wanted to hold her hand during the joyful Sabbath dancing. Trudy's wild hair blended with the porch's shadows and dripping plank walls, making her seem larger than life as she stood in the doorway.

"It's you," Ceci managed to say.

"Yeah. You were expecting maybe Barbra Streisand? Oh, the MIT scientist! I remember you from last night. So why weren't you at the Jewish lesbian workshop this evening? I know. You assumed we got rained out. We had it in the kitchen at the last minute." She paused, the door still swinging in her big palm. "You don't look so good. That's not to be rude, you understand."

"*Oy*," Ceci chuckled, rising to her feet. "I'm sort of on your porch unintentionally. I was feeling sorry for myself. I wanted a quiet place to think. I didn't mean to wake you."

Trudy had arms like strong young palm trees; they swung out akimbo as she edged onto the porch. Ceci looked up into a face that was ten serene years older than her own, a Jewish face more Russian than German, and beautiful teeth that flashed as Trudy demanded, "What's the matter? Someone hurt your feelings?"

"Well, this woman on my work shift called me a Jewish princess because I didn't know how to hammer a signpost. I'm better at indoor things…" Ceci trailed off, blushing. Did "indoor things" suggest she was an ardent lover? That wasn't what she had meant to say.

Trudy snorted her contempt for Ceci's workmate. "Listen, one minute. One minute. I took back some cookies from the kitchen tonight. They're hidden under my cot. Hang on." She disappeared into the cabin once more.

I must look hideous, Ceci thought frantically. She stabbed both hands through her thick brown hair, trying to rally her rain-plastered haircut and succeeding only in cutting herself on the left ear with her women's-symbol ring.

Trudy returned to the porch steps with a blanket and two enormous cookies. "They're kosher," she assured Ceci, who looked carefully into the dough. "I baked 'em myself."

"It's peanuts I'm allergic to," Ceci explained. "But these don't have any. Mmm, so *good!*"

"*L'chaim. La briut!*"

"To your health too," Ceci said shyly. They munched in silence, and then Ceci burst out, "I feel so *isolated* at this festival. I wanted to meet lesbians, but everything is so *outdoors* and *wet* and *stressful*. I've learned everything I know about lesbian culture through books, and I guess I'm just not ready for the embodiment." She smiled at both herself and at the joke, feeling better.

Trudy was nodding. "Everyone suffers from festival syndrome, though. You don't have to be a festie virgin or a sheltered nice Jewish girl to feel overwhelmed, pal. Did you go to Alix Dobkin's workshop? She's the most visible Jewish dyke here. Anyway, she says that part of being at a lesbian festival is being frustrated and miserable because our *ideals* are being tested. We create the matriarchy here bit by bit every summer, with no real blueprint to work by. We know what we *don't* want and so are critical of each other's mistakes or weaknesses." She paused to lick chocolate crumbs from her fingers. "This year I'm here at the festival as a worker, and so I get an actual bed in a worker cabin. A real mattress instead of a leaking tent makes a difference in *my* attitude. The first time you go you have no idea how to meet and maintain your own comfort level—or what the hierarchy of status in the worker scene is all about. Everybody's first festival is an over-whelming experience. Mine sure was."

"Tell me about it," Ceci suggested, luxuriating in the sensuality of chocolate.

Trudy shifted the blanket across their legs and gave a preliminary chortle. "Well, sister, I must say, the sight of you eating chocolate takes me back to my first festival. It was—hmm, I'm dating myself here—1980, and I was 21. Let me tell you that back then, when I was a festie virgin, women's music festivals were still in their infancy and offered even fewer comforts to the campers who came. I was just finishing college, but I was as out as the backyard and just aching for an armful of women. When I saw my friends' brochures for this festival, I packed my sleeping bag and canteen in like ten minutes—although the actual festival was still four months away.

"Our women's group chartered a Greyhound bus and driver to take us here, and the trip was at least 20 hours long. And every last dyke on the bus was in a couple except me, so I had to take that really attractive single seat in the rear by the bathroom. All through the night, women stumbled past me to pee, and two lovebirds tried to smoke a joint in there and got a stern lecture about 'foreign tobaccos' from our driver.

"We pulled into a truck stop for breakfast. So like 60 dykes poured into the restaurant for coffee and hash browns. We took over the bathroom, washing our faces, brushing our teeth, changing clothes, loading up on tampons from the dime dispenser. One woman, who had actually been my therapist for a year, washed out her menstrual sponge in the sink! The straight patrons were absolutely aghast. This trucker asked if we were on our way to a Girl Scout reunion. Other folks just stared. We had a dyke waitress, though; she ended up driving to the festival herself after work that night.

"I was so excited when we arrived that I didn't even bother to set up my pup tent. I slept in a community tent with women from all over the country and sang all night. But I wasn't prepared for the dreariness of the food! Fifteen years ago we didn't get nice, thick veggie burritos with sauce or lasagna with cheese or any of the amazing soups-for-1,000 you now enjoy. No, we had boiled gray potatoes with yogurt dip three times a day, livened up with the occasional old carrot. There sure weren't any concession stands selling ice cream and Oreos on the side either. The only type of snack for sale was popcorn, which you had to call 'momcorn.' Had I known beforehand I would have packed a muffin at least or some tea bags! So to make a long story short, I cruised a woman for no other reason than her giant bag of M&M's. I was desperate."

"What happened?" Ceci was fascinated.

"Oh, I laughed and talked and ate her chocolate for hours. We even wrote to each other for a while. Heh. Plenty of funny things happened at my first festival—like I was lying down in front of the day stage, wearing sunglasses and nothing else, and this woman swooped down on me and delivered a long, wet kiss. When I sat up and removed my shades, the poor lady gasped, 'You're not Claire!' and raced off in mortification."

Ceci and Trudy laughed together.

"And now you're laughing rather than feeling sorry for yourself," Trudy observed with satisfaction.

"Yes." Ceci had begun to yawn in spite of herself. She wanted to hear more stories from this fearless Amazon, who spoke with the same Yiddish lilt as Ceci's own parents. At the same time she longed to lie down and sleep in a warm, dry place. The prospect of returning to her damp, mold-coated sleeping bag in the woods was wildly unappealing.

"Tired? You can sleep in our cabin, Doc. We have an empty cot going to waste. It's pouring out there." Trudy stood up and stretched. "I have a spare sleeping bag you can use—I'm about to turn in anyway."

"Oh...no, n-no," Ceci stammered, feeling the back of her neck heat up like a cheap hot plate. "I know this is supposed to be the sleeping space for festival workers." She gazed longingly at the silent interior of Trudy's cabin.

"They're all *asleep*; they won't mind. You want to catch a cold, wandering around wet and miserable in those soaked jeans? Come on. Indulge yourself, sister; spend tonight on a mattress under a watertight roof."

This offer was simply too tempting for Ceci to decline. Trudy scooped up Ceci's knapsack, and together they tiptoed into the silent cabin.

From the beds around them came the soft breathing and assorted snorts of 20 slumbering lesbians. An occasional syllable of dream babble floated down from an upper bunk. Ceci heard her own rubber-toed sneakers squelch a wet trail into the rear of the cabin, where Trudy carefully moved an empty iron bed frame out from the far wall. "Here! Put this on." She handed Ceci a dry flannel nightshirt.

Ceci stretched out gratefully on the soft mattress. It was heavenly to be in something resembling a real bed after sleeping on hard, rooty ground for four nights. She felt her body relax for the first time in days and let out an involuntary moan.

"Is this your first camping experience?" Trudy whispered, sitting down on the next cot and removing her boots.

Ceci sighed into the dark, trying to speak as quietly as possible. "Yes. I've never had much outdoor experience. My parents certainly didn't take me camping; they were so over-protective! They were active Scouts themselves as kids, but later the woods held all sorts of terrors for them when they were hiding from the Nazis." She shuddered at this image.

"Your parents are survivors?"

"Yeah."

"Mine too."

"You're kidding!" Ceci leaned up on an elbow, astonished.

"Sure. It's not so unusual to find daughters of survivors at lesbian festivals. There are other women like us here."

Like us, Ceci thought, her heart pounding. *She's so big and strong, and she thinks I'm like her! How did I end up on her porch? I wished myself right into Jewish lesbian space!* She moved her face closer to Trudy's, straining to catch the whispered words.

"My mother grew up in Poland and during the war was hidden by a group of Catholic nurses at a regional hospital. It made such an impression on her that she spent years urging me to become a nurse. Apparently that hospital was a center of resistance activities, with nuns using drugs to bribe the Nazis to leave the kids alone. You haven't lived until you've heard my mother tell her story about picking the pocket of a totally stoned Nazi morphine addict."

"So did you do as she said? Become a nurse?"

"No. I'm a paramedic and drive an ambulance. Same thrill of saving lives, but I get to wear dykier clothes and map out traffic routes. I know what you mean about having overprotective parents, though. My mother's chief complaint about my lesbianism, for instance, is that I've somehow *willfully cho-sen* an endangered cultural identity, whereas she couldn't 'help' being Jewish. She doesn't get it that lesbian identity, like our Jewish roots, comes with a will to survive against odds, an ability to live as outsiders and insiders. I know she just wants to spare me from the hatred she put up with in her life."

"How was it…coming out to her?" Ceci wanted to know, thinking of her own parents' stupefied expressions the night she was caught making a valentine for Miriam Dinnerstein next door.

"Well, she's known for years and years. I wrote her a sort of manifesto in 11th grade. Her first reaction was to say she'd love me even if I were a murderer, which wasn't exactly the analogy I'd have liked. But we've grown closer since my father died, and she's met my partners over the years with open arms and steaming trays of kugel. She's really tried to love the women I've been with. But I'm, like…uh, not with anybody right now."

This last remark seemed to hang in the air.

Good God, thought Ceci.

She lay on her mattress watching her own heartbeat actually pushing the bedcovers up and down. What should she say next? Could they keep talking? Other women were trying to sleep. Ceci felt her teeth grinding together with frustration. *I don't know what to say. I really like her. I don't know what to say. She's the one woman I've met here who knows what I'm all about. She likes me just as I am. And I am hopeless! Hopeless! I can't move. I am utterly incapable of turning this situation to my advantage. A real lesbian would lean over and kiss her. Why must my*

mind be so much quicker than my body? Look at her: She is so hand-
some and strong. If I don't touch her, I'm going to implode with de-
sire. And there is no privacy. Women are sleeping all around us!

Ceci flinched as Trudy's elbow brushed against her.
"You're really tense. Would you like a back rub?"

Even Ceci knew this was the oldest line in the book. Or so
everyone said. Aloud she breathed, "Sure."

"Don't worry," Trudy whispered, pushing their two beds
together to form one large square and then rolling up the
sleeves of her faded festival sweatshirt. "I'm real good at this—
CPR training, you know." She deftly turned Ceci onto her
stomach and began kneading the muscles of her back and
neck with warm, skilled hands.

"O-o-oh," said Ceci.

"Sh," laughed Trudy. "This doesn't hurt? This feels all right?"

"Yes," Ceci responded, desire slowly gathering in the pit of
her stomach and pleasantly pinwheeling outward from there.
She breathed dizzily into the pillow.

"You have beautiful bones, nice bones." Trudy worked seriously, moving her palms with competent pressure around
Ceci's ribs and shoulder blades. In the darkness the only
sounds were women breathing and skin on skin.

Outside, the rain dripped sensuously from tree branch to
tree branch.

Abruptly Ceci rolled over and pulled Trudy on top of her.

For a moment neither of them spoke. Then Trudy whispered, "Are you sure this is what you want?"

"I want," said Ceci, wrapping her leg over Trudy's, astonished by her own bravado.

"How quiet can you be?" whispered Trudy.

"I don't know," Ceci answered truthfully, her fingernails pulsing. "I've never done this before. I really am a festival virgin."

Trudy paused.

"But I want you," Ceci said again, her voice barely audible.

Trudy slowly lowered her mouth onto Ceci's in the dark. The bedsprings squeaked approvingly.

"*Gevalt!*" gasped Ceci. She glanced wildly around at the beds filled with sleeping women. "I'm sorry. *Oy,* don't stop. I'll really try to be quiet!"

Trudy smiled, her white teeth shining. "No problem. Just keep your tongue in my mouth."

Outside, the rain gradually slowed to drizzle, then to a fine mist. Animals emerged from their burrows, sniffing the air, eager for a few hours of night foraging after the prolonged storm. Two raccoons lumbered onto the porch where Trudy's and Ceci's cookie crumbs remained.

Inside the cabin the temperature had risen several degrees.

Trudy had magically zipped their two sleeping bags together so she and Ceci could lie in a private cocoon of warmth. Ceci found herself naked against Trudy's bare hipbone. They both sighed at the mutual contact of warm flesh.

"Oh, my God," groaned Ceci.

"*Shah, shah,*" soothed Trudy into Ceci's breasts. "Listen. All around us, hear the sleep of sister passengers who travel with us on this journey. Deep in the belly of this ship, we all sail toward America. There will be women's land there—safety and warm dances."

"Yes," Ceci heard herself repeating over and over.

Trudy's hand cupped the back of Ceci's head and kneaded the tense little muscles there, then brought Ceci's face toward her own again.

As quiet as a pond, they exchanged tongues, feeling the tiny soft hairs at the corners of their mouths.

"A *shayne maidel*," Trudy said, exultant, and entwined her toes with Ceci's.

"Oh, please, yes. Speak to me in Yiddish. I can't believe you know my language!"

Trudy whispered the lilting, caressing words Ceci longed to hear and then said in a low voice, "Shall I make love to your Jewishness, my sister bride?"

The Song of Songs, Ceci thought. *She's going to recite the Song of Songs. I am so turned on.* Aloud she whispered, "Say it to me, as much as you know."

"Oh, that you would kiss me with the kisses of your mouth, for your love is better than wine," Trudy chanted, in Hebrew.

"Yes," gasped Ceci.

"*Ani l'dodi v'dodi li*—I am my beloved, and my beloved is mine; my beloved is unto me as a bag of myrrh that lieth between my breasts; my beloved is unto me as a cluster of henna in the vineyards of Ein Gedi. Behold, thou art fair, my love; behold, thou art fair; thine eyes are as doves."

"More," Ceci said, running her fingers across Trudy's lips.

"Behold, my love, our couch is leafy, the beams of our houses are cedars. I adjure you, O daughters of Jerusalem, by the gazelles and by the hinds of the fields, that ye awaken not nor stir up love until it please."

"It pleases me," Ceci affirmed, breathing unevenly. Steam began to form on the cabin window just above their beds. Trudy slid down, her tongue writing the passages of poetry across Ceci's erect nipples.

"Rise up, my love, my fair one, and come away; for, lo, the winter is past, the rain is over and gone, the flowers appear on the earth; the time of singing has come, and the voice of the turtle is heard in our land."

"Slower," Ceci gasped, watching Trudy's hand gradually disappear between her legs.

"Thy two breasts are like two fawns that are twins of a gazelle, which feed among the lilies. Come with me from Lebanon, my bride; thou hast ravished my heart, my sister, my bride; thy lips, O my bride, drip honey—honey and milk are under thy tongue."

"Slower."

Then, for a long time, no words, only motions and reactions.

Desire, longing, too much, shy, shy, start over. Now keep going.

Trudy curled against Ceci's body, stretching her warm tongue down to where her fingers had played.

"I sleep, but my heart waketh," Ceci panted.

"Open to me, my sister, my love, my undefiled, for my head is filled with dew, my locks with the drops of the night."

"Yes," moaned Ceci, her thighs trembling. "And I rose up to open to my beloved, and my hands dropped with myrrh, and my fingers with flowing myrrh. I opened to my beloved."

"This is my beloved, and this is my friend, O daughters of Jerusalem," wrote Trudy's tongue.

"Don't stop."

"The roundings of thy thighs are like the links of a chain; thy navel is like a round goblet, wherein no mingled wine is wanting; thy belly is like a heap of wheat set about with lilies; thy neck is as a tower of ivory; thy nose is like the tower of Lebanon..."

"I broke it in tenth grade," Ceci moaned.

"I will climb up into the palm tree, I will take hold of the branches thereof; and let thy breasts be as clusters of the vine; and the smell of thy countenance like apples; and the roof of thy mouth like the best wine, that glideth down smoothly for my beloved, moving gently the lips of those that are asleep."

"Amen," from Ceci.

"For love is as strong as death; many waters cannot quench love, neither can floods drown it."

"Keep going, keep going, don't stop; tell me more. It doesn't have to be from Song of Songs; I feel so close—"

"My heart overfloweth with a goodly matter; my tongue is the pen of a ready writer," Trudy recited.

"It sure is," Ceci breathed.

"And Ruth said: 'Entreat me not to leave thee and to return from following after thee...'"

"'For whither thou goest, I will go.'"

"'And whither thou lodgest, I will lodge. Thy people shall be my people.'"

"Slower. Slo-o-ower. Just a little bit more—"

"And Miriam took a timbrel in her hand, and all the women went out after her with timbrels and with dances, and Miriam sang unto them." Trudy raised her head and looked up at Ceci's flushed jawline. "Come into the Red Sea with me, girlfriend. We're crossing it, you and I, now. Hear it roaring on either side of us? No waters will ever close over our heads. We can run through it, come out alive, now."

Ceci heard the crush of parted water, the beckoning desert beyond both hard and hopeful. She saw on that far side Trudy dressed as Miriam, dancing with music, her brown feet bare. She felt her entire skin begin to tingle, a sensation so intense that it had a color all its own.

"Keep going. Keep go—*oh!*"

Water/hold me/the stone tablets of commandments smashing at our feet.

Thy people are my people, the lost tribe of lesbians.

Eventually Ceci became aware that she had not, after all, managed to keep quiet. Two festival workers were leaning over their bunks and staring down at her. Mortified, she ducked her head under Trudy's armpit. But secretly she thought, *I'm not a festival virgin anymore.*

"Say," said one of the awakened women. "Was all that from the Bible?"

"Hebrew Scripture, word for word," Trudy affirmed without a flicker of embarrassment at being overheard.

The awakened women looked at one another. "How come we never learned that stuff in Sunday school?"

Seduction.com

by Martha Equinox

Date: Wed, 15 May 1996 18:17:23
From: CecchiJ@pervert.com
To: ThompsCo@pervert.com
Subject: Networking for law offices conference

Hi, Corinne—Just wanted to touch base with you and tell you how much I enjoyed meeting you last weekend at the conference. It's possible I might be coming down to San Francisco in a few weeks, this time for pleasure instead of work, and I was wondering if you'd like to get together. My schedule isn't set yet, but the office owes me some time, and I might have a friend's place to stay in. I liked the little bit I saw of the city and of you. I'm interested in seeing more. Let me know.

Jean

Date: Wed, 15 May 1996 22:05:35
From: ThompsCo@pervert.com
To: CecchiJ@pervert.com
Subject: Your possible visit

Great idea, Jean—I liked what I saw of you too. I'm always interested in hot new play partners. I assume that's what you had in mind? Let's talk about this, see if we can make a good match. Usually I switch, but I haven't been bottoming lately. I know you're a top, but do you ever switch?

I am very interested in playing with you. I like smart, funny women, and you made legal billing problems a stand-up comedy act, yet still sold me your company's products. Your hands are marvelous. I couldn't help wanting to feel them on my body or wanting to run my fingers through the dark waves of your hair. I like your body: tall, solid, and butch, that feeling of strength and power coming from its pores. Did you notice that I kept touching you on your arm or shoulder to emphasize a point, brushing against you as I walked around your display? You have very sexy pheromones.

If we played together, what would you like to see me in? Neck-to-ankle black latex? A rose-colored silk teddy with garter belt and ankle-strap high heels? I think I'd like to see you in a white button-down shirt and button-fly jeans. I'd like to unbutton your shirt slowly, kneeling in front of you while you sit in a chair. I'd pull your shirt out of your waistband, trying not to be too clumsy. Do you wear undershirts? A bra? Well, since it's my fantasy, you'd have nothing on under your shirt, and I'd run my hands from your shoulders to your waist, looking at your breasts and skin. Your skin is such a beautiful rich olive, and I imagine it warm and smooth under my hands, your nipples and areolas a rich brown. I'd like to linger there, but I know too many butches who don't give their breasts to a lover until long after they've given everything else, so I'd just put my hands on either side of your waist, sit back on my heels, and look in your eyes. Then if you asked me what I liked, I'd tell you that I like dominance and submission play, points and sharps of all kinds, traditional beatings with canes and whips, and creative sensory play. I like to fuck my partners, and I like them to like fucking me.

What do you think ought to happen next?

Corinne

Date: Sat, 18 May 1996 09:35:07
From: CecchiJ@pervert.com
To: ThompsCo@pervert.com
Subject: My visit

I'm in my home office looking out the picture window toward the water and the mountains. I live on Capitol Hill facing the Olympic Peninsula and Puget Sound, and today is one of those perfect days when the snow on top of the Olympics is so bright, it hurts to look at it.

Sorry it took so long to get back to you. You took me a little by surprise, but I thought about our meeting and realized I shouldn't be. I'm always attracted to aggressive femmes. You girls are just so much fun to flip. Submission tastes sweeter coming from a woman who's used to being in control, and submission is what I want from you. I have a strong desire to see you on your knees naked, trying to find the words to beg me to touch you.

To answer your question, no, I don't switch, and don't think you're going to get my shirt off me so quickly. I'm a top, a sadist, not a masochist or a bottom. I don't like scenes where the bottom has a hidden agenda about flipping me. I've tried both sides, and I'm just not into pain or being told what to do. It always ends up feeling disrespectful and just pisses me off.

What did you mean, "I haven't been bottoming lately?" All I want from you is masochism and submission. Think you can give me that? I'd guess your head is the hardest part of your body to give up, but maybe I can help you with that little problem.

When I think of you, I see you restrained on a cross, facing me. I think I'll take the knife from my belt and cut your clothes off, then torture your tits for a while. Maybe I'll start with clothespins in rows across your pecs and upper tits and extend them up your inner arms. If you seem to be having a hard time, I'll slip my brass finger claws on, and with one hand holding your throat, I'll scratch the tender lower part of your breasts just deep enough to make bright red lines with a tiny bit of blood, then continue scratching down your belly, down your hips, into your inner thighs. If you object, I'll just tighten my hand on your throat until I'm sure I have your attention. Eventually, if you ask me sweetly enough, I'll take the clothespins off slowly, one at a time, enjoying the pattern of red bruises they leave behind. When they're all off I'll put the tit clamps on your nipples and slowly add weights, tightening the clamps a little more with each weight until your nipples are holding as much as they can carry.

By this time my hands will be sweating inside my gloves, so

I'll put new ones on, lube up my hands, and begin to play with your lips. I'd like to take a long time exploring outside your cunt before I go inside you. I think I'll move to stand beside you so I can play with your ass with one hand and your cunt with another while I tongue your nipples where they stick out of the clamps. Soon I'll slide one finger into your ass, and depending on how you respond, I might slip one finger into your cunt. Just one. I'll hold your eyes with mine while I slowly unscrew the clamps with my other hand. I want to watch your eyes when I pull your swollen nipple into my mouth as I slowly fuck you.

I think by now you ought to be begging for more, begging to be fucked deeper and harder. I like to think about fucking you, taking a long time to fill you up so that when I do, you're so hot that you burn my hand.

Maybe I'd take you down and put you over my knee so I could spank and beat your ass and back. I think that might be so pretty, I'd have to put my fist in your cunt again. I like the thought of holding you across my lap while I fuck you blind.

Let me know just what you're prepared to give up for me. I'm burned out on being some woman's marvelous fuck machine, so I want to make sure that you're very clear about how much I'll want from you, and I want you to give it up to me with grace and style. I'm very attracted to you, but if I'm going to go all the way down there to do you, I want to know that I can have whatever I want.

Jean

Date: Sun, 19 May 1996 21:13:47
From: ThompsCo@pervert.com
To: CecchiJ@pervert.com
Subject: ??scene??

I keep reading your E-mail, and each time it stops my breath and heats my cunt. I really like tit play. How did you know? I haven't gone under, gone into my deep masochism, in a long time, but the scene you described reminds me why I'm a masochist. It's been a long time since I've met a woman who makes me feel transparent and reminds me how hungry I am. I want this more than ever, but I don't know if I can get there. I'm having a lot of trouble with some aspects of bottoming right now. I don't think I can be submissive—just the thought of begging irritates me.

I've thought about this all weekend. I'm not being any good at giving up control lately, even though I really want to be able to give it up for you. My submissive side is on some sort of a sabbatical. Your fantasy about doing me made me weak in the knees, but you're right: The hardest part for me to release is my head. There've been some losses in my life recently, and death always pisses me off, you know? Maybe that's why my dominant side is so strong now. It's also probably why my masochistic side is so hungry.

We could have fun here if we can figure out a way to make this work. I have the perfect play space with my own (small) dungeon where we can make noise and be pretty out there. Do you know what an earthquake cottage is? After the '06 earthquake, a few hundred were built at the back of residential lots for families to live in while their homes were being rebuilt, and I've got one. It's completely private, at the back of a huge yard, and partially screened by bushes and trees. Everything around me is grass, flowers, trees, bushes, or the fences of the neighbors behind and beside. The smaller bedroom is my dungeon, and I just happen to have a cross that might fit your fantasy.

So here's what I'm thinking. I know you're a sadist, and that's what I want from you. I know I'm a masochist, and that's what I want to give you. It's just the dominance and submission part that I'm all fucked up about now, so I want to switch those roles. I am not talking about topping from the bottom but about dominant masochism and submissive sadism. I've done some of this kind of play, and I like it a lot; it lets both players go deeper into sadist/masochist play than they might otherwise get to go. The masochist has control over what kind of pain she gets, and the sadist is free to be extremely cruel without having to worry about pleasing the masochist or how close she is to the masochist's limits.

Please think about this. I am not talking about flipping you. There is no hidden agenda here, no expectation that you'll suddenly become a masochist, and no disrespect of you as a sadist. Just because I can't be submissive doesn't mean I stop being a masochist, and starting off in control lets me go there. Once I get really high, the tension of balancing dominance and masochism becomes unbearable, and I fall deeper into one side or the other. With a sadist who is also a true submissive, the scene can end with my beating her or fucking her. With a sadist who is really dominant, the scene ends with my giving up everything to the sadist, including my dominance.

I don't think I can get to my masochism without starting off in control. I guess the question is, Can you let go of dominance? Can I get you wet with the thought of torturing me, hurting me, doing everything you want to me with no responsibility for whether I like it? Can I make you hot by telling you I will give you my body and I will lay out the toys I want you to use on my body and I will move under your hands like no one ever has because your sadism and my masochism will be perfectly matched? The way it would work might look something like this:

We spend the first night fucking, rough trade, nasty and hard, getting to know each other's rhythms in that sweaty, intimate way. Waking up, we shower together, teasing and laughing but nothing serious. We eat, get dressed, and go for a walk, shopping for chocolate and fresh fruit. We talk about roles and what turns us on and anything else we want to talk about.

When we get back home we start to move into the scene. In the bedroom I take my clothes off for you, but you can't touch. I tell you to dress me and hand you one piece of clothing after another. I stroke your head and run my hands casually over your body but pull your head back by the hair when you try to take my nipples in your mouth. When my stockings are straight and my spike heels are on, we walk down the hall to the dungeon. While I pull a tall stool over to the cross and sit down, you cross the room to the sound system and set up the music. My toys are hanging on hooks on the walls, and we've added yours to the mix. I tell you to gather specific toys and put them close to the cross—a few whips, a nightstick and some canes, some scratchers and scrapers, and the case of blood-sports toys.

I tell you which whips are OK to start with and that I want you to begin on my back but to stay away from my ass for now. As I move to the cross, I turn my head away while you weigh the different choices, letting the falls drape over your forearm. I want to be surprised. I feel your palm flat on my back, pushing me gently against the cross, and I reach up to grab the chains over my head. For a moment, when your hand leaves my back, everything stops, waiting, then I hear the air rushing toward me. The soft, heavy weight of deerskin smacks against me, and heat suddenly blooms in my cunt and across my shoulder blades. As I fall into my masochism, you watch me begin to move and breathe with each stroke, and you change to a sharper, heavier toy. I look at you over my shoulder and see your eyes hot on me as we both start to sweat. I tell you to use the bull-hide slapper and arch up, crying with each stroke. Do you feel it, how much I like what you're doing? I want you to feel it in every part of your body.

When I'm ready for you to work on my ass, I stop you, grab your hair or throat, and kiss you, maybe slap your face or take your shirt off and pinch you, then show you the next toys to use on me. By now I'm panting, and my voice is a little hoarse. I lift up the back of my skirt and tuck it into the waistband so my ass is naked for you. If you make a mistake, I correct you. When I'm so hot that I can't speak, you'll still know what I want because I'll show you exactly what to do.

When the pressure of balancing masochism and dominance is too much for me to bear, maybe your dominant side will pull out my submission, and you'll take me further down than I've ever gone. Maybe you'll be so hot in your submission that I'll throw you down and fuck you till you scream. Maybe I'll let you fuck me, maybe I'll cry and beg for you to fuck me. You never know how it'll turn out.

Think about it and dream about me.

Corinne

Date: Thurs, 23 May 1996 19:03:27
From: ThompsCo@pervert.com
To: CecchiJ@pervert.com
Subject: ??scene??

I'm nervous that I haven't heard from you. If you're absolutely not interested, let me know, and maybe we can try something else. I'd hate to lose touch completely.
Corinne

Date: Fri, 24 May 1996 12:22:55
From: CecchiJ@Lawware.com
To: ThompsCo@pervert.com
Subject: Possible scene

Sorry I didn't get back to you, but you gave me a lot to think about. I've had a lot of strong reactions to the scene you described, so many that I don't know what I think. Give me a couple of days, and I promise I'll get back to you.
Jean

Date: Sun, 2 June 1996 08:43:48
From: CecchiJ@pervert.com
To: ThompsCo@pervert.com
Subject: Possible scene

All right, I think I know what I want to say—or at least some of what I want to say. I've never done anything like the scene you described. I've never even heard of anything like that, and at first it really pissed me off. I mean, I told you I don't switch. Are you guessing I can be flipped, or has someone been dissing me?

Switching has usually been a disaster. I've never been able to be submissive, but last week I realized that might be because I'm not masochistic at all, and submission has always meant masochism in the scenes I've done or watched. The possibility of being sadistic and submissive at the same time, without having to pretend to be a masochist, is wild.

I haven't been able to get you and your fantasy out of my mind. I keep wanting to see you panting with pain and lust and know I did that to you—no, know that you used me to do that to yourself. I don't know how to do this. I want to be deeply sadistic to you, I want to see your eyes dilate with desire and endorphins. I want you to need me, my cruelty and my passion, to get to your hottest place, and at the same time I want to be controlled by you. I don't think I know how to be submissive, but the thought of being told exactly how to hurt you, knowing I'm doing it exactly right, turns me on. I've never liked being slapped in the face, but I keep waking up in the middle of the night because in my dreams you walk up to me and slap my face and I come. Sadism is usually more head than cunt for me, but this stuff is hitting me in a really sexual place, and that makes me very nervous.

OK, OK, back up. Here's the practical stuff. What if I can't be submissive? What kind of dominant are you? I don't do humiliation, no contempt or bullying. That shit just pisses me off, and if I get pissed off, I will definitely not be submissive. And if I'm doing something, maybe whipping or caning, and you tell me I'm doing it wrong, I'm sure I'll get pissed off.

I don't know what to say anymore. Write me.

Jean

Date: Mon, 3 June 1996 20:33:07
From: ThompsCo@pervert.com
To: CecchiJ@pervert.com
Subject: Come here soon

I couldn't get to my E-mail last night until it was too late to write back, which meant I had to wait all day till I got home from work. It drove me crazy.

I like your dreams. I'd love to find out if slapping you at the right time can make you come. In fact, I can feel my cunt rise up just thinking about it.

I can tell that what I'm suggesting is working your nerves, but I like it that part of you is very excited by this. If it helps, no, I'm not into humiliation. I'm not into making you do something that offends you. What I want very much is to be masochistic for you in the only way I can right now. I want your sadism, and I want you, the flavor of you, the lust of you. I want to cry out in your hands. If you can give me your skillful cruelty, I can give you my pain and desire. If you can let go of this amount of control, I can open to you physically and sexually in a way that no one else ever has. I need a sadist who's confident enough to let go. I'm dependent on you for this. My lust and need have your name on them.

I don't want to own you or control anything about you outside of scene. I don't want a girlfriend or a best friend. I don't care what you call me. I'll call you Jean, unless you want me to call you something else that makes it easier for you. Do you want references? How can I entice you, convince you? I don't know what else to say except that I want you, and, yes, this is very sexual for me too.

I think you should come here soon. I was attracted to you when we first met and have only begun to want you more over the last few weeks. And, of course, I've checked you out, but no one has dissed you. Everything I've heard about you in scene and everything you've said to me in these letters makes me want to do this with you.

I can clear any weekend this month and take a Monday off work if I have some notice. You should have your own housing so we can have space if we need it, even though you might end up here the whole time. Gay pride is the 30th, if you're into showing off bruises. I know I'm just babbling, but as much as you can't get me out of your mind, I can't get you out of mine.

I keep thinking about you torturing my tits. I think about watching your face as you draw a razor blade across the top of my left breast toward the nipple, glance up at me, then keep cutting slowly and deliberately in a star-burst pattern around my whole breast. Your eyes are dilated and predatory, and the blood smell flares your nostrils. If one of the cuts stops bleeding, you gently spread the cut until it beads up, dark black-red in the light. I pant, and you press your other hand against my sternum to even out my breath, then cup the weight of my breast in your hand as you make another cut. The sounds coming out of my throat echo in yours. You bend to lick my breast, but I grab your hair and hold your head back, then reach to kiss you deeply and push my body into yours. My breast stings and bleeds more, and when I pull back, one side of your white shirt has lines and blotches of my blood in a circle. I hold you away from me with one hand and reach for the alcohol and matches with the other, then hand them to you. Slowly leaning back on the cross, arms up, I take a deep breath before I nod to you. You place a clean white towel across one of your shoulders, then dribble alcohol across the top of my breast. Staring into my eyes, you light the match, wait for me to drop my head back, then drop it onto me. As the alcohol burns blue and my skin turns red, you press the clean towel against me, then pull me to you and lick the tears off my face.

I really think you should come here soon.

Corinne

Date: Mon, 3 June 1996 21:51:19

From: CecchiJ@pervert.com

To: ThompsCo@pervert.com

Subject: Lust and lubricity

———————————————

I'm arriving SFO this Friday 6/7 at 9:12 P.M. on American

and return to SeaTac Tuesday 6/11 at 7:45 P.M. I've got a car reserved, so don't come to the airport. I'll come to you. I decided I wanted to drive if we go anyplace. I'll call you Thursday night to discuss what toys to bring and for the thrill of hearing your voice. I'll pack lots of white shirts.

Jean

Spelunking

by Wendy Caster

It was 1977, I had just come out, and I wanted desperately to get laid. At 23 years old I was the last virgin on earth. But I didn't know any lesbians.

I worked in a print shop as the "customer service rep," which meant I was the one you yelled at when someone in the back fucked up. My coworkers were all male. They were OK, but I was never attracted to men who keep pictures of air-brushed women with gigantic breasts on the wall. I was never attracted to any men. They had hair on their chests. They smelled funny. And they didn't have breasts. They didn't have vaginas.

You see, I wanted to go spelunking.

I had discovered spelunking at the library when I stopped in to see what there was about lesbians. I found a book called *Lesbian/Woman,* but I was frightened to be seen reading it, so I wrapped it in a *Life* magazine. Then I turned to the section on "what women do together," and before I realized it my hips were gently rocking back and forth on the small wooden library chair. I stopped my movement and looked around, but no one had noticed.

I closed the book, arranged the *Life* magazine over it, and tried to think of other things. It was embarrassing to feel hot in a library. But all I could think of were vaginas. The idea of putting my finger or tongue—tongue!—inside another woman sent sheets of lightning through my insides. The idea of a woman inside me was equally thrilling. But I was in a public place. This was not the time to think of vaginas. No vaginas, no vaginas, don't think of vaginas! For a second I made my brain blank. Then I saw a long pink tunnel. Then a cave. It was time for a walk.

I roamed through the stacks. The musty odor of old paper was enormously erotic. To distract myself, I grabbed the nearest book. It was called *Spelunking*. The subtitle was *The Art of Exploring Caves*. Yes, yes, yes! I wanted to explore caves! I checked the book out and went home.

The next day they hired a woman to run the press at work. This was considered a male job, but no man would accept the lousy salary we paid.

The woman's name was Terry, and she was tall, with short curly brown hair, almost iridescent green eyes, and a perfectly round face. She wore a blue checked work shirt, 501 jeans, and beat-up cowboy boots. The second I looked at her, I was fantasizing about spelunking again—and praying that she was a lesbian. And single. And attracted to me.

That afternoon, while the guys were at lunch, Terry did a wonderful thing. She went around the shop and removed all of their pinups, leaving the dirty green walls checked with light green rectangles. She treated the pictures gently, rolling them into one of the tubes we used for delivering posters and leaning the tube against the men's room door. Then she put a small picture of Virginia Woolf on the wall next to the press.

I was in love.

I fidgeted, waiting for the guys to return. I pictured Terry standing her ground, strong and proud, until they admitted they were sexist pigs and promised to change their ways.

Reality was less romantic. The guys came back in a flurry of "wha' the fuck," and "who the hell." It was obvious the culprit was Terry, so Joe, the boss, went right up to her.

"Did you take down our pictures?"

"Yes." Terry looked Joe so strongly in the eyes that he looked down at his shoes. Then he looked up again and said, "Why?"

"I refuse to work in a sexist workplace."

This was greeted with another chorus of "wha' the fuck." Joe said, "They're just pictures. They don't do any harm."

Terry replied, "They support the mistreatment of women."

The men's curses grew louder.

Joe said, without much conviction, "You'll have to put up with them or leave." He was probably praying she would stay; with no one to run the press, he would have to work 14-hour days.

"Then I'm gone." She turned to go.

"Wait!" I was surprised to hear myself speak. "Joe, she's right. Those pictures are awful. If she goes, I go."

Joe's mouth fell open. He turned to the men behind him. "Hey, fellas, what do you say we give the girls a little slack here?"

The chorus grunted their refusals.

Joe turned back to Terry and me. "Do you have to leave?"

"Yes." We said the syllable together.

Joe slunk to his office. Terry took her picture of Virginia Woolf and her denim jacket. I grabbed my windbreaker.

As we were leaving, one of the men said, "Hey, Julie, why are you quitting with that dyke?"

"'Cause I'm a dyke too."

I felt light suddenly but powerful at the same time. My chest felt like it was filled with helium, and I floated out of the shop. Outside, Terry grinned and invited me to her apartment for chamomile tea.

Her apartment was wonderful. Its two rooms were sunny and large, with walnut molding around the windows and doors. Pictures of women filled every inch of wall space. Amelia Earhart. Gertrude Stein. Greta Garbo. Terry had to tell me who some of them were. Jeanette Rankin, the first woman elected to Congress. Mother Jones. Emma Goldman. I had a few years of college under my belt, but I had a lot to learn.

The apartment didn't have much furniture. The kitchen had a table and two chairs, and the other room had a desk, a chair, a bookcase crammed with books, and a mattress on the floor, covered with a brown-and-lavender Mexican blanket. As Terry prepared the tea I sat at the kitchen table, and we discussed the asshole men at work.

"I knew it probably wouldn't work out," Terry said. "I almost never work with men. But I had a couple of weeks before I left town, and I thought I'd make some extra money."

Left town!

Terry was moving to the Northwest to live in a women's commune. "I'm sure you know all about lesbian separatist politics," she said.

"No," I told her. "I don't know anything. I just came out, and I don't know any lesbians."

She turned to me with two cups of tea and a big smile. "Well, now you do."

I took my cup of tea and put it on the kitchen table, but she motioned me into the other room. "It's lighter in there," she explained. "And you can see this great tree out the window." She went to the mattress and sat on it, her back against the wall. She patted the spot next to her for me to sit on.

I wanted to be near Terry, but I was scared, so I feigned great interest in a glass donkey on her bookcase. Terry watched me with an amused grin, then said, "Come on, sit down." She patted the mattress again.

My jeans slithered between my legs as I sat, and I realized I was wet just from being alone with a woman, this woman, this lesbian. Would I finally get to go spelunking?

Did I actually know how?

As we sipped our tea she told me about separatist politics and the importance of being woman-identified. She told me that some lesbians were heterosexually identified, particularly the butch/femme crowd, but they weren't real lesbians. They hadn't caught up with the present.

As we talked we watched the leaves sway on the giant tree outside the window, which tinted the room a glowing green. It was hard to concentrate on anything but Terry's shoulder next to mine.

Terry reached over and put our empty cups on the floor. Then she turned to me and ran her finger down my cheek, then across my lips. All the energy in my body flew to my face to be near her touch, and I blushed. She smiled, then kissed me. Her kiss sent intensified energy back into my body. My veins were tubes of red-flashing neon. She pulled me down onto the mattress and held me tight while gently stroking my tongue with hers.

There was a rush in my body as all my molecules clambered to be right next to Terry. My breasts were glowing. My toes were clenching and unclenching. And my brain was murmuring, "Finally, finally"—and also, "Oh, God, I hope I don't make a fool of myself."

Terry pulled slightly away from me and undid the buttons of my work shirt while kissing my neck. I wanted to undress her too, but buttons seemed impossible to deal with as my body went up and down and all around on its carousel. Instead I stroked Terry's back, then reached under her shirt. I was startled by the smooth warmth of her skin. I had never touched anything so sweet, so beautiful, so…touchable. I suddenly understood that matter and energy really were the same.

Terry rolled me onto my back. She leaned over me and kissed my clavicles, my breastbone, and then my breasts. I would have swooned, but I didn't want to miss anything.

Terry took my nipple into her mouth and the world stopped. There was nothing but my nipple and her mouth. The universe was focused on the tiny space where her tongue moved back and forth. I realized I was digging my fingers into her back and I stopped, scared I had hurt her—though she didn't seem to mind. She was crooning a sex song deep in her throat.

After a while she sat up, grinned at me, and said, "We have altogether too much clothing on here." She shucked her shirt and jeans, then her underwear. She was stunning. Her shoulders were big and broad. Her clavicles were deep and elegantly defined. Her breasts were tiny round pyramids with large brown tips. Her pubic hair wandered down a thin line from her belly button to a lush triangle of growth hiding the cave where I might soon be spelunking. I moaned, then blushed again. I had never made a noise like that before in my life.

Terry laughed. "Aren't you going to take off your clothes?"

I was so lost in her body that I had forgotten mine. My shirt was easy to remove, since Terry had already unbuttoned it, but I had trouble with my jeans. I couldn't remember how a zipper worked. I felt like a jerk—wasn't sex supposed to be smooth and graceful?—but Terry helped me get my pants off. My underpants made a loud slurp as she removed them from between my legs. I blushed yet again, embarrassed to be so extravagantly wet, but Terry seemed pleased. She seemed pleased about everything.

Terry lay down on the mattress, and I stretched next to her on my side. Slowly, carefully, I reached out and touched her breasts. My breasts were large and pendulous, but hers were petite and firm, and her nipples hardened to tickle the insides of my palms. My hands had never been so happy.

Terry moved my hands from her breasts, then pulled me on top of her. When I felt the full sensation of her skin against mine, I yelped. She giggled, then whispered in my ear, "I'm so glad I'm your first." Her breath made the fuzzy hair along my back quiver. We held each other tightly, breasts to breasts, belly to belly, thighs to thighs. So this was why the world was so obsessed with sex! I was surprised anyone ever got out of bed.

Terry started rocking slowly, so I rocked with her. Then she moved one of her legs so that her thigh was against my clit, and I moved one of my legs in the same way. We rocked together faster, then faster still, moaning and panting. Terry's moans changed to groans as we rocked and bucked. Then she roared, and I realized she was coming. Wow! I didn't know you could come like that! I felt her orgasm in my breasts and stomach and insides, and tears came to my eyes. Terry relaxed under me, then looked at me with a lopsided grin. "You're sure a sexy beginner," she said. I felt like I had won the Nobel Prize in Human Relations.

We held each other for a while, then Terry said, "Now it's your turn." She rolled me over onto my back, then started stroking me all over my body. I was like a kitten, raising each body part to her touch, purring, and wanting more. She kissed my belly and my hips, then my pubic hair. My cave swelled into a cavern, preparing a welcome for Terry.

Terry arranged herself between my thighs and resumed kissing me. She opened me with her tongue and drew circles around my clit. The whole mess of my 23 years of life now made sense; it was all so I could get to this moment. Energy spasmed throughout my body and my head rolled back and forth. A storm cloud was gathering in my loins, and lighting was going to strike. And my cave yelled, "Come inside me, please, please." Terry licked me and licked me. The storm cloud grew. My cave yelled, "Fuck me, please!" Terry didn't hear. Soon I didn't care about anything but her tongue and my clit. Soon after that, I came, a glorious, muscular, liquid come.

We made love two more times that evening, and it was incredible. But Terry never explored my cave, and when I tried spelunking her, she gently but firmly pulled my hand away.

Later she explained why. "You see, Julie, penetration is male-identified, so lesbians don't do it."

"All lesbians?" I asked.

"All real lesbians," she answered and handed me some books about woman-identified sex.

I didn't dare tell Terry how very much I craved spelunking, and for the next two weeks, we had nonstop sex—her way. It was wonderful, but I still wanted...more.

Terry moved to the Northwest, and I went job hunting. And lover hunting. After my adventure with Terry, I felt braver about going to lesbian rap groups. I read the books she gave me, and I learned a lot about lesbian behavior. Robert's Rules of Order seemed simpler, but I adjusted. After all, these women had carefully thought things through. Who was I to second-guess them? I thought.

I had occasional affairs but still no spelunking. When I masturbated, I would fuck myself furiously, but then I would feel guilty. I didn't want to be male-identified. I wanted to be a real lesbian.

A couple of months after I met Terry, I discovered the spelunking book, long overdue at the library, in the back of my car. I leafed through it and sighed, remembering when I believed that once I found women, my cave would get all the exploration it desired. Then I went to the library to return the book.

As I waited to find out how much I owed, a woman got in line in back of me. She was in her 40s and large and round. She wore a long skirt, an Indian print blouse, and a fedora. She smiled at me, and I was pretty sure we were both deciding the other was a lesbian. I'm not sure how I knew about her; she didn't dress the right way or anything. Maybe she didn't know the rules. Which meant, maybe, possibly, she did penetration! It suddenly felt warmer in the library.

"So what's spelunking?" she asked, glancing at the book in my hand.

"It's exploring caves," I answered. And I blushed. Not a little pink blush, mind you, but a big deep purple blush.

She continued the conversation as though my face were a normal color. "Do you explore caves?" Smiling, she dragged the words out slightly.

"Well, I'd like to." My blush did not, would not, recede. My earlobes were throbbing.

"Caves have always fascinated me," she answered, again with the slightest drag on each word. She was flirting with me. No, she was just chatting. Or was she? Her smile was lovely. Her eyes were dark and deep like a llama's.

The librarian said "Next," and I paid my fine and left the library, too scared to look back for the woman in the fedora. But outside the library I stopped. I didn't want to leave without talking to her some more. While I was frozen, deciding what to do, she came out.

Casually, as though we had known each other for years, she asked, "Want to get a cup of coffee?"

We settled into a booth in the back of a dingy coffee shop and quickly established that, yes, we were both lesbians, and yes, we were flirting. Her name was Jesse. She was a poet.

After we had discussed Emily Dickinson and Adrienne Rich, she asked me if I had ever been in a relationship. I told her about Terry and our wonderful two weeks. I told her about my dates. Something in Jesse's face made me feel like I could tell her anything—or maybe I was just bursting to talk. But the next thing I knew, I was telling her about my desire to spelunk. She laughed. "What an utterly charming word," she said.

"You don't think it's male-identified?" I asked.

"Honey," she replied. "I don't give a shit what men do. I don't give a shit what anyone does. And I don't need a decoder ring and membership papers to be a lesbian. I do what I like."

She paused. "And I'm just crazy about spelunking."

I was ready to go home with her on the spot. Hell, I was ready to marry her. But she wanted to go slower.

"I'm an old-fashioned sort of gal," she explained. (Gal! Terry would have had a fit.) "How about we date a bit and see if we actually like each other?"

We dated. I learned that Jesse was not a separatist, not a butch, not a femme, not anything you could label. She was 45 and had been a soldier, a nurse, and a sculptor. She wore fedoras because she liked them. She liked books, adventures, funny clothing, food. She liked almost everything, it seemed. Except rules.

We went to the movies. We held hands while Woody Allen and Diane Keaton battled a lobster, and Jesse drew little circles on my palms. I went home and masturbated. We went to a cheap bar, listened to jazz, drank beer, and sat shoulder to shoulder. I went home and masturbated. We took a long walk and made out in a quiet corner of the park. I went home and masturbated.

I had wild sex dreams. In one I wore a miner's helmet, with the headlight pointed into Jesse's giant glistening cave. In my sleep I started to fuck myself; half awake, I finished, with a roaring echoing orgasm.

One night we went dancing at our local lesbian bar. At first I was embarrassed to be seen with Jesse. In a sea of work shirts and jeans, her red Robin Hood blouse, purple troubadour pants, and ever-present fedora looked clownish. But after one slow dance, lost in her body, I saw how beautiful she really was. When the music ended she drawled, "Does tonight seem like spelunking weather?"

"Oh, yes," I squeaked.

We tore off our clothing as soon as we closed her front door. We stumbled around her living room, kissing and clinging. We dissolved down to the carpet, then touched and licked every inch of each other. Somehow, without discussing it, we agreed to leave our deepest parts for last.

Finally I could wait no more; my insides were crying "Fuck me, please!" But I didn't know how to ask out loud. Luckily, my hips did. They rubbed up against Jesse's leg like they would swallow the whole limb. Jesse murmured, "You sweet wanting woman," and put her hand between my legs. My lips fell open under her touch. She played with my opening, putting just the tip of her finger inside me and moving it almost imperceptibly. I moaned, half in pleasure and half in frustration. Jesse teased, "One must be very careful when exploring new caves," and moved her finger inside just the slightest bit more. I couldn't take it. I thrust myself at her hand until her finger was all the way inside me, and I rocked against her. She added another finger, and another, and fucked me with long rhythmical strokes. I stopped rocking and just experienced her fucking me. With each stroke I felt my insides grow larger and brighter. Jesse was bringing starshine to my lonely cave. Soon I was rocking again, meeting Jesse's hand with big, lovely slurps. Still fucking me, Jesse leaned down and licked my clit, her tongue matching the rhythms of her fingers. An orgasm tore through my body.

Jesse lay down next to me, her fingers still inside me. "Lovely woman, lovely woman," she murmured again and again, while postcome warmth pervaded my body. She nibbled my shoulder, and I kissed the top of her head. We breathed in and out together quietly.

After a while, when I had regained enough use of my body to start stroking Jesse's thighs, she said, "Have you ever considered simultaneous spelunking?"

I hadn't, but it seemed a wonderful idea. While Jesse stayed inside me, I stroked between her legs. I was tentative about going further, but Jesse used her free hand to guide me. Two of my fingers slipped into Jesse, and I gasped with wonder as they were swallowed in sweet, soft, slippery heat. Her cave walls were swollen and smooth and strong. I understood that caves were holy places.

I stayed in her. She stayed in me. We rocked together in a jumble of arms and legs. I had never dreamed anything could feel so spectacular. A roller coaster of feeling looped the track made by our intertwined bodies.

I was spelunking at last.

Petal Sweat

by Susan Kan

Rhonda Nickels never considered herself a poet, but lately she was drawn to the magnetic poetry kit on the refrigerator in the staff room at the women's health clinic where she worked. The lunchroom was a difficult place for her, she being shy and newly hired. Instead of trying to talk to the other nurses, most of whom spoke about their weekend escapades, dating dilemmas, or children, she would stand at the refrigerator, sipping from her milk carton. Rhonda was interested in their conversations, she had to admit, but she didn't know how to participate comfortably.

A recent graduate from a nursing school in a small Midwestern town, Rhonda's move to Boston had been a big change. Her family back home had been opposed to her leaving, but Rhonda felt the pull of the ocean, the salt spray, and the warm dunes calling out to her. Timid as she was, a kernel of adventurousness was burning inside her. At 31 years old she felt it was now or never.

At the clinic she was efficient and well-versed in the language of the body, but she interacted with the patients as though they had brought their cars in for tune-ups and repairs. She could say the words breast, vagina, cervix, fallopian tubes, and Pap smear as easily as mountain, elevator, door, subway, and lunch.

Rhonda pulled the tiny magnets around the refrigerator:

sit there and I can cook eggs and meat

Not very poetic. The next day she made a list of rhyming words:

make lake steak bake fake take

One day, about a month into her new city life, as she searched for words, she noticed on the side of the refrigerator facing away from the room a line of words all by themselves:

we am love by doing

Rhonda looked sheepishly around the room to see if anyone saw her. The others were absorbed in the latest *People* magazine, the one with *The First Wives Club* actresses on the cover. Turning back to the five simple words, Rhonda thought, *Bad grammar.* Then after thinking a moment she wondered, *We am love by doing* what?

Obviously, as a nurse, she knew. She knew what the books said. But as much as she hated to confess this, she had never been in love, and she had never done it. All day long she talked to women and girls, sometimes as young as 13, who said they knew love by doing. Rhonda coolly educated and examined them, but always a little tug wore at her soul. What was it like?

At night, lying in her bed, she tried to imagine. She had learned about masturbation but never cared much for touching herself. She tried, back when she was 17 and dating a boy named Jeffrey Wolf. In fact it was Jeffrey's idea. When Rhonda had refused to go all the way with him, he suggested that she watch him jack off and then he would watch her. The idea had been compelling enough that she had tried touching herself when she was alone a few times. But instead of letting him watch, she decided to break up.

And since she'd become a nurse, she spent a good bit of time looking at other people's private parts, and the whole concept had lost its allure.

We am love by doing. We am love by doing. Rhonda tried to guess who might have written that.

Every day, after that first discovery, Rhonda nonchalantly checked the refrigerator. A week later the sentence was gone, replaced with this:

worship a woman
picture her luscious bare fiddle
those easy moons

Rhonda blushed and scurried out of the lunchroom. In her haste she ran into Naomi Golden, a physician's assistant, in the doorway.

"Oh, I'm sorry," Rhonda apologized.

"No problem." Naomi's smile was so big, Rhonda thought she could see her molars. "What's your hurry? It's lunchtime." She gave Rhonda a little squeeze on the arm as they headed in opposite directions.

In the hallway Rhonda touched her arm where Naomi had touched it. *Odd,* she thought, *I haven't been touched in an affectionate way by anyone since I arrived in Boston.* Then the thought, which at first had seemed rather exciting, drooped like a wilted flower.

That night when Rhonda changed out of her uniform, she thought again of the poem. *Those easy moons,* she repeated, running her hands over her butt cheeks. Her skin was pale like the moon's face, she noticed as she inspected her body in the mirror. Then she looked herself in the eyes. Who could have written that? Everyone who works at the clinic is a woman. Who would be worshiping another woman?

As she drifted off to sleep that night, she held her arm where Naomi had squeezed it.

A few days later the words from the poem were pushed into the corner all messed up, and replacing them was this list:

> **tongue**
> **hair**
> **honey**
> **lust**
> **ask**
> **for**
> **it**

Rhonda got her milk out and, hoping her nervousness wouldn't show, went to sit at the round table with the other women. They were talking more seriously today about an antiabortion episode at another Boston-area clinic. Rhonda didn't like to think about the politics of abortion. The men who debated the issue seemed completely removed from the medical procedure and the women who came through the doors wanting services.

Naomi was very passionate about the issue, though, and Rhonda rather liked watching the way Naomi's hands flew up like birds around her face when she spoke.

"Our lives are at risk here," she invoked. "We can't just be passive."

The other women nodded agreement.

With the heightened tension around the abortion safety situation, the list of words stayed up for longer than Rhonda's patience lasted. She had memorized it, and every night in bed she recited it: *tongue, hair, honey, lust, ask for it.* She touched her tongue and hair as she said those words, and as she repeated the words they became like an incantation. One night her hand drifted toward her vulva when she said honey. *Ask for it. Ask for it.*

During her break the next day, she lingered in the lunchroom after everyone else had left. It was very hard to work fast with all the words randomly scattered across the door of the refrigerator, but she wanted to write something back, something to let the writer know that someone was reading her poems. Something also that would ask for more. She wrote:

**elaborate a moment as if you
are a blue lake sweating diamonds
gone enormous with beauty**

Rhonda stepped back from her words. *What does that mean?* She considered replacing sweating with drooling but only because that word was right there. But *drool?*

Just then the door swung open, and Naomi strode up to the fridge. Rhonda quickly smeared her words out of order.

"What are you up to, Nurse Nickels?" Naomi smiled her big grin. "A little poetry writing on the side, eh?"

"Oh, nothing," Rhonda lied. "Just trying to relieve a little job stress, if you know what I mean." Her armpits itched from the instant sweat she had broken.

"Me," Naomi winked at her, "I'm not much of a poet."

But the next day Rhonda found these sentences shaped into curving waves:

**whisper a lazy trip to the pink place in my forest
let me sing on the breast of your dress as we go
our cry a drunk light flooding after**

Reading these words made her wet between her legs, a sensation new and lovely. She looked over her shoulder with a guilty rush. Here under the fluorescent lights there was something both illicit and delicious about her feelings. She ran to the bathroom and hoped no one noticed her pink face.

Later that day when she was writing up reports, she found her mind wandering to the words on the refrigerator, again wondering who wrote them. She looked down at Grace Sheehan's chart and found that she had been doodling round shapes that looked remarkably like breasts with hard nipples. When Naomi breezed in, Rhonda sprung up, startled. Had Naomi always made her so jumpy?

She was eager to get home, to get undressed, to stand before her mirror and think her new thoughts. *Pink place in my forest.* She touched her tongue, swishing her finger in her mouth and over her lips. Then she lifted her hair high off her head and slowly let it drop. *Honey. Lust. Pink place.* She began to take a *lazy trip* through her forest, opening herself, stroking. Just before she closed her eyes, she saw in the mirror how flushed she had become. *Let me sing.*

But Rhonda stopped herself. *Let who sing?* And she didn't like the idea of a drunk light. That was not very good writing. Then it dawned on Rhonda that two women were probably writing these things to each other, that she was a voyeur, spying, in a sense, on their flirtation. She vowed she would stop.

The next day she did not look at the magnetic poetry.

The following day and all the next week, she stood at the window instead. Sometimes she would sit at the table, especially if Naomi was there.

"How was your weekend?" Naomi asked on Monday.

"Oh, fine, thanks," Rhonda answered, wishing desperately she had better conversational skills, that she could remember for the life of her what she had done over the weekend. All that flashed through her head when Naomi smiled and touched her shoulder was how she had opened her pink place and reached deep inside, how she had smelled her fingers, then quickly washed off the scent.

"How was yours?" she managed.

"Great! I went roller-skating along the river with a real cutie." She clapped her hands together. "Too bad I don't have time to tell all the details; I've got to get back to the health care biz. At least for now." She patted Rhonda's back, threw out her lunch trash, and went back to work smiling.

The room empty, Rhonda couldn't help herself. On the side of the refrigerator she read:

a
thousand
fast
waters
tongue
like
wind
on
winter
essential
as
storm
to
flood
as
woman
to
power
as
you
to
me

Rhonda's patients did not get her usual efficient and competent attention that afternoon. She kept thinking about one word in that poem, one word right in the middle of it: *essential*. She was feeling more and more intensely that she was missing something essential, something she didn't even have an inkling about back in her hometown.

That night she went to a movie, alone, in order to distract herself. But *essential* followed her, ranted in her ear as though the word itself were a force or had a voice. *As storm to flood. As woman to power. Storm, flood, woman, power.* Over and over.

She left the movie before the end, walked home in the rain, and arrived at her door drenched. She stripped off her clothes right inside the doorway, leaving them in a wet heap, and went to bed. She made herself put her hands under her back so they wouldn't move on her body, but even as she did this she felt her own easy moons of flesh.

The weather was misty and close to the ground when she awoke the following morning. She felt groggy, and her hand was in her pubic hair, her fingers combing it out before she realized what she was doing. She dressed quickly, had some toast and jam, took her vitamins, and was out the door.

rain girl raw with beauty
your skin sea honey and swim
let's boil petal sweat together
and cry a moon symphony

Whoever was writing the poems was having a more and more interesting time. And Rhonda realized that she had begun to associate the poems with Naomi. Maybe it was the word *raw*. There was something raw about Naomi. Or was that how Rhonda felt around her?

Rhonda was puzzled by the idea of boiling petal sweat. What could that mean? Throughout her day the words *petal sweat* ran around her mind. *Petal sweat. Petal sweat.* The clinic was backed up because Naomi had called in sick. Curiously so, given how well she appeared the day before. Her absence left Rhonda again to ponder who the poets were. If one was Naomi, who was the other one?

There was Samantha Graves, but didn't she always talk about her boyfriend, Joe, during lunch? There was Leslie Durante, but she had kids. There was the older doctor, Nikki Johanssen, but Rhonda couldn't imagine, for the life of her, her standing at the fridge moving magnets around. She couldn't think of anyone. And maybe she didn't want to know.

She liked the mystery, the distraction, the intrigue, and when she was completely honest, she loved the way she felt after she read the poems. She loved how her body flushed hot and sudden, how the moisture gathered in her panties, how her nipples pressed against her bra. Today she imagined that she was the rain girl; after all, it was just last night when she walked home through the downpour.

The thought of possibly reading another installment of poetry lifted her right out of bed the following morning and into the shower. With the hot water streaming over her hair and shoulders, she recited the bits of poetry that had stayed with her. *Tongue, hair, honey. Fast waters like wind. Essential. Bare fiddle. Pink place in my forest.* She stuck out her tongue and let her mouth fill with warm water and dribble out in rivers over her breasts. She tempted her nipples into hardness by teasing them with her fingers, both breasts at the same time. *Rain girl raw with beauty.* One hand kept up the nipple play while the other stroked up and down her belly, into her navel, down to her pubic hair. *My forest.* She was gushing between her legs, and when she touched there, opening herself, the slick wetness was not shower water. *Your skin sea honey and swim.* Rhonda, her face upturned into the spray, tugged and massaged her lips. *Oh,* she thought, *this is it, this is it. Here are my petals. Let's boil petal sweat.* More fingers exploring, stroking, now her clit. *The pink place. Drunk light.* She swooned and caught herself, held the shower wall as her body shook and delighted and pulsed from the explosion of that kernel deep inside her. *Cry a moon symphony.*

After she came she stood there, eyes closed, letting the new feeling in her body work its way out through every pore. Then she started to shiver. What time was it?

The rest of the week was a blur of work and refrigerator and private touching. She hated to admit it, but her patients' bodies took on new meaning; she looked at them differently. Not as parts made up of just bone and blood but of sensation and vitality.

Grace Sheehan was coming in again, and Rhonda was nervous to be in the examining room with her. Grace's breasts were shaped in such a come-hither way, like those portraits with the eyes that follow you around the room. Grace's nipples pointed straight toward Rhonda, it seemed, no matter which way she turned.

By the time Friday afternoon rolled around, Rhonda found that she had been getting great pleasure from stringing words together in her head. And even more pleasure from letting the words form pictures and sensations in her body. *Tongue. Peach. Mist. Smooth. Ache.*

Before leaving the clinic for the weekend, Naomi alarmed Rhonda by walking up behind her and saying in a low throaty voice, "I hope you do something nice for yourself this weekend."

Rhonda jumped from both her voice and the suggestion. Did her new explorations show on her face? She managed to reply, "Yes, thanks, and I hope you have a good weekend too."

"Oh, don't worry. I plan to. Life's too short, honey. You've got to get it while you can." She laughed as she flew out the door.

Within ten minutes everyone had gone, and Rhonda sat staring at the refrigerator. Then she walked over and began pushing the small magnets around. She stood back and read the arrangement of her words:

> **to feel you finger**
> **my peach from behind**
> **then swim around**
> **lie on top**
> **urging my bed springs to moan**
> **my petals to sweat honey**
> **take me please**
> **I want a heaving vision**
> **frantic as a summer storm**

She was breathing hard and smiling at her bravery. Then she quickly gathered her things and walked out to the parking lot. There were only a few cars left. She noticed the one near hers in the back row. Two people were sitting close together in the front seat. As she neared the car she realized they were kissing, so she lowered her eyes. She had to pass right in front of them to reach her own car, and it was then that she turned to look. Someone was waving hello. It was Naomi, and pressed against her was Leslie Durante looking flushed and tousled. Rhonda surprised herself by smiling broadly at the two women. She believed they had let her in on a secret, had answered a question they didn't know she had, and she felt a rush of relief and pleasure. In fact, she responded as if she knew what they felt when they touched each other. Well, she almost knew.

That night, after relaxing in a hot bath, Rhonda crawled between her soft flannel sheets. When she closed her eyes and stretched out her legs, she imagined Naomi standing naked at the foot of her bed. She saw her warm smile and easy posture. Then Rhonda opened her eyes. "Wait," she said out loud as if to Naomi, and she scampered out of bed in search of a candle. "Wait, wait, wait," she repeated as she opened drawers looking for matches. Eventually, she was back in bed with the shimmering flame, and, yes, Naomi had waited.

Naked from the waist up now, Naomi pulled down the covers and slowly ran her strong hands from the soles of Rhonda's feet up to and along her thighs, around her belly, across her breasts, and down her arms. Naomi stopped at Rhonda's hands and gently lifted them up to her own breasts. They were smaller than Rhonda's, with silky curves around the bottoms and sides. Then Naomi took one of Rhonda's fingers and led it on a journey over the map of her body: nipples pursed and heedful, neck sleek and pulsing, armpits hollow and tangy. Rhonda looked at and touched and tasted this new territory, so like her own and yet not. Her own breath, panting and reaching. Her own rocking, on her back, glistening with sweat. Her own sweet, slick petal sweat. And as all the sensations heightened, her own words washed over her. *Take me, please. I want a heaving vision.*

And that night she had one.

The Place Before Language

by Lucy Jane Bledsoe

Picture me in my Class-A National Park Service uniform: the polished-to-a-luster shoes, the green trousers with the razor-sharp crease, the belt with the embossed pinecones, the short green jacket with the shiny badge and brass buttons, and the wide-brimmed Smokey the Bear hat. The whole bit. You see a woman who can name every wildflower on Mount Rainier, who has climbed at least eight major peaks, and who knows the secret life of glaciers.

You think you see a woman in control.

You see a femme at heart hoping to find relief in a butch getup.

You see me, a woman whose summer job as a ranger on Mount Rainier had not stopped her raging fantasies about murdering Donna's new girlfriend. Graphic pictures—of my hands around her neck, of my green Park Service truck colliding wit her bulk—lit the dark recesses of my mind like little nuclear explosions. I couldn't stop them. I didn't want to.

She—the new girlfriend—was dog ugly and had a personality that lurked in dark corners. She looked like she needed a vigorous trot in country air. Near the end of our ten years together, Donna had called me a bulldozer, and compared to this beige, papery moth, I suppose I did come across forcefully. I never denied being a high-maintenance girlfriend. I knew I wasn't an easy person. But then I had trusted "easy" wasn't what Donna was after.

No, it wasn't my bright obsession with violence that disturbed me. If I'd had the chance to act on my fantasies, I don't doubt that I would have. What really bothered me was the feeling that my grasp on everything I'd always known to be true was slipping, that a vital part of my brain had shaken loose and was rattling around in my head like useless machinery. You see, until that summer, I had believed in the power of language. As a writer, I lived with the conviction that everything could be said. Words were life's cradle, the way to name, shape, hold, and, yes, control one's world. I had always believed that as I sharpened my verbal skills so too would my world view come more crisply into focus. Language to me was like a massive database where one filed away experience—relentlessly, day after day. Even as I was living each moment, I was assigning words to it, writing it, wrapping it up in a neat package of verbiage.

This word castle crumbled when Donna dumped me. Even my agent, whose job was to promote my words and who'd treated me like the next Willa Cather just a few months before, quit returning my phone calls, as if she'd been in cahoots with Donna. I felt hollow and formless when I started the summer on Mount Rainier. All I had were visions of human roadkill flaring up in my gut like a forest fire, hot and out of control. That and this uniform.

I was stationed for the summer at Sunrise, a set of cabins just above tree line on the east side of the mountain. When I arrived there in mid June, a roommate had already moved in.

"I've taken the bottom bunk," she said, "but if you prefer it we can draw straws."

"I'm usually a bottom," I answered to amuse myself, "but I need a change. I'll take the top."

In those first couple weeks I hardly used the bunk at all. I tried to work on short fiction in the evenings, but nothing ever came. I couldn't sleep, either, so I spent the nights haunting the trails around Sunrise. Up there the mountain was so close it filled up half the sky, and even when the moon wasn't out, the stars were so abundant and the mountain so bright with glaciers that I could go anywhere without a flashlight. I would climb out to the end of Sourdough Ridge or explore the Silver Forest, a shadowy grove of smooth silver snags left over from a fire long ago. The meadows were full of columbine, aster, paintbrush, phlox, heather, monkey-flower, and lupine, and where the snow was just melting, glacier lilies, their colors rich and magical in the starlight. Sometimes I would hike out to Frozen Lake or down to Sunrise Lake.

These night prowls provided no insights, no answers, no inspirations, and no relief from wanting to murder Lurking Dog. I felt eclipsed by the massive glowing mountain, as if I didn't exist at all against its commanding backdrop. And yet, looking back, I see that these hikes were a kind of boot camp of the soul. I was getting ready.

On the first of July three teens turned up missing on the mountain. Two boys, 17 and 18, and a girl, 16, had begun climbing Rainier the day before. They were expected back at the White River camp by late afternoon. They never arrived.

I'd seen the kids earlier in the day. The Sunrise visitor center has enormous glass windows facing the mountain, and from there climbers look like tiny strings of ants. With strong binoculars you can make out their ropes, ice axes, and wool caps. That morning I'd seen the three dots and had been impressed because they were climbing quickly—and also because no one should have been on the mountain. The clouds, full and still, were turning that polished gray color that means a storm is brewing. The Park Service had put out an advisory against climbing. The kids, according to their friends at the White River camp, had come all the way from Wisconsin to climb, and they had to be home at the end of the week. They decided to take their chances.

By 10:00 that night, Jack Keeney, the head backcountry ranger, was putting together a search-and-rescue party. Night had swept in around the mountain along with a stiff wind and spitting rain. Up there it would be snow. I drank coffee in the visitor center with the rest of the interpretive staff and listened to Jack, who was next door in the ranger station on the short-wave radio, summoning as many climbers as he could find.

The voices on the radio were all men's save one. Elise Sawyer's. The Mount Fremont lookout, where Elise had been stationed every summer for the past ten years, was primarily a fire tower. But it was also positioned for relaying messages around to the other side of the mountain. I'd heard Jack say how Elise had never missed a single fire. She was more dependable than any man he knew. Most fire lookout people had been replaced by patrol planes. But as long as she wanted it, Jack had said, Elise could have her job.

I remembered meeting both Elise and Jack a month before at the beginning-of-the-season cookout for summer employees. Elise had looked like the only prospective dyke in the crowd, so after getting my food I followed her to the shade of a Douglas fir, where she joined a tall, auburn-haired woman and a man who looked like an Army sergeant. Elise looked the man dead in the eye, without smiling, and shook his hand firmly, saying, "Jack. Good to see you." Only then did she turn to the woman and say, "How're you doing, Barbara?" All three of them ignored me. I could have left, but then I'd have to try to break into some other conversation. At least here I had the chance of meeting a dyke. So I introduced myself. Balancing my limp paper plate of ribs, corn on the cob, and green salad in one hand, I shook their hands with my other. Elise was less than friendly, almost sulky, but I liked Barbara and Jack. Besides her bronze hair, Barbara had formidable cheekbones and a mouth that looked vulnerable, as if she were ready to kiss someone. Jack had a flattop crew cut, big dimples, and a lean, muscled body. Together they broadcast a feeling of capability, like they were a team more than a marriage. I imagined them having athletic sex.

As the conversation stumbled along—tensely, I thought— I tried to make significant eye contact with Elise. She appeared not just disinterested in me but almost hostile. I got the feeling she wanted Jack and Barbara to herself. Shit, I thought, I wasn't trying to flirt with her or anything. Could a little lesbian camaraderie hurt? I left to get more ribs, thinking this was going to be an even lonelier summer than I had expected.

I had not spoken with Elise since those few words at the cookout a month before. Tonight, her butchy voice on the radio stirred me. Her competence, her complete control of the situation impressed me. I wished I could help. But despite my extensive climbing experience, women were not considered for search-and-rescue teams.

I remained quiet as my fellow Park Service employees clucked and shook their heads at the reckless climbers. They'd wanted only to climb the mountain. They'd driven all the way from Wisconsin. They'd wanted it badly. I found myself respecting those kids, who'd ignored good judgment, and hating these folks around me, who doled out their lives like treats that had to last a long time. Good judgment suddenly felt as slippery as a trout in hand. Was death really a fair punishment for ignoring storm warnings?

I felt restless, so I went back to my cabin and pulled on a sweatshirt, my down parka, and my Gortex suit. I set out in the thick mist, treading the mile out to Frozen Lake where the trail forked in three directions. One went up to Burrough's Mountain, one down to Berkeley Park, and the third over to the lookout tower on Mount Fremont. I climbed in the opposite direction of the lookout tower. The dense clouds made the night black and cold. Patches of snow still nestled against the leeward slopes.

The frozen mist engulfed me until I reached the top of Burrough's Mountain, where I could climb out of it. I breathed hard, feeling utterly alone. But something was different tonight. My insignificance in the face of this immense universe pleased me. By abandoning good judgment, those three kids had been cut loose. They were free agents in the cosmos. As much as I worried about them, I also envied them. What did good judgment have to do with anything?

From where I stood I could see the lookout tower on Mount Fremont, glowing with a warm yellow light. I pictured Elise stationed at the radio, relaying flawless messages from Jack to Paradise on the west side of the mountain. I didn't plan to do what I did next. Shivering, I headed back down Burrough's Mountain, cold and tired and hungry, thinking I would go home to bed. Instead, when I got to the junction at Frozen Lake, I started up Mount Fremont. As I approached I could see Elise's silhouette in the all-glass room at the top of her tower. Although I was still a quarter of a mile away, Elise came out on the tiny balcony that surrounded her glass perch. They were right when they said she missed nothing from her tower. I didn't call out or wave. So what if she was frightened by the approach of someone in the dead of night. That's what she got for being unfriendly at the cookout.

When I got to the base of the tower, neither of us had spoken yet. I was a bit disappointed to realize that she wasn't one bit scared. She looked annoyed. I climbed the stairs and met her on the balcony. She wore a red-and-gray flannel shirt over a white T-shirt and Levi's. Clearly Elise didn't relish my intrusion.

"Did Jack send you?" she asked gruffly.

"No. I went out for a walk and landed here. Can I come in?" I was surprised at how aggressive I was being. For a femme out of uniform, anyway.

She turned and entered her tiny room, leaving the door open. After I followed, she went back to shut the door and then filled a beat-up tin pan with water from a metal tank on the floor and put the pan on a propane burner.

"I won't bother you. I mean, I know you're relaying messages for Jack.

"The search-and-rescue party just left. They won't need me anymore," she said, fingering the radio. "They've got six climbers. They're hoping to make the top of the Inter Glacier by midnight. Another party is going up from the Paradise side. Apparently the kids had talked about maybe going down the west-side route and hitching back to White River."

Jack's voice came across the radio. It was fuzzy and distant, but I could pick up some of the words. "Bob, I want you to personally check the carabiners on each...Then we'll..." His voice faded out again.

"Where'd you learn to use that thing?" I asked.

She stopped to listen to Jack and didn't answer me.

Besides the radio, her tower was equipped with a map table, a direction finder, and high-powered binoculars. Jack's voice faded in and out as I looked over her instruments and maps.

"Jack knows exactly what he's doing," she said. "There's never a spare word in his communication. It's always tight and to the point."

So this was a mutual admiration party of two. She spoke of Jack with so much veneration I began to wonder if I'd been wrong about her being a lesbian. Maybe she was one of those types that was nothing, neither straight nor lesbian. She felt lesbian to me, though. She definitely had dyke essence.

"Listen to him," Elise said, sitting down. She stirred instant-coffee crystals into two tin mugs. "He's perfect."

"That's a strong statement," I said, thinking about Jack's auburn-haired wife, the fire in her eyes. The way she stood next to perfect Jack, her fingers curled around his biceps.

Elise nodded absently. "Want chocolate in your coffee?"

"Sure."

"Are you hungry?"

I was very hungry and nodded.

Elise smiled. Oh, I felt as if I'd seen an endangered species. That rare smile melted the knot in my throat.

She opened a plastic bag of mixed dried fruit and put it on the map table. Then she put on another pot of water. "I'll make soup."

In response to my questions, Elise showed me how the direction finder worked. She pointed out where the biggest fires of her tenure had occurred and explained exactly how she'd spotted them and what techniques had been used to smother them. Until she hurt her back she'd been a smoke jumper for the forest service, a firefighter who jumped from helicopters into burns too deep in the wilderness to reach by foot or road vehicle. She told me about the black bear she'd known since it was a cub and visited her several times a summer. It had a brown spot on the right side of its nose, and its paws were even more pigeon-toed than other black bears. This summer the bear had brought her own cubs for Elise to see. Tears came to Elise's eyes as she told me this. No, of course, she hadn't named the bear. It was a bear, not a person. And, of course, she never fed her. It was cruel to teach bears to rely on people.

I had the feeling Elise thought it was cruel to teach people to rely on people.

Elise seemed a bit like a bear to me. She had that round, solid build and bright eyes. She contained her strength rather than strutting it. She also had a clean, direct way of talking that moved her stories straight to my heart. I hadn't expected her to be a talker, especially not to a middle-of-the-night intruder. But she seemed blasé about my unexpected arrival, as if she had visitors on many nights. After we'd drunk two cups of mocha each, she ladled chicken noodle soup into my cup, without rinsing it, and set a box of crackers next to me. She had a way of offering food that was both clumsy and tender. It made me feel shy about looking her in the eye. We didn't talk as we dunked crackers into the soup and slurped up the noodles.

From the tower all I could see was the black night, and yet the light shifted minute by minute as the clouds moved, thinned, and then thickened again. The hot drinks and our warm bodies heated the room, and soon I was toasty.

"If you have to pee," she said, breaking the silence, "the outhouse is down the stairs and to the right."

I did. Outside, I felt something stir in the night and turned, half expecting the bear and her cubs. But it was something bigger. It was the wilderness itself stirring in my gut. When I returned, Elise was sitting on her cot where she'd been when I left. Her back was against one of the glass windows, and her legs lay open, one along the side of the cot and the other hanging off the edge. Instead of sitting back down on the stool by the map table, I sat on the cot and leaned back against her leg. Neither of us spoke for a long time. I let my body sink more deeply into her cot, against her leg, settling so I was more *between* her legs. She picked up the foot that was on the floor and moved her legs so they loosely encircled me. Outside, the forest of green-black trees extended for hundreds of miles in one direction. In the other, Mount Rainier rumbled gently in the night, three kids lost in the clouds blanketing her flanks, hot molten lava gurgling in her heart. Again, I felt the wilderness seize me, as if she were a lover.

I was going to ask something about the bear and her cubs, but Jack's voice came, suddenly clear, on the radio. "Camp Sherman, come in."

Another man's voice, small and tinny but still audible, replied, "Roger."

"Have you looked over the western ridge of Steamboat Prow? Over."

"Negative. But we have to turn back, Jack. It's snowing harder and harder. I can't risk the lives of the whole crew. Seeking permission to turn back. Over."

There was a long silence before Jack answered. Then, firmly, "Granted. Come on back. Over."

"Ten-four. We'll stay at Camp Sherman tonight and try again in the..."

The voices faded again.

"The kids haven't got a chance," I whispered. "Not overnight."

"Maybe," Elise answered. "Sounds like the searchers are going to camp at 11,000 feet and try again in the morning. People have survived nights on the mountain. Maybe it will clear."

"Maybe," I agreed.

Elise reached up and pushed her fingers through my hair, starting at my neck and moving to the crown of my head. "I love curly hair," she said.

"Oh," I answered, surprised to hear her say something personal. She placed her other hand on my knee and pulled so that my legs were open. Then she traced the inseam of my jeans with her middle finger, moving from my knee up. "Your jeans are almost worn out," she said, touching the frayed places on my Levi's. Her hands were beautiful. They were strong and rough, the fingernails bitten.

I wished I could have answered with something just as casual, but I didn't trust my voice. The wind whistled across the roof of her tower. The windows shook. She scooted forward so she was pressed against my hip, and then she tightened the grip of her legs around me. I had never wanted anyone in my life as badly as I wanted this woman.

Her fingers moved gracefully as she undid the buttons of my shirt and pulled it off my shoulders. I sat on the cot in my worn Levi's and bra while she slipped onto her knees on the floor and unbuttoned my pants. I realized then that she wasn't even going to take off her boots.

I felt myself giving in to something dangerous, as if I were about to enter the mountain blizzard as foolishly willing as those three kids. I held myself back. I said, "I didn't come here for this." Elise didn't answer. Her strong hands tugged my jeans down over my hips. The voices on the radio scratched on and off as the steam on the windows of the glass walls sealed us in. I began to disappear into the hollow of my belly, somewhere much deeper than my own body.

Elise pushed me back on the cot and leaned down to take a nipple, through my bra, into her mouth. Her hands cradled my neck for a while, as if this were going to be very tender lovemaking. But soon she slid them across my collarbone, briefly gripping my shoulders, and then moving down my sides and over my hips. She handled me roughly now, as if she were desperate for the nourishment my breasts, belly, and thighs gave her. I struggled to stay in my body, but I could no more return from this journey than those kids could find their way down the mountain this stormy night. As I came the first time, my mind slipped away, disappeared altogether, and I found myself in a foreign land. It was like the universe, black with stars all around. It was like the top of the mountain, desolate and empty, yet all I could ever need. It was a land that predated all I knew to be true. As if creation were happening all around me. In and through me.

At some point, I don't know how many orgasms later, I returned to the lookout tower. Elise was rocking between my legs, her fist still in me. My head hung so far off her cot it nearly touched the floor, but she had one arm securely behind my shoulders to keep it from hitting on the wooden planks. Seeing I had come back, she effortlessly lifted my head and shoulders onto the cot. I know I looked at her with uncompromised worship. "Don't," was all she said. And I knew she was right. It wasn't Elise; it was that land on the other side that had made me reverent.

Outside, the sky had lightened. The tiny room smelled musky and hot. The back of my throat ached with desire, an aftertaste I knew would never go away. Elise cracked open the door to clear the windows. The clouds had fled, and a scattering of stars still remained in the paling sky. I lay on the cot, not moving, and watched the mountain turn peach and then bright yellow as the sun rose. The storm had lifted. Could the kids still be alive?

I loved Elise for not saying "You better go," though she was already at her instruments, measuring wind speed and direction, reading her barometer, recording the morning's temperature, writing down the exact moment of sunrise.

Messages were singing across her radio. She seemed to ignore them until suddenly she pivoted and took up the radio. A voice was calling urgently, "Fremont, come in. Fremont, come in."

"This is Fremont. Go ahead." Elise was all business.

"We found 'em. One mile from Paradise." The voice paused. I heard a sharp exhale of breath. Then, "All three dead. Transmit to Jack and stand by. Over."

"Ten-four. Verify message for Jack: Three climbers found dead one mile from Paradise. Over."

"Ten-four. Over and out."

"Over and out."

Elise didn't even look at me. She called Jack. "Communication from the Paradise search-and-rescue: The three climbers were found dead one mile from Paradise. Over."

Jack was silent for a long time. "Shit," he said into the radio. Jack, who never broke a rule, yelled, "Shit, shit, shit."

Elise waited. Then she spoke: "Jack, is there anything you want to relay? Over."

"Negative. Stand by. Over and out."

"Ten-four Over and out."

I dressed quickly, then walked over and put a hand on Elise's shoulder. "I'm going now," I said. My hand was shaking.

"OK, then." Elise stood up and put her hands in her front pockets. She looked me dead in the eye, as she had with Jack at the cookout. I felt inadequate in the face of that look. I knew my own eyes swam with sleeplessness and utter fulfillment, that my hair was foolishly smashed to one side.

"The kids," I said. I wanted to cry so badly.

Elise nodded.

They only wanted to climb the mountain. They came all the way from Wisconsin. I left, running down the wooden stairs of her tower, crying hard as I jogged the five miles to my cabin at Sunrise.

★★★

I couldn't think of anything but the three dead teenagers. And Elise. Night after night, I kept myself from stalking back out to her lookout tower. I tried to use up my energy by running out to the end of Sourdough Ridge and roaming through the Silver Forest. One night I even swam at midnight in Sunrise Lake, stroking through the black and icy glacial water. The lake was deep, and at the bottom lay a thick mud where all kinds of slimy worms and crustaceans lived. I flipped over on my back and floated, touching myself and thinking of Elise. Even that icy water wouldn't put out the fire she'd lit in me.

Donna and Lurking Dog—as well as my visions of homicide—became ancient and vague memories. Thank God that Donna left me, I found myself thinking, so I could be here for this. Even the anxiety that my pool of stories had dried up, that I'd never write again, disappeared. What did stories matter when I thought about those three dead teenagers? When I thought of Elise? Everything had become unbearably immediate.

And yet, as badly as I wanted her, I knew that to return to Elise would be to miss the point. The coordinates of time and space had brought us together for a moment, and it was this coincidence that made it work for her, maybe even for me. I should let that moment explode like a star, hot and bright, a thing unto itself. But I couldn't. I wanted to be touched by her calloused hands again. I wanted to see her dark brown eyes that looked like soil, like hard work. I wanted to touch her strong back and feel her skilled strength deliver me outside myself. On the seventh night I tracked back out there, moving like a shadow. My plan was to stop at a distance and only watch her. If I was lucky, she'd be up with her lantern lit.

As I approached I saw that her lantern was indeed lit. I scuttled along the trail, keeping my eyes lowered so wouldn't attract her attention, and ducked behind a large boulder about a hundred yards from the tower. I was breathing hard and was afraid she'd already detected my presence. Slowly, I eased my head around the side of the boulder to look.

There was someone in the tower with Elise. Two women were silhouetted against the night. One woman had her hands braced behind her, on what would be Elise's map table, her head thrown back. My view gave me a perfect profile, and I could see the woman's open mouth and her hair hanging freely behind her head. Her breasts lifted up toward the ceiling of the tower. Another head was between her legs. "Sweet Jesus," I murmured, sinking back behind the boulder.

The moon was bigger now than it'd been the week before, and it cast long shadows. The brightness of the mountain made it feel like daylight out here. I shifted my weight and an old piece of wood cracked, sounding like an explosion in the stillness of the night. I froze. I counted to ten. Then I slid my head around the rock again to see if I'd caught their attention. Hardly. Elise's head was still decidedly between the woman's legs. She stayed like that for what seemed like hours, the other woman's mouth opening and closing in what appeared to be gasps, her hips rocking back and forth in Elise's hands.

Finally, the woman pulled Elise up by her collar, and they sunk into a long kiss, the woman lying back on the map table now and Elise pressing on top. After a while the stranger pushed Elise off her and reached for something on the floor. Her shirt. Elise helped her get her arms in it and then tenderly buttoned it up for her. With me, Elise hadn't been so much tender as she'd been deft. Even at this distance I could see that Elise became malleable in the presence of this other woman.

The woman moved quickly now, as if she were late. She pulled on her jacket, kissed Elise again, and hurried out of the glass room and down the stairs of the tower. Shit! I hadn't thought about being discovered by the stranger! There was no way I could escape without being seen. I had to wait behind the boulder and pray she would not see me as she passed on the trail just three yards away. I watched the woman approach. She hadn't come very far along the trail when I recognized Jack Keeney's wife, Barbara. Sweet Jesus! What was going on here?

I pressed myself against the back of the boulder, held my breath, and watched her half-run past me on the trail. She looked beautiful. Her hair bright in the moonlight, her gait loose and easy. When she was out of sight, I looked back at the tower.

I couldn't help myself. I waited a respectable amount of time and then stepped out from behind my rock and headed up to the fire tower. For once, Elise wasn't aware of everything that came within a hundred yards. As I approached I saw her blow out her lantern. I drew close.

I still could not believe what I'd seen. All I'd ever heard from the other rangers was how much they envied Jack and Barbara's marriage. They shared so much together: a love of the outdoors, a clear decision not to have children, a simple close-to-the-bone existence. Barbara, I'd heard from male rangers, was the perfect woman, both gorgeous and able to keep up. I just couldn't believe this. And the way Elise nearly worshiped Jack. Her boss.

I started up the stairs. My footsteps echoing on the lumber must have startled her. She called out, "Barbara?" She thought her lover had returned.

She had, but not the one she expected.

"Barbara!" This time her voice was urgent.

I paused a moment. Then I called out, "It's me."

Elise appeared at her door in her long underwear. She looked softer than I'd ever seen her. I wanted her more than ever. But a vulnerable butch is something you don't mess with. I stopped my approach, like an animal who understands territory. She was speechless.

I said, "I saw everything." Trying to lighten the mood, I added, "So how many women traipse out here for your services, anyway? I thought your job was putting *out* fires."

Elise looked me over good and long, still speechless and maybe even frightened. She knew next to nothing about me, and I had first-class blackmail information on her.

"Can I come in?"

She stepped out of the doorway and let me in.

Elise had been crying. I noticed the wet patch on her pillow, the red blotches on her face, her eyelashes clumped together with tears. I stood awkwardly next to the map table, not knowing what to do but unwilling to leave.

She suddenly began sobbing. "I don't cry," she forced out between sobs. "I don't cry in front of people."

"You are now," I said softly. "You are now."

I filled her tin pan with water from the tank. Then I fiddled around trying to light her propane burner, which provided her the opportunity to get up, push me aside, and do it herself. That helped. She paced for a while, looking more like a bear than ever.

"Ten years this year," she began, wiping her nose on her sleeve. "Barbara and I have been lovers for ten years, ever since my first summer up here." She laughed hoarsely and ran her hands through her short hair. "Oh, we've broken it off a million times, sometimes me and sometimes her. One summer we made it through the whole season without having sex once."

"Why doesn't she leave Jack?"

Elise looked at me as if I were crazy. "Jack doesn't have anything to do with it."

It seemed to me that Jack would have everything to do with it. "Does he know?"

"Of course not. But they have a perfect relationship. Jack...Jack, he's..." For a moment Elise seemed at a loss for words. Then, "Jack is so solid. No woman in her right mind would ever leave Jack. You know, he was a POW in Vietnam. He's the kind of person that every year you know him you learn more. I love Barbara too much to ever want her to leave Jack. Ever." Elise was almost growling now.

After a long silence she whispered huskily, "But..."

I waited.

"But every time she leaves me, it's harder. Every single year it gets wilder, bigger, deeper." She turned off the boiling water and started to make coffee. "I spend every winter ravaging women at home in Michigan, looking for one who can call up the passion Barbara calls up in me. But Barbara, she's this rock in my heart." Elise was fierce. "Do you understand?"

I nodded. I thought I did. I wondered how many of those ravaged women in Michigan felt as awed by Elise as I did now.

"You're the only person I've ever told."

"I swear I'll never breathe a word to anyone."

Elise smiled softly, nodded a little.

I waited for her to say something more, but she was quiet. She made only one cup of coffee. I could tell she wanted to be alone. I was no replacement for Barbara. I stood to go.

"You know, Elise," I said, "you're about the best thing I've come across in my whole life."

She looked startled, ready to fend me off.

"Don't worry," I said and glanced out of her glass tower at the clean, bare surface of the nearly full moon. Something inside me rocketed past the ache at the back of my throat to that starry wilderness she'd shown me. It was the place before language. The place where all stories come from. Where life comes from.

"You've made me hungry for myself," I said.

About the Contributors

Deborah Abbott likes to get wet as often as possible; thus, she is apt to be found on or in wet places such as rivers, lakes, oceans, swimming pools, bathtubs, and lesbians. She is a rafter, kayaker, swimmer, psychotherapist, mother, lover, and writer. She is the director of the University of California at Santa Cruz's Gay, Lesbian, Bi, Trans Resource Center. Her poems, stories, and essays have been widely anthologized. She coedited *From Wedded Wife to Lesbian Life: Stories of Transformation* (The Crossing Press).

Lucy Jane Bledsoe is the author of *Sweat,* a collection of short fiction, and *The Big Bike Race,* a children's book. Her work has appeared in several anthologies, including the *Women on Women* Series. She also edited *Heatwave: Lesbian Short Fiction* (Alyson, 1995).

Maureen Brady, author of *Folly, Give Me Your Good Ear,* and *The Question She Put to Herself,* teaches writing at New York University and The Writer's Voice. She lives in New York City and the Catskills.

Wendy Caster wrote *The Lesbian Sex Book* and has also published dozens of opinion columns, along with short stories, reviews, and articles. She lives in New York City, where she is working on her first novel. Wendy makes her living as managing editor at a medical education agency.

Ouida Crozier was born, raised, and schooled in Florida. Following college graduation she moved to South Carolina, where she lived for ten years while working and attending graduate school. In her mid 30s she moved to Minnesota, where she continues to reside. Ouida has published poetry, nonfiction, short stories, and one novel. In addition to being a writer, she is a psychologist and an educator.

Linnea Due is a novelist (*High and Outside, Give Me Time, Life Savings*), nonfiction writer (*Joining the Tribe: Growing up Gay and Lesbian in the '90s*), and editor (*Dagger: On Butch Women*). Her feature articles have covered the gamut, from sex clubs in San Francisco to feral cats in Berkeley, from Queer Nation to the Jewish Film Festival.

Martha Equinox has worked as a waitress, ice-cream-truck driver, auto mechanic, psychic healer, astrologer, law-office manager, and accountant. Her published work has appeared in *Coming to Power* (Alyson, 1987) and *The Rock,* and she has written and performed autobiographical work on death and loss, aging, and lesbian sex roles.

Lynne Yamaguchi Fletcher coedited the anthology *Tomboys! Tales of Dyke Derring-do* (Alyson, 1995), with Karen

Barber. Her poetry, fiction, and essays have been published in various journals and anthologies.

Julie Anne Gibeau lives in Covington, Ky., and works as a computer tape librarian for the Internal Revenue Service. She is a graduate of the University of Iowa. Julie loves erotica's capacity to illustrate personal growth through sexual expression. *"Le Main"* is her first published story.

Lisa Ginsburg recently moved to West Hollywood, where she is pursuing her writing and film career and hoping, as she was promised, that there really are butch women in Los Angeles—you just have to know where to look.

Nicola Ginzler's work has appeared in many magazines and some books. She has performed, in one way or another, in San Francisco, Los Angeles, New York City, and London. Watch for an interactive CD-ROM featuring her story "Consent," forthcoming from *Skin Two* magazine.

Susan Kan writes stories, poems, and book reviews. Her work has been published in small literary journals. She works as a freelance copy editor and makes her home in Shutesbury, Mass.

Catherine Lundoff is an activist, writer, top, and clerical temporary. She lives in Minneapolis with her wonderfully patient and supportive girlfriend and considerably less supportive cats. Her stories have appeared in *Cherished Blood, Pillow Talk, Xoddity,* and *Lesbian Short Fiction.*

Lee Lynch's latest novel is *Rafferty Street* (New Victoria Publishers). She has produced ten other books, including *The Swashbuckler* and *Morton River Valley*. With Akia Woods she edited *Off The Rag: Lesbians Write About Menopause*, also from New Victoria. Her column The Amazon Trail appears monthly in magazines across the United States. She lives with Akia in Oregon where she earns a living in the social services.

michon says she's a "black chick writing to survive, working to sustain, living to love new baby, chocolab pooch, and girlfriend, buttacup ("buttacup sunshine")...and still learning how to be an adult...working on a vampire story and a collection of short stories."

Bonnie J. Morris is a women's studies professor and the author of three books, including *Eden Built By Eves* (Alyson, 1999), a tribute to women's music festivals. When not in the classroom or working at festivals, she can be found touring the country with her one-woman play, *Revenge of the Women's Studies Professor*. Her work appears in more than 30 anthologies.

Lesléa Newman is the author and editor of more than 25 books, including *Girls Will Be Girls: A Novella and Short Stories* (Alyson, 2000), *Out of the Closet and Nothing to Wear*, *The Little Butch Book*, and *Heather Has Two Mommies*. She is also the editor of six anthologies, including *The Femme Mystique*, *My Lover is a Woman: Contemporary Lesbian Love Poems*, and *Pillow Talk: Lesbian Stories Between the Covers*. Her literary honors include five Lambda Literary Award nominations, a Massachusetts Artists Fellowship, and the *Highlights for Children* Fiction Writing Award.

J.M. Redmann lives, works, and frolics in "that swamp known as New Orleans." She is the author of four novels, *Death by the Riverside, Deaths of Jocasta, The Intersection of Law and Desire,* and *Lost Daughters.*

Mariana Romo-Carmona is the author of a novel, *Living at Night.* She coedited *Cuentos: Stories by Latinas,* and her work has appeared in many anthologies and periodicals. She teaches in the fine arts program at Goddard College in Vermont. Born in Santiago, Chile, she has lived in the United States for more than 30 years.

Stephanie Rosenbaum is a freelance journalist who writes about food, fashion, and culture for a variety of Bay Area publications. Her fiction has been published in *Beyond Definition: New Gay and Lesbian Writing From San Francisco, Virgin Territory,* and *Tangled Sheets: Stories and Poems of Lesbian Lust.*

Marcy Sheiner is editor of *Herotica 4, 5, and 6.* Her stories and essays have appeared in many anthologies and publications. *The Oy of Sex,* erotica by and about Jewish women, will be published by Cleis Press in spring 1999. She is now working on a book called *Sex for the Clueless,* to be published by Citadel in fall 1999. Visit her Web site at www.sexsense.com.

Judith Stelboum is coeditor of the forthcoming book, *The Lesbian Polyamory Reader: Open Relationships, Non-monogamy, and Casual Sex.* Her fiction, poetry, and essays have been published in various anthologies.

Robin Sweeney is a Bay Area writer, editor, troublemaker, and activist. To pay the bills, she still temps but is working on a novel she hopes will change that.

Lindsay Taylor is a native of Connecticut. She earned her BS in mass communication, magna cum laude, from Boston University in 1985 and has resided in the San Francisco Bay area since then. In her day job she is an administrator at the University of California, Berkeley. In her passion she is an author. Her exposé "Engendering Perspective" is featured in the Lesbian Herstory Archives in New York City. Her short story "Life With B: Erotica in G, Opus 33" first appeared in the anthology *Heatwave: Women in Love and Lust*. A revised version of the work has been reprinted for this anthology.

Jess Wells has had seven volumes published, including the anthology *Lesbians Raising Sons*, the novel *AfterShocks,* and the short-story collection *Two Willow Chairs*. Her work has appeared in numerous anthologies, including *Women on Women: An Anthology of American Lesbian Short Fiction, The Femme Mystique, Lavender Mansions, Lesbian Culture,* and *When I am an Old Woman*. She also edited the anthology *Lip Service: Alluring New Lesbian Erotica,* forthcoming from Alyson.